WISHES FOR CHRISTMAS

Books by Fern Michaels:

About Face
Perfect Match
A Family Affair
Forget Me Not
The Blossom Sisters
Balancing Act
Tuesday's Child
Betrayal
Southern Comfort
To Taste the Wine
Sins of the Flesh
Sins of Omission
Return to Sender
Mr. and Miss Anonymous
Up Close and Personal
Fool Me Once
Picture Perfect
The Future Scrolls
Kentucky Sunrise
Kentucky Heat
Kentucky Rich
Plain Jane
Charming Lily
What You Wish For
The Guest List
Listen to Your Heart
Celebration
Yesterday
Finders Keepers
Annie's Rainbow
Sara's Song
Vegas Sunrise
Vegas Heat
Vegas Rich

Whitefire
Wish List
Dear Emily
Christmas at
    Timberwoods

The Sisterhood Novels:

In Plain Sight
Eyes Only
Kiss and Tell
Blindsided
Gotcha!
Home Free
Déjà Vu
Cross Roads
Game Over
Deadly Deals
Vanishing Act
Razor Sharp
Under the Radar
Final Justice
Collateral Damage
Fast Track
Hokus Pokus
Hide and Seek
Free Fall
Lethal Justice
Sweet Revenge
The Jury
Vendetta
Payback
Weekend Warriors

Books by Fern Michaels (Continued):

The Godmothers Series:

Classified
Breaking News
Deadline
Late Edition
Exclusive
The Scoop

E-Book Exclusives:

Desperate Measures
Seasons of Her Life
Upside Down
Countdown
Take Down
To Have and To Hold
Serendipity
Captive Innocence
Captive Embraces
Captive Passions
Captive Secrets
Captive Splendors
Cinders to Satin
For All Their Lives

Fancy Dancer
Texas Heat
Texas Rich
Texas Fury
Texas Sunrise

Anthologies:

When the Snow Falls
Secret Santa
A Winter Wonderland
I'll Be Home for
    Christmas
Making Spirits Bright
Holiday Magic
Snow Angels
Silver Bells
Comfort and Joy
Sugar and Spice
Let It Snow
A Gift of Joy
Five Golden Rings
Deck the Halls
Jingle All the Way

FERN MICHAELS

WISHES FOR CHRISTMAS

KENSINGTON PUBLISHING CORP.
http://www.kensingtonbooks.com

KENSINGTON BOOKS are published by

Kensington Publishing Corp.
119 West 40th Street
New York, NY 10018

Copyright © 2015 by Fern Michaels.
Fern Michaels is a registered trademark of KAP 5, Inc.

All Kensington titles, imprints and distributed lines are available at special quantity discounts for bulk purchases for sales promotion, premiums, fund-raising, educational or institutional use.

Special book excerpts or customized printings can also be created to fit specific needs. For details, write or phone the office of the Kensington Special Sales Manager: Kensington Publishing Corp., 119 West 40th Street, New York, NY, 10018. Attn. Special Sales Department. Phone: 1-800-221-2647.

Kensington and the K logo Reg. U.S. Pat. & TM Off.

Library of Congress Control Number: 2015937822

ISBN-13: 978-1-61773-632-2
ISBN-10: 1-61773-632-5
First Kensington Hardcover Edition: August 2015

10 9 8 7 6 5 4 3 2 1

Printed in the United States of America

Contents

And the Angels Sing

Chapter 1

What had started out as a simple, run-of-the-mill luncheon had somehow turned into a major culinary event sponsored by Maggie Spritzer for her Sisters, known to their many adoring fans as the Vigilantes.

Normal luncheons with the Sisters were usually done on the fly and, for the most part, held in favorite cafés or restaurants. When Maggie first came up with the idea, it was because she had a serious matter to discuss with the Sisters. She knew the luncheon would go into overtime, and at a public eatery, they would be rushed, hence this luncheon was in her own home in Georgetown.

It was well known that Maggie was not a cook, not even a fair to middling one. Oh, to be sure, she could throw things together and manage somehow to make the result edible, but she much preferred takeout, which she warmed up and pretended that she'd prepared. She did, however, have one dish that always garnered praise, a broccoli, three-cheese casserole that was beyond delicious. She always served it with a crisp garden salad, warm, tiny, spongy garlic rolls, and a peach cobbler straight out of the supermarket freezer section.

No one ever complained, and there was never enough

left to save, so Maggie was confident her luncheon menu would meet with the Sisters' approval.

Maggie took one last look at her dining-room table. She knew she should have used her once-a-year good dishes, but she'd just been too lazy to take them out and wash them, so she had opted for colorful hard plastic plates with an autumn theme. All gold, orange, and rustic brown. Her centerpiece was an arrangement of fall leaves that matched the plastic plates. All in all, she was satisfied. And she also knew the Sisters wouldn't complain even if she served the food on Styrofoam plates, because things like that simply were not important.

The timer in the kitchen went off just as the doorbell rang. Talk about timing. She grinned as she ran to the door with Hero, her cat, right on her heels.

As always, the Sisters oohed and aahed over the delicious aromas as they hugged and squealed over seeing each other.

Coats and jackets were hung up. It was the end of October, and there was a definite chill in the air.

The women all headed for the kitchen and were surprised when Maggie said, "No, we're eating in the dining room today. And guess what? Today we are having fresh apple cider. I picked it up this morning. Someone pour while I get the food on the table."

The moment everyone was seated, Maggie held up her glass and said, "Happy harvest, everyone! Tomorrow is Halloween. And, by the way, I personally carved that pumpkin you all saw on the front stoop. I just love autumn."

The Sisters all toasted Halloween, then sat back and waited, because they all knew Maggie's casserole had to set for ten minutes before it could be scooped onto plates.

"Are we celebrating something today, or is this just a get-together, dear?" Myra asked.

"Both," Maggie responded smartly.

"Well, speaking strictly for myself, I am all ears," Kathryn said as she eyed the golden brown casserole sitting in the center of the table. Everyone knew and teased Kathryn that she had the appetite of a truck driver because she was an overland driver who handled her eighteen-wheeler like the pro she was.

"Me, too." Yoko laughed. "Spit it out, Maggie, or do we have to eat first?"

"Why don't we be devilish today and break Charles's golden rule that we don't talk business while we eat?" Annie suggested. The others hooted that they were in agreement.

"Any reason why you didn't invite the boys?" Nikki asked.

"Well, yeah, this is girls only. I thought we agreed to do that once a month," Maggie said as she toyed with the serving spoon that would scoop up her casserole.

"Okay, I get it. This is that once-a-month social gathering, *plus* some business, right?" Alexis grinned.

"A hint, a clue, something would be nice," Isabelle said as she popped a tiny garlic roll into her mouth. She rolled her eyes at the delectable delight.

"Does whatever you have in mind involve just us girls or the boys at some point?" Nikki asked, the lawyer in her wanting details and facts.

"To be decided," Maggie said, waving the spoon. "It's just an idea. An idea I've had for a long time. With the holidays fast approaching, it always takes over my mind at this time of year, and I simply cannot stop thinking about it."

"What? What?" Annie exploded as Kathryn reached over to take the serving spoon out of Maggie's hand. Reaching for the plates, she put spoon to casserole and filled them.

"The money from my husband's insurance. I tried to give it to Gus's nephew, but he refused to take it. I never spent a dime of it. I couldn't. I want to give it away this

Christmas. I want you all to help me. And then I took it one step further and thought, wouldn't it be nice if you all kicked in some money to match it and . . ."

"And what, dear?" Myra asked.

"Make someone's world brighter and happier. Save someone's life. Do something for someone, or more than someone, who otherwise would stay in whatever position they're in at the moment. This year, for some reason, I want . . . no, I *need* to make the angels sing. I want to *hear* them sing. Does that make sense?" Maggie asked fretfully.

"Of course it makes sense. I think it's a wonderful idea. Count me in," Annie said. "Now, you know if you include the boys, the fund would grow substantially higher," she said slyly. The others agreed as they all started to eat.

"Not so fast," Myra said. "Dear," she said, addressing Maggie, "did you forget we have an organization that Abner is in charge of that donates yearly, very generously and very heavily, during the holidays? Any new charity or person is always welcome. I thought we all had agreed to that. Last year alone, we donated—anonymously, of course—over one billion dollars, which we confiscated from that monster, Angus Spyder. So, I'm not quite sure what it is you want us to contribute to, and while I have no problem with that at all, I guess I just don't understand the end result here."

The women stopped eating long enough to stare at Maggie, waiting to see how she would respond.

"I guess I didn't fully explain, because I'm not clear in my own mind. Sometimes late at night, when I can't sleep, I think about my life, my childhood, my family and wonder, as I think most people wonder, if I could do things over, what would I do differently? Is there some wrong in my past life that I never made right, for whatever reason? Just think about that for a minute. I have an instance, and I've never forgotten it. I don't know if money can or will right that situation, but I want to look into it and try. It's not the same as what Abner is doing with Spyder's money and all those other people's money we helped ourselves to. This is *personal*. That's the best way I can explain it to you all. Does it make more sense now?"

"Well, yes, dear, it certainly does," Myra said. "I think you might be on to something. Let's run this up the flagpole. Now that I understand where you're going with this, I think we should include the boys in this."

"I agree," Isabelle said. The others were quick to agree.

"We can't call them now. It's too late," Yoko said. "They'll be miffed that they weren't included in this luncheon."

"Then we'll do a repeat tomorrow at my house," Nikki said. "That's when we'll run it up the flagpole, and they'll never know this was a rehearsal for tomorrow. How about that for sneaky? Do you all agree?"

"What are you going to serve?" Kathryn asked, her mind jumping ahead to the menu.

"How about a little of everything that is takeout?" Nikki laughed.

"Works for me." Alexis giggled.

Not surprisingly, it worked for everyone.

"So, let's get to the dessert, Maggie," Annie said.

The women talked nonstop as they devoured the peach cobbler, the main topic being that memories, for the most part, were a wonderful thing, be they sad or happy.

"How much money are we talking about?" Yoko asked. "The reason I ask is that Harry and I are going to China next month, and that always puts a big dent in our budget."

"It doesn't matter how much, Yoko. If it's fifty dollars, that's fine. If it's two hundred fifty thousand dollars, that's fine, too. The point is it has to be our own personal money, whatever we can afford. Gus's insurance money is just the cherry on top. I'll be putting my own money in, too. It will all go into one fund, and then, when we're ready to distribute it to whoever needs it, we'll vote on it. I think that's fair. If you all want to keep your amounts secret, that's okay, too. We should vote on that tomorrow. In the end, it might not even come down to money. Maybe there is someone out there from our past who needs something other than money. Something we can provide for them that no one else can. That kind of thing."

"I think this is a wonderful idea," Myra said. "I can't wait for tomorrow. Thank you so much, Maggie, for bringing this up. Sometimes I think we forget that it's better to give than to receive. Oh, this is going to be such a wonderful Christmas. The true meaning of it. Truly, truly."

Annie swiped at her eyes. "Myra's right. This is just what we all need. We've been getting complacent. I agree with Myra. I can't wait till tomorrow."

Twelve minutes later, right on schedule, Maggie's kitchen and dining room were back to normal, with just the autumn centerpiece in the middle of the table. A second round of fresh coffee was served as the girls talked nonstop about what was going to transpire the following day.

"It's going to take a lot of research to track down people from our past," Isabelle said.

"And who better to do that than our four intrepid reporters, meaning Ted, Dennis, Maggie, and Espinosa?" Nikki chortled.

"We need a name for this project," Alexis said.

The group threw out names and titles, but it was Yoko who came up with the one they finally agreed to. Bright Star.

The Sisters all clapped, making their newest project official.

Nikki was as good as her word. Lunch consisted of all takeout—Thai, Chinese, Italian, deli, and Japanese. Dessert was individually wrapped fortune cookies. The food was served buffet style for the simple reason that Nikki and Jack's dining-room table could seat only ten. It didn't matter. The group adapted to everything and anything when they were up against the clock or a new mission was unfolding.

Harry and Yoko were the only ones with glum faces. It took all of Annie's and Myra's expertise to convince them that despite the new project on the drawing board, it was all right to still make the trip to China to see their daughter. They reminded them both that faxes, e-mails, and text messages, along with Skyping, would keep them in the loop and in the thick of things. Yoko accepted it much better than Harry did, but in the end he came around to the group's way of thinking. Yoko beamed her pleasure at Harry, who literally melted in front of everyone.

Jack Emery smacked his hands together. "So, when do we start?"

"How about right now? Or we can wait a few days and meet up over the weekend out at the farm, which will bring us to the start of November. Our research may go fast, or it may go slow. There are a lot of us, so every day is going to count. Not to mention we need data to start. You guys . . ." Maggie was about to say, "You just came into the picture, whereas us girls have had all night and this morning to think about it," but she didn't.

Dennis reached for the last sushi roll and popped it into his mouth. "Who's in charge of the fund? I'm willing to do it if no one else wants to. And when does the money have to be in hand?"

"The job is yours, then, kid," Abner said, "because that will free me up to do other things. Anyone object? Speak up now." No one spoke up. "Okay, then, I'll open up an account and text you the info."

Dennis looked around at the group. "Don't worry. I'm good with money."

"Okay, that's one less problem we have to worry about," Ted said.

The rest of the hour was spent talking about the past, individual memories, the upcoming holidays, and, of course, Harry and Yoko's trip to China.

Cleanup took precisely twelve minutes, as always. The moment it was done, the group left to come to terms with righting a wrong from their respective pasts, leaving Jack and Nikki alone.

"Happy Halloween, Jack," Nikki said, squeezing her husband's arm.

"Happy Halloween, Nik," Jack said, gathering her in his arms. "You know what, Nik? As much as we talked about the past—and if we had to do things over again, would we or wouldn't we?—I wouldn't. Because if I did, maybe even for a few seconds, that might have thrown off my timing, and I never would have met you."

"Jack, that is absolutely the sweetest thing you've ever said to me, and I feel exactly the same way."

"Let's go for a walk, Nik. Let's hold hands and enjoy the afternoon, okay?"

"For you, Jack, anything."

Chapter 2

Sunday dinner at Pinewood was always a delight, and the gang never missed a chance to get together for one of Charles's memorable dinners because he never disappointed. Today was no exception.

Today's menu consisted of a vermicelli soup, garlic-roasted beef tenderloin, melt-in-your-mouth sweet potato puffs, green currants in a secret sauce, which the chef refused to reveal, and creamed cucumbers with young onions. For dessert, there was fig pudding with peaches and cream. Fresh homemade buttery cheese rolls completed the meal, along with hazelnut coffee, which Charles firmly believed was just as good as a dessert.

Belts were undone as the gang groaned and moaned about how it was going to take them a whole week to work off all the calories they'd consumed in one sitting. Charles showed them no mercy by saying, "I only prepared what you asked for."

Cleanup took sixteen minutes, as opposed to the usual twelve, because, as Alexis put it, "We're all sluggish," and the figs scorched the bottom of the pan, and so it had to be scoured.

"We know, dear," Myra said as she worked alongside the girls. "And Charles really outdid himself today. Now we have to go down to the war room and *work*. We have only fifty-four days until Christmas Eve."

Jack grumbled under his breath, but Harry heard him say, "Whose bright idea was it to eat first, then work? It should be just the opposite." Harry gave him a shove to move forward, then needled him that he could already see the five extra pounds added to his gut. Jack was too miserable to respond, other than to say, "I never eat like that, but it was so good."

"Yeah, yeah, yeah," Harry continued to needle.

In the war room, Espinosa pressed a button, and the new table that Isabelle had designed, and that Avery Snowden and his men had crafted, opened, and the extra leaves slid into place, expanding the table so that everyone was comfortable. Yoko slid the grungy old shoe box to the center of the table. Everyone eyeballed it, but no one said anything.

Charles was on the dais, and it was good to see him back there. "I think we are really back to normal now," Nikki whispered to Kathryn, who nodded in agreement.

"We need to look alive, people," Myra said. "As I said earlier, we have only fifty-four days until Christmas Eve, and you all know how fast the season goes once it gets under way. First, though, I have a bit of news to share with you all. It was just confirmed, or I would have told you all sooner.

"It concerns Nellie and Elias. As you all know, Elias has advanced Alzheimer's. Nellie refuses to place her husband in a care facility, and rightly so. We take care of our own. As long as we can. Even with all the help she has, she has her own health issues. One of her new hips isn't working properly. She's looking at surgery and some serious recovery time. She has opted to go into an assisted living facility, a very nice one, I might add, where both she and Elias will have twenty-four-hour care if they need it but will still technically be on their own. Annie and I offered to move in with her, but she wouldn't hear of it, which isn't surprising, because she is so independent.

"Having said all that, she can take her beloved cats, all four of them, with her. She's turning the farm over to Nikki and Jack. She said it is perfect for them now that Cyrus has his five pups. At some point, if they want to buy the farm, that might happen. So Annie and I will have a new neighbor. Nikki and Jack are going to rent out their house in Georgetown."

The gang all clapped to show their approval.

"Guess who is going to rent our house?" Nikki said. At the blank looks, she laughed and said, "Jack Sparrow. The perfect tenant. He's never home, so there won't be much wear and tear on the house, and he's a bachelor. Win-win for everyone."

"With that business out of the way, let's get down to why we're here on a Sunday night. As Myra said, we have only fifty-four days to follow up on Maggie's suggestion. So, let's talk. You go first, Nikki," Annie said.

"Jack and I think it's a great idea. Here's the 'but.' Jack made a point that if we were to go back in time, then time would change. Jack, tell them what you told me last night."

Jack sat up straighter. "It's the time chain. Twelve years ago, I lost a case to this obnoxious lawyer who should be ashamed to call himself an attorney. He's a bottom-feeder if ever there was one. And the only reason he got his client off was on a technicality. I was so angry, so bummed out, I was going to follow him out to the parking lot and knock him silly. I was streaming down the hall and ran into Nikki, or she ran into me. Then two other attorneys who were right behind me collided with me. All our folders and files went flying. Took us a good ten minutes to gather up what belonged to each of us. Now, if I hadn't been on the verge of running after Singer—that's his name—I might never have met Nikki. Would I want to relive that moment? Change it? The answer is, 'Absolutely not.'

"Speaking strictly for myself, it's all a nonstarter. Looking back, yeah, things went wrong, some my own fault, some not. But not worthy of trying to make it right in this day and age. I'm thinking—and again, this is just my opinion—we should look for a cause or a person or persons who, as Maggie said, could use our help. I'm up for everything and anything. Nikki agrees with me."

"All right, then, let's run this up the flagpole and see what we end up with," Myra said.

Two hours later the final vote was in. No one had anything in their life that they would do differently, for the very reason Jack had outlined. Dennis West summed it up perfectly. "If we did that, none of us would be sitting where we are now, having this discussion. Life has to go on. The past is past."

Maggie felt like crying. She had been so sure everyone had something, like she did, that they wanted to make right. A tear rolled down her cheek. Annie saw it.

"Why don't you tell us what *you* want to make right, Maggie? Just because the rest of us don't want to upset the time chain doesn't mean you can't," she said. "We all have regrets. If I didn't have that horrible headache the day my husband and children went boating, maybe they would be alive today. They wanted to stay with me, but I told them to go and enjoy the day. For nine long years, I regretted that decision, and I still do to this day, as does Myra for not telling her daughter to stay with her instead of going back to her car for the camera. They're regrets. As Dennis said, if we had acted differently back then, none of us would be here today. Now, tell us what we can do for you, Maggie."

Maggie stiffened. "It was a mistake. I just got carried away there for a few moments. You are all right. So now we have to come up with a cause and make it work for us. Fifty-four days is not all that much time," Maggie said with a smile on her face that didn't reach her eyes. It was evident to everyone in the room that she was bummed out and was trying desperately to cover up the feeling. She wasn't going to say another word.

The silence in the room was deafening as all eyes watched Maggie. She was too stiff, too flat. They all felt like they had failed her somehow. They also knew that for now they had to let it go and revisit the issue only when Maggie was ready to revisit it. If ever.

The conversation turned to childhood Christmases and all the stories that went with them, from childhood to adulthood. The stories were upbeat, as only those about childhood escapades could be. It was a good way to wind down the meeting, and so they did, with a promise to meet up the following week back at Pinewood.

Maggie woke early. She hated it when that happened, especially when it was a Saturday, and she could sleep in. Hero hopped on her chest, purring loudly. Maggie loved it when he purred just for her. She stroked his thick coat and tussled with him for a few minutes, something he was absolutely crazy about. Finally, she swung her legs over the side of the bed. Hero scampered off to do whatever it was he did until his mistress was showered and on her way to making his breakfast—salmon flakes and crunchy morsels.

In the kitchen, Maggie followed her normal routine. She craned her neck to see the thermometer outside the kitchen door. It read thirty-five degrees. She shivered. She had no plans for the day. She could have coffee, she could go back to bed, she could sit around and read a book, or she could watch the idiot box and eat snacks all day. But none of those options appealed to her.

Maggie fixed her gaze on her kitchen calendar. Tomorrow was Pinewood, but she didn't have any great hopes that the gang would come up with something that would please her in regard to her original idea. Then again, perhaps they would.

Maybe she could get a head start on her Christmas decorating. Not that she did much, but she always made sure she put up a Christmas tree. An artificial one that looked more real than the ones she used to get at the farmers' market. This year, with the trip to China looming, Yoko had decided not to do Christmas trees.

Normally, Maggie did her decorating the weekend after Thanksgiving. So, she'd get a head start this year. It would give her something to do.

The decision made, she settled down and ate her scrambled egg with two slices of bacon and toast with jam. Always mindful that she was of an age now when she had to pay attention to her cholesterol, she ate bacon and one egg only on Saturday. The rest of the week she ate yogurt, fruit, and bran muffins. Her blood work at her last checkup was perfect.

Christmas! She really didn't like the holiday and was sick and tired of pretending that she did. Everyone called her Scrooge, but she didn't care. The truth was, she didn't hate the holiday; she just dreaded it. How many times had she wished she could go to sleep in November and not wake up till January 2? Not January 1, but January 2. Way too many times to count. Way too many. Since it was now November, she could feel the old uneasy feeling start to settle over her, the way it had every year since she was ten years old.

As her thoughts drifted back to her childhood, Maggie

busied herself cleaning up the breakfast dishes. She did like a tidy kitchen. She knew she was stalling as she cleaned Hero's litter box and took out last night's trash. She built a fire. You always needed a fire when you set up a Christmas tree. And music. You needed Christmas music to complete the picture. Snow would help, but a gloomy gray day would work just as well.

Maggie dragged her feet as she made her way to the walk-in closet off the family room, where she stored seasonal items, mainly the Christmas tree, which came in three parts. When she'd bought it originally, years before she started getting a real tree from Yoko's nursery, the salesman had told her that even an idiot could put it together. She'd narrowed her eyes at that statement, and the salesman had hastened to say something less offensive, which was, "Even a ten-year-old could set up this tree." She recalled trying to say something, and in the end, she'd fled the store in tears. Two days later, she'd gone to another store to buy the identical tree. The same tree she was now going to set up in her family room. She had to agree with the first salesman, though: any idiot could set up the tree and plug it in.

And that was what she did. The tree sprang to life with, if she recalled correctly, a thousand tiny colored lights at the tip of each branch.

Maggie stood back to stare at the tree. She fluffed out a few branches, looked at it from various angles, and decided it was as good as it was going to get. She looked over to see how her fire was going, and it was blazing. Two down and two to go. She turned on her stereo. She rooted around for her Christmas album and pressed a button. The sound of "Jingle Bells" flooded the room. Hero perked up, did a crazy dance, then leapt up and onto the back of the sofa, where he hissed and snarled. Maggie turned down the volume, and the fat cat immediately relaxed and went to sleep.

Three down and one to go, meaning it was now time to decorate the tree. Another trip back to the walk-in closet for the ornament. Ornament, as in *one* ornament—a single, solitary ornament. It was all she ever decorated her tree with. There were no heirloom Christmas balls, no tinkling bells, no fluffy angels, and no star on top of the tree.

Maggie swiped at her eyes as she reached up for the old cardboard boot box on the top shelf where she kept the ornament stored year after year. Her hands were trembling as she tried to smooth out the creases in the old box, to no avail. She carried it over to the sofa where Hero was sleeping and sat down to open it. So many layers of tissue and bubble wrap. Anyone watching Maggie would have thought there was a priceless, fragile treasure underneath all the layers of tissue.

Maggie peeled away the tissue and stared down at the Santa she'd made when she was only ten years old. It was made from an empty toilet-paper roll and was covered in red, black, and white cotton balls that Miss Roland had supplied. Over the years, she'd had to get out her glue gun to keep the colored balls intact. How well she remembered the hours that she, along with her entire class, had spent dyeing the white cotton balls red and black and waiting for days for the balls to dry before they could glue them onto the paper holder.

Maggie recalled how happy she'd been the day Miss Roland, her teacher, said it was time to finish their Santas and glue all the cotton balls in place. She was so excited when Miss Roland praised her for not getting the Elmer's glue on the fluffy red and black cotton balls like the other kids. Miss Roland was always stingy with praise, and Maggie had reveled in it that day. She could hardly wait to get home with her Santa so her mother could see it, and she actually got a stomachache. She felt even worse when her mother smiled and hung it on the back of the tree, out of sight.

Maggie leaned back into the depths of the sofa and let the tears flow. If she hadn't gotten that stomachache that day, if she'd gone straight out to the bus, she wouldn't be sitting here crying like she was. If only . . .

Chapter 3

Nikki Quinn fished around in her pocket for her key chain, where she kept a spare key to Maggie's kitchen door. Maggie had a key to Nikki's house, too, in case of an emergency. She let herself in and stood stock-still when she heard Bing Crosby's mellow voice singing "White Christmas." She looked around, a frown building on her face. She felt something brush against her ankles and saw Hero.

"Hey, Hero. How's it going this morning?" Like the big fat cat was going to answer her.

Nikki called out as she walked through the kitchen out to the hall and into the family room, where she saw Maggie crying on the sofa. "Maggie, what's wrong?" Nikki said, rushing to her friend and neighbor.

Maggie looked up, stunned to see Nikki standing in front of her. She wiped her eyes on the sleeve of her sweatshirt. "I didn't hear you come in. What's going on? Is something wrong?"

"That was my question to you, Maggie. It's eight o'clock on a Saturday morning, and you're crying. Not to mention you put up your Christmas tree and are playing Christmas music. You don't usually do that till the weekend after Thanksgiving. So, I'll ask again, what's wrong?"

Maggie swiped at her eyes again. "Nothing. I just thought

I'd get an early start this year. You know how good I am at procrastinating. As you can see, I'm all done. I just have to hang my Santa on the tree. Then Ted and I are supposed to go to brunch at that new eatery on the main drag that everyone is saying such good things about. What brings you over here so early?"

Nikki wasn't buying Maggie's story for a minute. "Jack and I are heading out to our new digs. I just wanted to ask you to keep an eye on the house till Jack Sparrow moves in next week. We put all the lights on timers, to go on at five o'clock. We locked everything up tight. You know where we keep everything, so if Sparrow needs something, he'll most likely call on you. Like the snowblower and all the winter stuff."

"Sure. No problem. You excited to move into Nellie's farmhouse?"

"I am. I think Jack is more excited. We can ride every morning and exercise Nellie's horses. We'll be closer to Myra and Annie out there. Sometimes, I really hate driving all the way out there. Going into the District once a week will do it for me from here on in. I think I'm going to love living out there. Ah . . . Maggie, I'm a good listener. Do you want to talk about it? I know something is wrong, so don't push me away, okay? Talk to me. Get whatever it is off your chest. That's what friends are for."

Maggie fingered the Santa in her hand. She held it up for Nikki to get a better look at her creation. "I made this when I was ten years old. The day I finished it, I was so excited I made myself sick. I almost missed the bus."

"Why?" Nikki asked. "I mean, why did you almost miss the bus?"

Maggie bit down on her lower lip. "My mother didn't think my Santa was as beautiful as I did. She hung it on the *back* of the tree. You know, it wasn't easy making this ornament. First, we had to dye the cotton balls and let them dry. It took days for them to dry. I was so careful not to get glue on the colored balls. Miss Roland complimented me. She was my favorite teacher. She used to sub for my class, but that year she was my full-time teacher. She liked the stories I wrote in class, and told me that someday I was going to be a writer. Do you believe that?"

Nikki had no idea where all this was going, so she just nodded and said, "And look at you now. You are a writer. I bet Miss Roland is proud of you. Did you stay in touch?"

"When my dad was transferred to California, I took only two things with me, this ornament and my pillow. That's sad, don't you think?"

"Not really, Maggie. Why take a bunch of junk and shove it somewhere? You took what meant the most to you. Some people don't take anything. The past is past, and it's all about moving forward."

"We moved around a lot, with my dad in the military. We were supposed to move in October of the year I was ten, but something went awry with my dad's orders, and we didn't move till two days after Christmas that year."

"It's hard to make friends when you move around, and it's even harder to adjust to a new school," Nikki said. "Did you get to say good-bye to everyone? You said you moved two days after Christmas, so school was out."

"Good-byes are sad. The answer is, no, I didn't. I didn't want to move. Miss Roland was the best teacher I had ever had. God, how I loved that woman. That year was her first year teaching full-time. She wasn't pretty or anything. Actually, she was very plain, but she was always neat. Funny how, as a kid of ten, I could tell that. She had a clubfoot. She wore this ugly built-up shoe and had to drag her foot along. The boys in class used to make fun of her. I never did. I swear to God, I never did."

"I would never think that for a nanosecond, Maggie."

Bing Crosby was now crooning "Silent Night." Nikki wished she could turn the stereo off, but every instinct in her body warned her not to move or do anything that would interfere with Maggie's pouring her heart out. "We all know children can be cruel sometimes."

"Even adults. As young as I was, I knew that even the janitors made fun of her. I told my mother, and she told me to mind my own business, because I was just a kid, and she didn't want to be called into school. She had more important things to do, like play cards and drink wine with the other military wives. I never really got along with my mother. Did I ever tell you that, Nikki?"

"I kind of suspected it when you never talked about your parents. But you weathered it all."

"No, I didn't. I'm just a good actress."

Nikki blinked. "Talk to me, Maggie. Get it off your chest. Whatever it is that is torturing you, it's time to lay it to rest. I'll keep your confidence. You know that. Sometimes, if you tell just one person, it feels like you've taken a load of bricks off your shoulders. I won't judge you, Maggie. I promise."

Maggie raised her head to stare into Nikki's eyes. Nikki thought she'd never seen a more tortured, miserable human being in her life.

"You see, that's the problem. *I should be judged.*"

"For what, Maggie? What happened to make you think and say that?"

Maggie sat up straighter, squared her shoulders, and took a deep breath.

Dean Martin replaced Bing Crosby and was warbling about being home for Christmas as Nikki waited for whatever it was that Maggie was going to say next.

"It was the last day before Christmas break. We'd finished our Santas that very morning. We'd started on them after Thanksgiving. We'd worked in shifts, with dyeing the balls and setting them out to dry, then fluffing them out and finally gluing them. There were thirty kids in my class. That's why it took so long to finish them. I don't know why I was so excited or what it was about this, but I was," she said, holding up the toilet-roll Santa. "And, of course, Christmas was just around the corner, and we were going to be moving. Again.

"I don't know what it was about Miss Roland, but I adored her. It was her first year teaching full-time. I remember she used to sub a day or so a week. Over the years, I tried to figure out how old she was that year, and I decided she was two or three years out of college. I hated looking at her foot. I really did. And I tried not to, but I was a kid. Anyway, it was about two forty-five, and class was about to be dismissed. I had a bus to catch, like all the rest of the kids. My bus left at three-oh-five, so I thought I had time, but I started feeling sick the minute the bell rang. I had a Timex watch, and I knew how to tell time, so I waved to Miss Roland and ran to the bathroom, not sure if I was going to be sick or not.

"I was sick. I cleaned myself up and left the bathroom. Everyone was gone, and it was real quiet. I looked at my watch, and I could see my bus moving up the line. Then I heard this noise, this sound, like someone crying or moaning. It was coming from the supply room two doors up from the girls' bathroom. I looked in and saw Miss Roland lying on the floor. Her clubfoot looked real funny, the way it was positioned. I asked her if she had fallen, and she asked me to help her. I didn't know what to do. I started to holler and shout for someone, and one of the janitors, the son of the older one, came out into the hall. I said, 'Miss Roland fell and needs help.' I saw my bus move up to the number one spot, so I had to run. I knew if I missed the bus, I would have a five-mile walk, because my mother would be too drunk to come pick me up. I ran out to get the bus.

"That night I told my dad what happened, and he said he would check to see if Miss Roland was okay. She wasn't okay, he told me the next day. She was in the hospital. Then he said she wouldn't be teaching anymore. It took me years to figure it all out. I tried to find her, Nikki, not when I was a kid, but later in life. I never did. It was like she had dropped off the face of the earth. I should have stayed with her, even if I missed my bus. The office was closed and locked, and that's where the phone was. I left her there and ran out. *I left her there!*"

"Oh, Maggie, how awful for you. I am so sorry that happened. You were just a child at the time. There was nothing you could have done. You do know that, right? And you told the janitor's son. There was nothing else you could have done. Don't you see that?"

"What I see now is that this son is the one who did whatever happened to her. I asked her attacker to help her. That's what I did. No one else was in the building. I was just a kid, and no one was going to believe anything I said. I guess I instinctively knew that somehow."

"Oh, Maggie, you can't know that for certain. Did you ever hear what happened to the janitors?"

"At that time? I don't know. Christmas was just two days away, and then, two days after Christmas, we moved to California. When I finally, years later, started looking into it, the little school had closed. There was no way for me to get hold of any records to find out what the janitor's son's name was or his father's name. I wasn't a reporter then. Didn't know the first thing about how to find out information. Now, when I do know how, I come up blank."

"You're blaming yourself for all of this, aren't you?"

Maggie nodded. "Wouldn't you if you were in my place?"

Nikki nodded. "Okay, here's what we're going to do, Maggie."

"What?"

"We're going to find your Miss Roland. Tomorrow we'll present this to the Sisters and the boys, and we'll get right on it. How does that sound?"

The stereo suddenly went silent.

Nikki sighed with relief. "I think you should hang up your ornament. And may I say, it is one beautiful ornament, made by a very caring ten-year-old little girl who grew up to be one of my very best friends in the whole world. Now, run upstairs and wash your face and get ready to go to brunch with Ted. You are now in good hands. Oh, this is going to be the very best Christmas in your whole life. I guarantee it!"

The two women hugged one another. A promise was a promise.

"See ya tomorrow. Keep your eye on my house now."

Maggie smiled through her tears as she gave Nikki a thumbs-up as she walked out the front door.

Maggie stared through her tears at the colored lights twinkling on her Christmas tree. She continued to smile as Hero investigated the lower branches by swatting at them. When one of them bounced back and smacked him in the snoot, he scurried to Maggie and leapt into her arms. She laughed out loud.

Fingering the red satin ribbon attached to the Santa hat, Maggie looked for just the right branch, then nestled her treasured ornament perfectly front and center. She stood back to look at it. "I think it's perfect, Hero. Just perfect. I think I might have a good day, after all. Nikki's right. I'm in good hands now."

Maggie reached out to touch the cotton-ball Santa. "I'm going to find you, Miss Roland. And I'm going to give you the best Christmas of your life, and that's a promise from me to you. My gift to you. Merry Christmas, Miss Roland." She was glad there was no one in the room but Hero to hear the sob that caught in her throat. She crossed her fingers the way she had when she was ten years old that she could make good on her promise.

Thirty minutes later, Maggie had changed into a pair of warm gray flannel slacks and a cherry-red turtleneck sweater. She was drinking coffee while she waited for Ted to arrive. She'd banked the fire, filled Hero's water bowl, and set down a small bowl with some dry cat food in case she stayed out for more than a few hours. With Ted, you never knew. Ted's idea of a shopping Saturday was walking through hardware stores, looking for the newest and latest gadget to make owning a home easier. She didn't get it, since Ted lived in an apartment, but she didn't say anything, because eventually all the gadgets found their way into her garage.

Maggie was singing "Jingle Bells" for the tenth time when Ted bounded through the kitchen door. "I could see from the street that you put your tree up already. What got into you to do it this early?" he asked curiously as he stared at the woman he loved more than life itself.

"You know what, Ted? It's a long story, and tomorrow out at the farm, I'll go through it all for everyone. Right now, I just want to go outside and walk in the fresh air. Where are we going, by the way?"

"I made a reservation at the Mellow Mushroom, that new café everyone is talking about. Don't you remember? Then I thought we'd take a spin through Finnegan's Hardware Store. We should get some rock salt. You have only half a bag left over from last year. They deliver, so we won't have to lug it around. And didn't you say you needed some glue sticks for your glue gun?"

"You remember my saying that?" Maggie asked in surprise. Ted had a memory like an elephant.

"C'mon, let's hit the road. By the way, how many ornaments did you put on the tree this year?"

"Just one. But you know what, Ted? One is just enough."

Ted laughed. Outside, in the brisk November air, the couple held hands as they walked down the street.

Maybe it was going to turn out to be a good day, after all.

Chapter 4

Maggie Spritzer felt like she was on top of the world. Her very own private world, that is. The reporter instincts that she always relied on were telling her that her long-held secret was now out in the open and that only good things would follow. Her gut also told her that her Sisters never failed on a mission. Throw in the Christmas season, and she was as good as home free.

Already her shoulders felt lighter now that she'd unburdened her secret to Nikki, who had then informed the entire gang that for the first time since they had banded together as the Vigilantes, they had a Christmas mission, and had said, "You all know how much we all love Christmas."

Humming "Jingle Bells," her favorite upbeat holiday tune, Maggie tripped her way to the war room, where the others awaited her. She was late today because Hero had had a hair ball stuck in his throat, and she'd had to run him to the twenty-four-hour emergency clinic. All was well now, and Hero was out for the count and sleeping peacefully on her pillow. She'd called Nikki and explained and told the others to start without her.

Her peers looked at her, questions in their eyes because each and every one of them was an animal lover. She assured them Hero was fine and was sleeping soundly when she left.

"We'll bring you up to date, dear," Myra said. "Actually, there isn't much to bring you up to date on, but here is what we have at the moment. Your teacher, one Miss Alma Roland, obviously doesn't believe in social media. She is nowhere to be found. Abner is scouring colleges and universities, but he has had no luck to this point in time. Charles is looking into alumni reunions. Even if Miss Roland gave up teaching, there would still be a record of her somewhere. People simply do not drop off the face of the earth, unless they are those the Vigilantes have made arrangements for. Someone, somewhere, has to know her. Or know of her."

Annie doodled on a yellow pad in front of her. "It is possible she got married and has a new name. Abner is trying to hack into the Social Security database but so far has not come up with anything. We *will* find her, Maggie. It just might not be today or tomorrow," Annie said.

"Think, Maggie. Is there anything you might have forgotten to mention to Nikki? Even if you think it's not important or silly. Any little thing might help us," Isabelle said.

Maggie's face scrunched up. "It was so long ago. I was only ten. Actually, I had just turned ten. Miss Roland told the best stories. Instead of circle time, she would tell us a story. Then, just when the story was getting good, she'd stop and make us come up with an ending. The kids liked that better than hearing a story being read from a book. We would all come up with a different ending. She said one time she was going to write a children's book. I remember that."

"Where did she live? Do you know?" Yoko asked.

Maggie shook her head. "I took the bus to school, and she was always in the room when I got there. I don't even know if she had a car. But how would she have driven with a clubfoot? It was her right foot, too. I do remember that."

"Wait a minute! We should be looking into that. She would have had to wear a special kind of built-up shoe. We need to look into places that do that sort of thing," Kathryn said.

"I'm on it," Charles shouted from the dais. "I can check every orthopedic manufacturer out there."

"Maggie, I know you were just a kid, but did you get the feeling your teacher came from that area or from somewhere else? Like, did she talk about growing up there, anything like that?" Jack asked.

Maggie shook her head no.

"What about orthopedic doctors?" Dennis asked. "We could start in the town where Maggie went to school, then broaden our search. I can do that."

"Do it, then, young man," Charles shouted again from the dais. Everyone smiled. It was good to have Charles back in the fold. He had been gone too long.

"Hospitals," Espinosa said. "I say that because I'm thinking about the way she would walk. It would put pressure on her hips. I'm no doctor, but I've seen people like your teacher and the way they walk, tilted to the side, for want of a better explanation. She had to have a doctor."

"I'll take that on," Ted said. "I've got some sources I can call."

"Maggie, you said your dad told you Miss Roland was taken to the hospital that day. Maybe we can get some information from that particular hospital. Or from her insurance carrier," Myra said. "By any chance, do you know the name of the hospital?"

Maggie shook her head. "We lived in the town of Albright. It was small, and the military base was close by. We lived off base. The school was very small, K through sixth grade. Only military kids went there. There had to be a hospital there, or if not in the town of Albright, then close by."

"Okay. I can check that," Alexis said as she tapped furiously on her laptop.

Annie reached across the table for the grungy old shoe box that had held their secrets over the years. "Not to change the subject, but we need to put our checks in this box. We all voted before you got here, Maggie, that all the monies would go to your Christmas project. I want you all to think about that poor woman and what she has endured, and I hope you can all be generous. So, get out your checkbooks!"

Ever practical, Dennis raised his hand. "What if she won't take it? Some people are too proud to accept charity. Then what do we do?"

Annie sniffed. She hated it when someone threw a wrench into a plan. "Look around, young man. Do you see how many of us there are here? Miss Roland is just one little lady. Maggie did say she was tiny. I think we can convince her that it isn't charity and that she should accept our generosity."

"Okay," Dennis said agreeably. "That makes sense. I guess," he mumbled under his breath.

"I heard that, Dennis. Of course it makes sense, because I'm the one who said it," Annie snapped. Dennis grinned and went back to tapping the gizmo in front of him. Annie eyed it suspiciously. A techie she was not.

Both Myra and Annie leaned back in their chairs as they watched their chicks write out their checks, fold them neatly, and slip them into the old shoe box. They didn't know it then, but on the message line of each check the guys and girls all wrote, "Merry Christmas."

"I have a good feeling about this. What about you, Myra?" Annie said.

"I do, too, Annie. I don't know if I want us to succeed

more for Maggie to take that burden off her chest or for the faceless Miss Roland and the life she's had to lead since that awful day. Maggie will be devastated if we can't find her."

"I hesitate to remind you that the word *failure* is not in our vocabulary."

"I know that, Annie. We all know that. Now, having said that, there is a first time for everything. Obviously, Miss Roland was severely traumatized. If she went off the grid, it is entirely possible that she changed her name and moved. She could have opted to do the kind of work where she didn't have to produce her Social Security number. As you know, that happens a lot. Some people can hide forever. Sometimes in plain sight. Rest assured that we will leave no stone unturned in our quest to help Maggie."

"I think I have something!" Alexis said, waving her arms about. "There is a hospital in a town called St. Stephens. It's nine miles from Albright and is a one-hundred-bed hospital. It serves the tricounty area where Maggie went to school."

Abner was off his stool in a nanosecond, peering over Alexis's shoulder. "Good work, Alexis. I might be able to crack their firewall. Send that to me as an e-mail, okay?" He was back on his stool in a second, his fingers poised to pounce on the keyboard. All eyes turned to Abner and stayed there, transfixed on his fingers as they flew over the keyboard.

Maggie was chewing her cuticles until Ted reached over and took her hand away from her mouth.

No one noticed Charles stepping down off the dais. He leaned over and whispered to Myra that he and Fergus were going upstairs to start dinner. "There's nothing more I can do for the moment. I'm waiting for responses to all my inquiries. Dinner will be ready in ninety minutes." Myra nodded.

Fergus squeezed Annie's shoulder. She reached up and patted his hand.

If there was one thing Jack Emery hated in life, it was being inactive and silent. One eye on Charles's and Fergus's backs, the other on Abner, Jack leaned toward Harry and whispered, "You guys ready for your trip to China tomorrow? Whatever you do, do not forget to take Lily's presents out of my car. You have to Skype me the minute you give Lily Julie Wyatt's gift. She took this great picture of Cooper rocking her granddaughter's cradle. She even made the frame. Tell Lily the paw prints are Cooper's, just for her."

Harry smiled. Harry never smiled except when it came to his daughter, Lily. Just saying her name to him made his eyes light up, and he would grin from ear to ear. Then, after the grin, he'd just smile.

"Lily never asks about Cooper. Yoko and I always bring him up and tell her the latest tidbits that Julie shared with us. She just smiles and says, 'I know, Daddy. I talked to Cooper last night or yesterday or an hour ago.' Something along those lines. Don't look at me like that, Jack. Then she'll tell me something that Julie will tell me two days later. We are never going to figure it out, so let's quit while we're ahead, okay?"

"Um . . . yeah, okay, Harry. Damn it, I want to know how they do that. Kid and a dog . . . He got inside my head that last day before she left. I wanna know, Harry. Stop bullshitting me. You want to know, too, and don't say you don't."

Yoko leaned over and whispered, "No, he doesn't, Jack."

And that was the end of that.

"Okay, ladies and gentlemen, I cracked the hospital records. Believe it or not, that little rural hospital converted all their files and records to computers fifteen years ago. We are good to go." To prove his point, Abner raised his hands, cracked his knuckles, then flexed his fingers for a full five minutes before he lowered his hands to the keyboard. "This might take a little while, because I have to go back so many years. If it's here, I'll find it."

Isabelle preened like a queen at the king's words. This was her man saving the day. That got smiles around the table.

While Abner did what he did best, the others focused on Yoko and Harry and their trip. Mostly, it was about the presents everyone had bought for Lily.

Jack shrugged. "It's a girly thing," he said to the others.

"You should see Lily fence. She even beat out the boys' class. She's at the top of her age class. Her master said she is one of the best that he's ever trained. He said he had only one other student who, at the same age, was as advanced as she is," Harry said, pride ringing in his voice.

"And that student's name is—drumroll please—one Harry Wong! Like father, like daughter!" Yoko said, clipping Harry alongside the head. Harry actually blushed.

"No kidding!" Dennis said. "Wow. That is awesome. You must be so proud, Harry. The best thing in the whole world is being a good dad, and I think you're the best. Oops, that's wrong. I *know* you're the best dad in the whole world."

Harry turned around and gazed at Dennis with a strange look on his face. Dennis started to shake. "Dennis, that is the nicest thing anyone has ever said to me in my entire life. Thank you for saying that."

All Dennis could do was nod, because he didn't trust himself to speak. Harry was . . . Harry was . . . Harry was Harry.

"Heads up, everyone! You may applaud now. The wizard of Pinewood has performed once again!" Abner shouted at the top of his lungs.

Everyone clapped. Maggie ran to stand behind Abner to stare down at his computer. The others followed.

"Okay, people, here it is. I'm printing out copies for everyone, but I'll read to you what her file says. Alma Ann Roland was twenty-four years old when she was admitted to St. Stephens Hospital. She was taken into the emergency room. The doctor of record was James Montgomery. The file says she had been brutally attacked. She also suffered a concussion. Probably from a fall on the tile floor. She had head lacerations, a split lip, and a broken nose. She needed sixteen sutures. She also had two cracked ribs. It says here that she put up a fight. She was in the hospital for seven days, then released.

"Her insurance carrier was Blue Cross of North Carolina. The address where she lived at the time is in the file here. It must be an apartment, because it says she lived in two-B. The apartment complex is called Myler Gardens, and Myler Gardens is in Albright, which we know is where the school was located. Roland was discharged and left the hospital on her own. She was given a prescription for painkillers and the name of a well-known counselor and was told to see her own physician the following week. That physician's name is Hector Morales. That's all, folks."

"That's a lot, actually," Maggie said. "Now we have a starting point. I'm up for going there tomorrow, if it's okay with you, Annie."

"Of course, dear. Whatever it takes. Take Ted, Joseph, and Dennis with you. That way you can all cover quite a bit of ground in the shortest time possible. And now I think our ninety minutes are up, and I'm sure that our dinner is waiting. We can discuss this more after dinner if you like."

Dinner was a boisterous affair now that the gang had something they could sink their teeth into. To Charles's chagrin, business, which was never to be discussed at the dinner table, was the main subject of conversation.

Myra looked her husband square in the eyes and defiantly said, "While you were gone, dear, we all voted on a few changes, and talking business at dinner was one of those changes, so grin and bear it."

Charles grinned because it was an order. Even though he didn't like the new order, he would have cut out his tongue before he said a word.

"It's a wise man who knows when to keep his lip zipped, my friend," Fergus hissed out of the corner of his mouth.

"Amen," Charles said, the smile still plastered on his face.

Chapter 5

"The sign says MYLER GARDENS—APARTMENTS, so I guess this is the place," Ted announced as he turned right, then followed a sign that said VISITOR PARKING.

"Looks like any other apartment complex anywhere in the good old U.S. of A. Seventy-five units, tops," Dennis said as he peered out the window of their airport-obtained rental car.

"The place has been here for a while, that's for sure. But it looks to be maintained," Maggie said as she hopped out of the car and headed for a building that had a small sign by the door that read MANAGEMENT.

A bell tinkled when Maggie opened the door. Two women sat behind desks, one typing on a computer and the other pouring over a ledger of some sort. The ledger reader looked up and asked if she could be of help. She went on to say there were no vacancies, but one would open up, a two-bedroom unit, on March 15. She was a pleasant-looking woman of sixty or so, with fashionable reading glasses.

"Actually, we aren't here to rent. I'm looking for someone who used to live here around twenty-seven years ago. I know that's a long time ago, but any help you can give us would be appreciated," Maggie said.

"Well, that lets me out," the woman whose name tag said her name was Donna Lyme said cheerfully. "My husband and I took over management twelve years ago, when the owners moved to Florida for the warmer weather."

Maggie pulled a face. She could feel anxiety start to build. She knew it was a long shot, but she asked, anyway. "Is there anyone living here now who might possibly have been here back then? The woman we're trying to find is named Alma Roland. She lived in apartment two-B on Magnolia Court."

Donna Lyme pointed to a map on the wall. "Let's see. A staff sergeant, a bachelor from the base, lives in two-B now. He's been here about five years. Ruth Ryder lives in four-B. She's lived here, like, forever. I think someone once said she and her husband moved here when they got married. It would appear she never left. She is a widow. Her apartment is a three-bedroom. I'd love it if she'd move to one of our one-bedroom units, but she won't hear of it. Seems she raised two kids here, in that very apartment, and she isn't leaving. Nice lady, not that I know her that well. We have a nice family mix here.

"In six-B there is a young couple who moved in two years ago. Does that help you? Mrs. Ryder is the only tenant that's been here forever, like I said. The other units have all turned over since my husband and I took over. I can give you directions to Mrs. Ryder's apartment building. She's on the first floor. You can walk from here."

Maggie copied down the instructions and scooted out the door, which Ted was holding for her. "I hope the lady has a good memory," Maggie kept saying over and over as they hurried along a slate walkway, as if the sooner they got to Mrs. Ryder, the more likely she was to remember something.

Espinosa jabbed at the doorbell. They could all hear a

musical chime inside. The door was opened by a tall, thin, gray-haired woman wearing an apron.

"My goodness' sakes, come in, come in. It's cold out there."

The little group entered and stood awkwardly in what was a short hallway or foyer that led into a living room. It looked to be a pretty comfortable room, done up in chintz and maple. And it was neat as a pin; nothing was out of place, except maybe a book and a pair of reading glasses on the coffee table. The place smelled wonderfully of cinnamon and vanilla. Maggie's mouth started to water. She did love sweets.

Maggie rushed to explain why they were there.

"Lord, have mercy. Now, that calls for coffee and some cinnamon buns. Come along, youngsters. We'll eat in the kitchen. I'm a kitchen person, and I like to sit over a nice cup of coffee to do my talking."

Mrs. Ryder proved she could multitask as she set up cups and plates and talked about Alma Roland. "She was the sweetest, kindest young person I've ever met. Such a shame what happened to her. I remember it like it was yesterday. All of us who lived here back then did what we could to help her, but in the end, it wasn't enough. She said she had to leave, but she would stay in touch. I think she meant what she said at the time, but she never followed through. That young woman carried such a burden."

"Tell us what happened and what you remember," Maggie said, leaning forward so as not to miss a word once they were all seated around the kitchen table.

"To begin with, I and everyone here at the time were surprised when so little coverage was given to the whole thing. But then, that's the military for you. It was their school where it all took place. By the same token, Alma really didn't want to talk about it. She was like a zombie. Strangers who didn't know her the way we did seemed only to focus on her clubfoot and say that was the reason she was attacked. People can be so very cruel to those who have handicaps. Alma was very sensitive about her handicap, even if she didn't talk about it.

"We all went to see her in the hospital. When I say 'we,' I mean three other neighbors who Alma knew, plus myself. We took flowers, books, and candy. She was . . . Today the term would be, I guess, *zoned out*. After about a half hour, she asked us to leave so she could go to sleep. We did, and we all cried on the way home. She looked so pitiful, lying in that hospital bed. She stayed in the hospital about a week, maybe a day or two longer. She locked herself in her apartment and would open the door only to me because I was taking her food.

"It was so sad. She'd decorated her apartment for Christmas. It looked so pretty and bright and cheerful. She had presents under the tree for me and the neighbors. The decorations on her tree were all made by the children in school. She treasured those because she said innocents had made them. She even had a fresh balsam wreath on her front door. I wanted her to talk about what had happened, not because I was being nosy. I just wanted to help the poor little thing. She was an orphan, you know, no family. She told me once that when she was born, her parents didn't like that she was deformed, so they threw her away. They just threw that baby away. Who does such a thing? Who?" Mrs. Ryder asked, outrage written all over her face.

Her voice was so choked, Maggie could barely get the words out of her mouth. "What did she tell you happened to her?"

"She said she was one of the last to leave the building that day, and she was returning something to the supply room. She said someone came up behind her, threw a rag over her head, and knocked her around. She had to have a lot of stitches, and they had to shave all her pretty curly hair. That broke my heart to see her half bald. One of the neighbors knitted a hat for her, and she did wear it."

Maggie felt like she was going to black out any second. She gripped the edge of the table and held on for dear life.

"What else did she say?" Ted asked gruffly, his eyes on Maggie.

"She said one of her students saw her lying on the floor and tried to help her, but all she could say to the little girl was, 'Go get help.' She said the child was terrified . . . then something about the bus. Anyway, she said the janitor's son found her and called for an ambulance. Or his father did. The boy just helped his father at the school when he got home from school. I think he was a senior that year. I don't know where I heard that, or maybe it was in the paper. That's pretty much it. Alma simply didn't want to talk about what happened. Who could blame her? I tried saying all the right things, but while she heard the words, she didn't *hear* them, if you know what I mean."

"When did she leave? You said she left," Dennis said.

"About two weeks later. She went to two, maybe three counseling sessions and said she wasn't going back. She said she felt dirty when she left. A few days later, she was gone. She had an old, rickety car, but it did run. She didn't take any of her furniture or bedding. Just her personal things. She left me a lovely, sweet note, thanking me for trying to help her and for being her friend. I cried for days."

In a strangled voice, Maggie said, "I was that little girl. I've been trying to find Miss Roland for years. I *need* to find her, Mrs. Ryder. Do you have any idea where she might have gone?"

"Dear Lord, how awful for you. I wish I could help you, but I don't have any other information to give you. I wish I did."

"What about her friends? Did she have any? Do you know where she went to college?" Espinosa asked.

"She really didn't have any friends to speak of, at least that I knew of. The young people around here at the time liked to party. There was no place for a girl with a clubfoot at a party scene. Alma went to Duke University. On a full scholarship. She didn't have to pay a dime. She worked in the admitting office at Duke to earn spending money. She was so proud of her academic achievements. She told me she graduated second in her class and had a four-point-oh GPA."

"And they never found the person who attacked Miss Roland?" Espinosa asked.

"No. And let me be the first to tell you they didn't look very hard, either. I always thought that the janitor or the son did it, but Alma couldn't identify anyone. Then, when the school term ended, the military closed the school, and the father and his son were out of a job. About a year later, the boy was killed on his motorcycle. There was a big to-do about that in the paper at the time. Drugs and alcohol." She sniffed. "I don't know what happened to the father. I guess the police closed the book on all of it."

Maggie was so sick to her stomach, she wanted to cry. All she could do was stare at the plate of cinnamon buns. She looked down into her coffee cup. She hadn't tasted anything at all.

"Did Miss Roland ever talk about her clubfoot? By that I mean, did she have to go get fitted for a new shoe from time to time? I'm sorry I'm so ignorant on that subject. How does it work? Do you know?" Ted asked.

Mrs. Ryder frowned. "Now that you mention it, yes, she did go somewhere. Let me think." The frown deepened. "I can't absolutely swear to it, but I think there were two places where Alma went. One, I know for sure, was in

Spring Lake, on Bragg Boulevard. I want to say they went out of business, but it might be the other one that closed. The other shop or clinic, whatever it was, was in Fayetteville. And I am virtually certain that one of the two of them closed down. There had been something wrong with the last fitting, and Alma had terrible blisters. She said the shoe felt extra heavy, something about inferior leather. I don't know the name of either place. I'm sorry. I'm sure the one that is still there is in the Yellow Pages. Maybe they would know something about the one that closed down."

Maggie knew that was all they were going to get. She stood up, anxious to head to either place to see what else they could find out. "Thank you so much for your help, Mrs. Ryder. If we locate Miss Roland, I'll ask her to call you." She handed over one of her business cards, then scribbled her cell phone number on the back. "Please, if you think of anything, call me, even if it's the middle of the night." Mrs. Ryder said she would do that.

Mrs. Ryder swiped at the corner of her eye. "If you find Alma, tell her I have all her Christmas decorations. I packed up what she left behind. I thought she might come back for them someday. Wouldn't it be nice if she showed up at Christmastime? Now, that would be what I call a Christmas miracle."

Maggie sniffed and tried not to cry. "That's what I would call it, too," she said in a soft whisper.

"We're going to find her, Maggie," Dennis said once they had all stepped outside. "I promise."

"Okay, Dennis. That's good enough for me."

Mrs. Ryder waved from her doorway. As an afterthought, she called out, "I know it's way too early, but Merry Christmas."

*   *   *

It didn't take long to discover that the Bootery, the shoe clinic Alma Roland had used in Spring Lake during that time, had gone out of business. A discount cosmetic emporium was located where the Bootery used to be. All thanks to Dennis and his magic fingers and social media.

"We might as well head to Fayetteville. Find us an address, Dennis," Ted said as he pulled into traffic.

"There is only one place that might, I say might, be what we're looking for. It's called Step & Step. It says it caters to proper shoe fitting and everything is custom made and they use only the finest leather." Dennis rattled off an address, which Espinosa fed into the GPS system.

"Twenty-seven years is a long time to keep records," Maggie grumbled. "I'm not feeling hopeful here."

"Stop being so negative," Dennis said. "Look. They're hanging Christmas lights up ahead. I bet it's a pretty town during the holidays, with all the colored lights." If he thought that was going to cheer Maggie up, he was dead wrong. He could see that her eyes were leaking. Like a little kid, she bent over and wiped her eyes on the sleeve of her jacket as the robotic voice of the GPS instructed Ted where to turn. He wished there was something he could do or say to make Maggie feel better, but his heart and his gut warned him to leave well enough alone.

Fifteen minutes later, Ted made a turn based on the robotic voice's instructions and said, "We're here. Street parking. Small shop. Looks like it's been here forever. We just might get lucky, Maggie," Ted said, trying his best to sound cheerful as he pulled into a parking space.

They bailed out of the car the moment Ted turned off the engine. Maggie was the first one through the door of the shop. The overpowering smell of new leather and shoe polish washed over them. Some kind of buzzer under the floor mat sounded. A man who looked to be in his midthirties, wearing a rubber apron, appeared from a back room. His hands were rough and callused. Maggie got right to the point.

"Well, now, miss, that was a long time ago. My dad ran the shop back then with his brother. They're both retired now. The records here at the shop only go back, I want to say, fifteen years. When I took it over, I hired some whiz kid from the military base to input all the files into the computer. My dad took a lot of the old ones home and put them in the basement because I needed the room for a new leather machine, and the file cabinets took up too much room. Then a pipe broke in his house, and the basement flooded. He chucked it all. Just a big, soggy mess."

"Can you call your father and ask him if he remembers Alma Roland?"

"Of course. He has a memory like a steel trap." He held out his hand to Ted and said, "Josh Appleton." Everyone held out a hand to shake his. "The phone's in the back. Have a seat while I make the call."

Maggie paced the small shop and for the first time noticed a decorated Christmas tree on a stand in the corner. It was a live tree, which surprised her even more. And it was decorated with toy cars. Obviously, Josh Appleton had a son or possibly a nephew who liked toy cars. So at least she wasn't the only one who was getting a jump on the holidays. The thought left her even sadder than she was before she walked into the shoe shop.

The others watched their friend, wishing there was something they could do or say, but they knew that Maggie would rebel and lash out at them if they stepped over her invisible line.

"Miss Spritzer, my dad said he doesn't recall the name, and he really doesn't recall the young woman. What he did say was he only had two female customers back during the time in question. You might not know this, but more males are born with clubfeet than females. What he did remember was that both those females were referrals from the Bootery. That was our competition back then, but before my time here in the shop.

"Dad said they closed down because a shoe they made for a customer did the customer so much damage, the person had to have his foot amputated. The firm couldn't come back from that kind of bad publicity. So while my dad used the word *referral*, I don't think he meant it in the true sense of the word. Like I said, my dad is pretty sharp, and if that's all he can remember, then that's all there is. I'm sorry."

"Where do you think she might have gone?" Maggie asked.

Josh Appleton shrugged. "This is a dying business. By the time my son is ready to hit the job market, there will be no need for a shop like this. I can't even begin to guess where she might have gone. Orthopedic doctors these days have their own shops—they call them clinics—where they do the special shoes themselves."

Maggie nodded and tried to smile. "Is that the same son whose little cars are on the Christmas tree over there?"

Appleton laughed. "My wife is a Christmas fanatic. November first, we are up and decorated. Our house is all done. Teddy loves the holidays, so she wants to get the most out of them. Two full months. What she never tells anyone is that by the end of November, she has to take down the trees and put up new ones because the old ones dry out no matter how much you water them." Maggie did smile then, a genuine smile.

"Plus, my wife gets to take Teddy back out to the Christmas tree farm to pick out a second tree and watch the men cut it down. I really am sorry I can't help you. I hope you find your friend. What I can do this week is ask around at our monthly chamber of commerce meeting to see if any of the owners or businesspeople remember your Miss Roland."

Ted nodded and handed over his business card. "Call anytime. Thanks for your help."

Back at the rental car, the foursome climbed in and sat looking at one another.

"What is our next move, people?" Dennis asked.

"I don't think we have a next move," Espinosa grumbled. "There's no point in going to the local hospital, since they won't tell us anything, because of the privacy laws. Abner will have better luck hacking into the system. No sense going to the police station. Jack already obtained the police report. They'd just stonewall us, anyway. We might as well head for the airport and go home, unless you guys have a better idea."

The guys looked at Maggie, who simply nodded.

Chapter 6

Nikki looked across the breakfast table at her husband, Jack, and smiled. Cyrus and his pups romped through the farmhouse, yipping and yapping at their new surroundings, which they were just getting used to. Jack laughed out loud as one of the pups skidded across the tile floor, a look of stunned surprise on its face.

"I love it out here, Jack. Tell me the truth. Do you love it as much as I do, or did you agree to move out here just to please me? I know you're a city boy, and for the most part, I am a city girl. But you can't beat the beauty and the peace and quiet out here. We can ride every day, we can watch the grass grow, and the dogs have acres to run, even though they stay close to home."

"I do. I will tell you what bothers me the most about our lives. Technically, we've retired from our lives as lawyers. I still want to practice law but not right now. I like what we're doing, which is *breaking the law,* if we're being honest."

Nikki reached for Jack's hand and squeezed it. "Weigh the good we do against the bad out there. That's how we have to look at it. We're all okay with it. We all know and recognize that one day it will somehow all come crashing down on us. We signed on for whatever happens. I'm not about to switch up now. I think both of us will know when our time is up and will act accordingly. Now that we've put that to rest, I think we should follow in Maggie's footsteps and get an early start on our Christmas decorating. This old farmhouse has so many possibilities. I want to gussy it up from top to bottom, and then I want us to have a big Christmas party. Let's go cut down a Christmas tree! Today is the perfect day—it's flurrying out, and it's *cold*. The dogs can help."

Jack grinned. Like he would say no to anything his wife suggested. "Sounds like a plan. Guess we need to dig out our long underwear."

Nikki giggled. "I got it out last night. Just let me get our dinner started in the Crock-Pot, and I'm your girl. How does that West African peanut soup I made last month sound? I'll load it with shrimp, and when we get back, I'll bake the bread. I mixed it up before you came downstairs, and it will be good to go once we get back with our tree."

"What's for dessert?"

"Twinkies. Your absolute favorite." Nikki laughed.

"Nik, I just had a thought. Won't Yoko be upset if we cut down our own tree? We always get everything from her nursery."

"Jack! Did you forget Yoko and Harry are in China?"

"You know what? I did forget there for a minute."

"I'm so far ahead of you, Jack, you are never going to catch up," Nikki teased. "I called Yoko's nursery manager, and today they are going to deliver the balsam wreaths. I ordered twenty, complete with red satin ribbons. It's your job to hang them on all the doors and windows. Oh, this is going to be such a great Christmas."

"Maggie . . ."

"We're going to make that happen, too."

Jack wasn't so sure, but he nodded. If his wife said it was so, then it was so. It was that simple.

While he stood a few minutes later under the steaming water in the shower, Jack relived all the phone calls of the night before with Abner, Ted, and Myra. He wondered how Nikki could be so sure that they would find Maggie's old teacher after so many years. While Maggie and the boys had made a little headway, all things considered, they still had nothing to go by in their search to locate the elusive Alma Roland.

As he toweled himself dry, Jack recalled Abner's frustration last night, when he said there was no bank account in Alma Roland's name to be found anywhere. And there was no record that she had filed an income tax form in twenty-six years. She had filed one for the last year that she worked at the military school and not another one since. Even though they had her Social Security number, nothing was showing up in any database. How had she survived? Maybe the question they all should be asking was, did she survive? He made a mental note to ask Abner if he'd checked the obituaries. Knowing Abner, he was certain he would have already done that. Where was Alma Roland?

Jack pulled on his long underwear and a pair of corduroy trousers, thermal socks guaranteed to keep his feet warm even in subzero temperatures, stout Timberland boots, and two sweaters. He felt like a lumberjack as he made his way downstairs. Nikki was waiting at the bottom.

"I made fresh coffee. See you in a bit."

Instead of heading for the kitchen and coffee, Jack wandered through the rooms of his new home, Nellie and Elias's beloved homestead. He loved the old farmhouse; loved the carved moldings; loved the worn, shiny pine floors, the floor-to-ceiling paned windows, and the fieldstone fireplaces, of which there were six, all of them big enough to roast an ox. He knew that he and Nikki would be happy here. Not that they hadn't been happy at their house in Georgetown. They had been, but this was different. This house had character. People had been born here, had died here, had raised families and lived and loved. And now he and Nikki had been given the chance to do the same thing, and today was the start of it.

Getting ready for Christmas. The thought excited him. Cyrus appeared out of nowhere and nudged his leg. "We're putting down our roots, boy. This is home now."

Cyrus yipped happily as he sprinted out of the room to corral one of his unruly offspring. Jack laughed. Yep, this was home.

In the kitchen, Jack checked the fireplace. He laid a pile of maple logs on the grate. When they returned, all he would have to do was strike a match. Then he realized that he and Nikki would also be in the family room, putting up the tree, so he trotted off, laid a fire, and stood back to admire his handiwork. *Not bad for a city boy. Not bad at all.*

Abner Tookus knuckled his eyes. He was bone tired. And he was frustrated. Not to mention downright angry. He was supposed to be the go-to guy with all things computerized, and here he was, with zip to report. He looked down at what the others called his magic fingers and winced. "Magic, my ass," he mumbled. Nothing in his makeup allowed for failure. Nothing. No one—he didn't care who it was—could drop off the face of the earth and not leave some kind of footprint. Not in this digital age.

Abner swiveled around when he heard a loud plopping sound. "What are you doing, Isabelle?"

"I'm getting a head start on Christmas, like Maggie did. Nikki called earlier and said she and Jack were doing the same thing, but they're going out on their very own property to cut down a real, live tree. I'm going to put up this ratty artificial tree you have, and I'm going to decorate this place. You want to help?"

Did he? No, not really. Abner grappled for an excuse. "It isn't even Thanksgiving yet. The Christmas season doesn't start till the day after Thanksgiving."

"I know that. I'm hoping that doing it early, like Maggie and Nikki are doing, will give me some insight somehow so we can help Maggie." Intuitive as she was, Isabelle looked at her husband and said, "You can't find her, can you?"

Abner rubbed at his eyes again. He needed some Visine. And he needed some sleep, not to mention a shower and some clean clothes. "No, I can't find her—as much as I hate to admit it. Isabelle, knowing what you know about Alma Roland, and if you were in her shoes, what would you have done at that time? Think about it. Where would you have gone? What would you have done?"

"That's not really a fair question, Abner. That was a different time. People were different back then. They had prejudices, hang-ups, and they worried about things we don't give a second thought to today. For instance, couples living together who aren't married. Prenuptial agreements, having babies out of wedlock. Today no one cares about things like that.

"Now if you absolutely, positively need me to give you an answer, I think I would have looked for a safe harbor. Someplace I could go to where, hopefully, no one would know what happened to me. Or, at the very least, they wouldn't judge me. At that point in time, I would imagine Alma Roland would have wanted to hide from the world. And don't forget, she was carrying that baggage of her clubfoot. You said she was an orphan. Maybe she went back there to that orphanage, to the only home she knew. Maybe she went to a convent and became a nun. If they took her in and let her live there for room and board, and she helped out, then there would be no reason for a bank account or filing her income tax returns. I just don't know. I think that's what I would have done. Now, are you going to help me set up this Christmas tree or not?"

Abner bounded off his chair, crossed the room in three long strides, picked up Isabelle, and swung her around. "Isabelle, my darling, you are beyond a doubt the smartest woman I know, and I love you! That's it! That's it! Hey, honey, you'll figure out how to get that tree up, because you're really smart. I have work to do right now." His dirty clothes, his smelly body, and his tired eyes were forgotten in an instant when Abner sat back down at the computer and started to tap the keys.

Charles Martin watched his wife doodle on a pad at the scarred old oak table in the kitchen. She looked to be a million miles away in her thoughts. He hated it when she was like this. He'd tried tempting her with a BLT, but she'd said she wasn't hungry. He'd then suggested a trip to town to browse the stores, pointing out that the town was already decorated for the holidays and Christmas merchandise was already in the stores. She'd said she wasn't in the mood. He'd offered to drive her over to Nikki and Jack's, but she'd said they were busy settling in and didn't need visitors. As a last resort, he'd offered to call Annie to invite her and Fergus for lunch. She had said that wasn't a good idea but hadn't explained further. All she'd done was turn the paper over and doodle on the blank side.

So, here they sat, staring at one another.

"Want to talk about it, Myra?"

"No. Yes. There really isn't anything to talk about, Charles. Unless you count the fact that we're all stymied. This is not a good thing. We're surrounded by all these fine minds, and I'm including yours and mine among those fine minds, and we cannot find one little lady. We can't even find a clue.

What does that say for us, Charles? Are we slipping? Are we losing our edge? What? Are we going to have to admit to failure? I don't like that word, Charles. And don't you dare tell me that there is a first for everything."

"I wouldn't dream of it, old girl. Nor is that word in my vocabulary. We have a lot of irons in the fire, Myra. We just have to wait for them to get red hot. We will find Alma Roland. Trust me on that. This is just taking us longer than it normally would.

"I know you're worried about Maggie. Don't be. She's a tough little cookie. Speaking of Maggie, I have an idea. Why don't we do what she did and get an early start on Christmas? Let's bundle up and go out to the field and cut down a tree. I can put it up. Then we can call Annie and Fergus and invite them to come over and help us decorate it. I'll make us a nice dinner and . . ."

"Okay, Charles, let's do it. Maybe we should ask Annie and Fergus to go with us to cut down the tree. I'm thinking it will take all of us to do it. We aren't twenty years old anymore."

Charles pretended to be relieved. "I thought you'd never get around to mentioning that. Superb idea. Call Annie while I warm up the pickup and sharpen the ax."

The phone was in Myra's hand before Charles could stop speaking. Annie picked up on the first ring. Annie started to babble immediately.

"Whatever it is you're calling for, the answer is yes. I am going out of my mind here. What are you calling for, by the way?"

Myra told her.

"We'll be there as soon as we can put on our long johns."

Myra was up and off her chair like there was a spring attached to her rear end. She literally ran up the stairs, pulled on her long johns, and added an extra sweater. As Charles said, she was good to go. She barreled down the stairs, whistled for the dogs, then waited by the kitchen door for Annie and Fergus. The dogs were going to love riding in the back of the pickup, a treat Charles had initiated on his return from Spyder Island.

Until now, Myra hadn't realized that it was flurrying. Perfect weather for tromping the fields to cut down a Christmas tree. Absolutely perfect.

The dogs barked shrilly, something they always did when Annie blasted through the gates at ninety miles an hour. She laughed at the fear showing on Fergus's face. You'd think he'd be used to the way Annie drove by now. Obviously not.

Myra opened the door, and the dogs ran to Fergus, who handed out treats from his mackinaw.

Annie wrapped her arms around Myra. "Thank God you called me. I think I was beginning to get a brain freeze. I'm ready. What are you waiting for, Myra?"

Myra laughed. "For you to let go of me, so I can put on my jacket. This is going to be so much fun, Annie, and it's just what we need. Charles said he would cook us a fine dinner while we, I assume, as in you and I, decorate the tree."

"Like old times, eh?" Annie said, linking her arm with Myra's just as Charles rolled up in the farm's old, rusty pickup. Fergus lowered the tailgate, and the dogs leapt up and started to bark. Translation: an adventure was about to unfold.

Chapter 7

Kathryn Lucas almost lost her balance on the escalator as she whirled around at the sound of her name being called. She spotted Alexis Thorne, who was almost at the bottom of the down escalator. "Alexis!" She stepped off and waited while Alexis headed her way.

The two women hugged, as they always did, and immediately started to jabber. They were in Neiman Marcus at the Galleria. Alexis suggested a restaurant where they could go for coffee.

"It's past lunchtime, so we won't have to wait for a table. I haven't had any lunch, and we can grab a sandwich." Kathryn readily agreed, as she, too, had skipped lunch.

"The stores are already decorated," Kathryn said in awe as the two friends walked along.

"Where have you been, Kathryn? The stores have been decorated since Halloween. Oh, I forgot, you are the queen of catalog shoppers. So what are you doing here?"

"Believe it or not, looking for a Christmas present for Bert. I thought I'd get an early start because he is heading to Macao to check out the new casino that Annie opened in China. He's going to be there the whole month of December."

Alexis and Kathryn walked into the restaurant and the hostess immediately seated the two women and handed them a menu.

Kathryn shrugged. "Bert's married to the casino business. Cosmo Cricket is going with him. That means Lizzie and Little Jack are coming east for the holidays and staying with Myra. She's happy about it. Myra, that is."

"You didn't answer my question, Kathryn. Are you okay with Bert going over there for a whole month?"

"Yes and no. I'm staying here in my little house. I have Murphy with me, so I won't be alone. Bert did ask me to go with him, but I said no. I said no mainly because of Maggie, but I've really had enough of Vegas for a while. It gets to you after you've been there too long. I want to help Maggie, if it's possible. Damn, I had no idea everyone was jumping the gun this early for the holiday season. Meaning the stores, the merchandise, all that, plus Christmas music, and it isn't even Thanksgiving. It's kind of disconcerting. Heck, if they don't even wait for Thanksgiving anymore, why not start right after Labor Day? How about the Fourth of July? Let's just have Christmas all year long."

Alexis laughed. "They started early because all those doom-and-gloom financial pundits are predicting a slim shopping season given the poor economy. The retailers want to get the most they can get out of the season. They said Halloween sales were a bust, so they rushed right into Christmas. Everyone in my opinion has lost sight of the true meaning of Christmas. It's just a money thing these days."

Kathryn thought about the cashmere sweater she was going to buy Bert. Mentally, she scaled the sweater down to a tie and matching socks. She felt relieved at her decision.

"I talked to Nikki last night, and she told me that she and Jack are cooking this Thanksgiving. She said she didn't tell Charles yet, but oh, too bad. She's going to call everyone today to invite them. They both want to christen their new home. They positively adore it, by the way."

"I bet they do. All that room. All those dogs. Makes for happiness," Kathryn said.

"Speaking of doom and gloom, you don't exactly look like a happy camper, Kathryn. Why is that?"

"Part of it is Maggie and how desperate she is to find her old teacher. Then there is my leg. The doctors told me I'd be able to drive my truck the first of the year, but it's simply not true. I still need a boatload of therapy. That in itself is depressing. On top of that is Bert's and my inability to commit to marriage. There's a strain between us that both of us pretend isn't there. I don't like living year-round in Las Vegas, and he loves it. And Christmas is sneaking up on me faster than I would like. It's me. I know that. I have to change my attitude. I will, but I don't know when that will be. Enough about me. What are you doing here? You don't like to shop any more than I do, so what's up?"

Alexis winced. She sat back so the waiter could place the sandwich plate in front of her. When he was gone, she asked, "What do you buy your prospective mother-in-law who doesn't like you because you are black and are marrying her son? Ah, I can see you are as stymied as I am."

Kathryn blinked. "How do you know she doesn't like you?"

"Kathryn, I can tell. She's a sweet lady, and Joseph is the apple of her eye. She wanted him to marry a nice Spanish girl who would produce a lot of babies. I don't quite fit that mold. I do a lot of pretending, but it's starting to get to me. Joseph is oblivious, and you know how he loves and adores his mother, his whole family."

"You aren't marrying the whole family, damn it. You're marrying Joseph."

"Now, you see, that's where you are wrong. I will be marrying the whole family. That's how it works. I turned myself inside out to be nice to them, to go the extra mile. She's aloof, pleasant, but she has never smiled at me. Not once. She's nervous around me. Joseph said it's because I'm a lawyer. She is in awe of me. I'm not buying it. She just doesn't like me. What does my being a lawyer have to do with marrying her son? Nothing, that's what."

"So what are you going to do?" Kathryn asked as she bit into her sandwich.

"I'm going home, and I'm going to decorate my house. That's what I'm going to do. Maybe that will help. Nikki and Jack went out today to cut down a real, live tree. We've all got *Maggieitis*. And before you can ask, no, the Valentine's Day wedding is probably not going to happen. Now, let's talk about Maggie. You got any ideas?"

Kathryn leaned across the table. "You know what, Alexis? I do have an idea. I was going to call you later, and Isabelle, too, to see what you thought. I tried to put myself in Miss Roland's shoes. You know what I would have done? I would have gone to some church, whatever her faith was, and asked for help.

"The minute Maggie shared her story with me, I had this strange feeling that I knew something that could help her. I just couldn't nail it down. It was just a flash of something. Then, this morning, I remembered what it was. I used to deliver to the Home Depot in the Fayetteville area. I remember a delivery I made years ago. While my truck was being unloaded, I passed the time by walking around the garden center. At the far end you could see the buildings across the road. The biggest sign to be seen was THE GUARDIAN ANGELS MISSION. A storefront kind of place.

"I struck up a conversation with one of the workers who was watering the plants, and she said the place was wonderful and was run by some ex-military guy from Fort Bragg. I can't be sure, but I think she said he was a chaplain. She said that they donated plants to them and that in the back he had a massive garden, which his flock tended. She gave me the lowdown, but at the time it was just conversation, and I didn't pay all that much attention. I do remember that she said the guy never turned anyone away. No matter what, he'd find room for one more lost soul. They exist mainly on donations. Restaurants donate leftover food. That kind of thing. They feed the homeless three times a day."

Alexis reared up. "And you think maybe that's where Alma Roland might have gone, right?"

"Yeah. Wanna take a ride there tomorrow? Or we could fly up in the morning and come back the same night. I think Isabelle is free, so she could go with us."

"Why aren't we telling the others?" Alexis asked.

"In case I'm wrong. No sense getting everyone's hopes up, in case I'm way off base here. Especially Maggie. Oh, Alexis, think about it. What if I'm right, and we actually find the elusive Miss Roland?"

Alexis pushed her plate away and motioned the waiter for a coffee refill. "Count me in. Send Isabelle a text. You better explain the secrecy part. I'll check with the airlines. I'm not in favor of a long car ride. The earliest flight they have, right?"

Kathryn nodded as she sent out a text to Isabelle.

Isabelle's return text arrived at the same time the restaurant's complimentary brownie arrived, along with their coffee refills. "She said she's in, too."

*   *   *

Alexis drove around the block three times before she was able to park her rental car. Alexis, Kathryn, and Isabelle climbed out of the car and headed toward the entrance to a storefront. It was cold, and a light snow was falling. The women shivered as they picked up their pace.

At the entrance, Kathryn turned and said, "Look across the road, at the far east end. That's where I was standing. Now look up at the sign. It's weathered since then, but you can't miss it."

Isabelle and Alexis nodded. They stepped to the side to allow Kathryn to open the door. A bell tinkled, a pleasant sound.

It was warm inside, and the enticing scent of something cooking permeated the air.

"Chicken soup," Alexis said.

"Vanilla. Either chocolate cake or chocolate pudding," Isabelle said.

"The Christmas tree is up and decorated," Kathryn said, sniffing as she pointed to a corner of the big room they were standing in. There was a long table where six men were playing chess. Next to their table, another table was set up with easels, and three women were splashing paint on different canvases. Another group sat by the fire blazing at the end of the room. A stack of wood that reached almost to the ceiling guaranteed that the warmth would last as long as it was needed. The sound of someone playing a piano somewhere out of sight could be heard.

Alexis whirled around at the same time Isabelle did and said, "We don't have a story, an explanation as to why we're here," they both hissed at the same time.

All three women spun around when they heard someone ask if he could help them. The voice belonged to a tall, gray-haired man wearing a religious collar. "Pastor Tennyson. Can I help you?"

Kathryn's brain raced. She held out her hand. "Kathryn Lucas. This is Alexis Thorne, and this is Isabelle Tookus. Ah . . . I think it's the other way around. We want to know if we can help you. Um . . . we belong to an organization that . . . that takes on a cause, and your . . . ah . . . mission came to our attention. We'd like to help. It is the Christmas season, you know," she said, finishing lamely.

"Well, look around, ladies. I'm not proud. I never turn down an offer of help. Would you like to stay for lunch? Chicken noodle soup with real chicken, thanks to the Chicken Emporium. Homemade bread made by these hands," Pastor Tennyson said, holding up his hands. "And chocolate pudding for dessert, thanks to Coburg Dairy, which provided the milk to make the pudding."

"That's very kind of you, but we don't want to impose," Alexis said.

"No such thing. Anyone who walks through these doors is welcome. This will be my thirtieth year at Guardian Angels. I hope I can be here for another thirty years. So, you'll stay?"

The girls nodded.

"Can we help?" Isabelle asked.

"I never refuse help. My wife is home with a bad case of bronchitis, so I'm here alone today. It's not a problem. My people are patient, and sometimes, they even help. Come along, ladies. We can talk as we ready the tables. We still have an hour till my flock arrives for lunch, and you can tell me about the organization you represent."

Kathryn was quick on the uptake this time. "Of course, but turnaround is fair play, so we want to know how you came to be here and why."

"Deal," Pastor Tennyson said, handing over three pristine white aprons. "We use paper tablecloths from that roll on the shelf. We use paper plates when we can to help with the cleanup. Everyone has to wash up first, and then we say grace and our guests get in line. We encourage everyone to eat as much as they want and to not go hungry. Mostly, they oblige. Then they come back to sleep here if they have nowhere else to go. My wife and I are proud of the fact that we've never turned a soul away. They might have to sleep on the floor, but they're warm and safe inside these doors."

The girls had golf ball–sized lumps in their throats as they listened to Pastor Tennyson. If Kathryn's guess turned out to be wrong, and Alma Roland wasn't here, this was going to be Annie de Silva's next project.

"And you and your wife do this alone? That's a tremendous undertaking. I don't think I know anyone who could do what you're doing," Alexis said.

"Of course you could. If the need is there, a soul can do whatever it takes. My wife walked through those doors many, many years ago. I could see by the look on her face that she was at the end of her rope. She never left, and within a year, we got married.

"You hear a lot today about movie stars and the like saying they have finally met their sixth or seventh soul mate. Those people do not know the meaning of those words. My wife is my soul mate in every sense of the word. I would have closed up shop a long time ago if it weren't for her."

Kathryn felt light-headed at what she was hearing. It had to be Alma Roland he was talking about. Still, she wasn't ready to ask the pastor for his wife's name.

"Tell me about your organization, ladies," the pastor said as he handed out plastic silverware and hard plastic throwaway bowls.

Alexis took the floor. "I'm a lawyer, Pastor Tennyson. I do a lot of the legal work for what has to remain an anonymous benefactor. It's not exactly a charitable organization. She relies on our recommendations. So, if you could tell me what your wish list is, we'll try to accommodate you."

"A wish list, is it? Lord, have mercy, ladies. It's endless. I'm not greedy. I'll take whatever you're willing to give us, and I'll pray for you all night and day, as will my wife."

"Still, everyone has a wish list. What would make this place better than it is?" Isabelle asked. "Or if we were to ask your wife, what would she say? Is it possible her wants would be different than yours?"

Pastor Tennyson laughed. "Alma would ask for one of those industrial bread-making machines. The oven on our stove is about gone. She'd ask for one or two of those extra big washing machines."

Kathryn swayed dizzily. She risked a glance at Alexis and Isabelle, who looked exactly like she felt.

"We need more cots, more blankets, a deep freezer. Sometimes we get too much food, and if we don't cook it right away, we have to discard it. As I said, the list is endless. We pride ourselves, Alma and I, on how clean we keep this place. Detergent is very expensive, and not many people donate cleaning supplies. Suddenly, I am feeling very selfish here. But you did ask." Pastor Tennyson grinned.

Kathryn smiled. "That we did. And we can guarantee it all. Do us all a favor, Pastor, and call your wife and ask her now. I'd like to take a full list back with us. Please tell her not to be shy about what you all need or want. Whatever it takes to make this place even better. Can you do that?"

"Of course I can. The phone's in my office." Pastor Tennyson eyed the clock. "Set the table, ladies. Condiments are on trays, and there are two to a table. Bread is to be sliced, and the butter isn't butter but margarine, and it's in the fridge, which is also on its last legs."

The minute the pastor was out of sight, the threesome hugged and did a jig.

"Oh, my God. Oh, my God, we actually found her. Kathryn, thank God for your memory. Maggie is absolutely going to go over the moon when we call her. We found her! We honest to God found Alma Roland!" Isabelle squealed happily.

The front door opened just as Alexis set the last bowl on the table. Since the food was served buffet style, Pastor Tennyson's flock lined up and started to help themselves from the huge serving pots.

Pastor Tennyson motioned for the girls to come closer. He looked flustered and apologized before he even conveyed his wife's wishes. "It would seem my wife's list is something I never thought of. She said if we have a fairy godmother with a magic wand, then we need three new toilets. Industrial dryers to go with the industrial washers. She also said if we had an industrial dishwasher, we could save on all the throwaway products we have to buy if we don't get donations. Of course, that means we would have to buy dishes and silverware. She wasn't shy. Is it too much?" he asked anxiously. "Oh, she also said it would be nice if somehow we could get our piano tuned."

"Consider it done, Pastor," Kathryn said as she stepped to the end of the line. She could hardly wait to dig into the chicken soup.

An hour later, hands were shaken as the lunch guests cleaned up the tables.

The pastor smiled. "One of the rules is that it's not totally free. You eat, you clean up."

"We'll be in touch. I hope your wife feels better soon," Alexis said as she tucked her scarf inside her coat.

"Thank you for the lunch. It was delicious," Isabelle said.

Outside in the cold November air, the women ran to the car. Once inside it, they high-fived each other and laughed until they had to hold their sides.

"We found her! Oh, Maggie is going to be so happy. What a perfect Christmas present," Kathryn said happily. "Next stop, the airport, ladies!"

Chapter 8

Snow was falling heavily when the girls exited the airport and headed for the parking lot. They were so excited, they barely noticed.

When they finally became aware of the weather conditions, Kathryn looked around and said, "I live the closest, so let's head for my house and have a sleepover. I'm starved, for one thing. All we had to eat today was that soup at the mission and those stale pretzels on the plane. What do you say, girls? A good old-fashioned sleepover? I have some real cozy flannel nightgowns."

Isabelle's head bobbed up and down as she danced from foot to foot, shivering in the frigid temperatures as Kathryn searched for her car keys.

"That works for me," Alexis said.

Finally, with the windshield cleared and the engine running, the girls huddled, teeth chattering, as they waited for the car to heat up.

"Did either one of you get in touch with Espinosa or Abner? Where do they think you are?" Kathryn asked.

Alexis shook her head. "I didn't tell Joseph anything. We do not have the kind of relationship where we have to check in and announce our whereabouts. I don't ask him where he goes or what he does, and he tries—I say tries—not to ask me. I'm good. When we get to your place, I'll send him a text to say good night."

Isabelle laughed. "That works for you because you aren't married. Yet. Abner always wants to know where I am and what I'm doing. Today I told him I was going out with you two and didn't know when I'd be back. He was okay with that, but I always go home at night. Meaning I don't spend the night away from home. He'll be okay with it. He is so into trying to find Alma Roland, he can't think of anything else. When he gets like that, I could set the place on fire, and he would never notice till he started to choke from the smoke."

Ten minutes later, they were on the road and headed for Kathryn's house. It took them almost an hour with the slow-moving traffic, but they finally made it.

Kathryn unlocked the door and led the girls into her toasty, comfortable cottage, which was just big enough for her and her dog, Murphy, who came on the run, barking happily at his mistress's return, together with friends who did belly rubs in the bargain.

"You all know where everything is. Turn up the heat a few notches, lay a fire, and get some food ready while I walk Murphy."

Noticeably absent in the tiny cottage was any sign of the upcoming holidays. Isabelle commented on it. Alexis just shrugged.

Outside in the frigid night air, Kathryn said, "Make it quick, boy, and you get some real bacon for dinner. And eggs. You know how you like scrambled eggs. It's your reward for having to stay alone all day. Quick! Quick! Murphy."

Understanding the words *bacon* and *eggs,* the shepherd did what he had to do, then barked to say he was ready to go back. The dog sprinted ahead, but Kathryn limped. Her leg ached fiercely from sitting so long on the plane. The cold weather didn't help, either. She longed for a steaming hot bath and the liniment she rubbed on her leg to ease the ache. She felt tears forming in her eyes. She knew her leg was never going to be the same, no matter what the therapists and surgeons said. It was her leg, and she knew. She had serious doubts that she would ever be able to take to the highway in her eighteen-wheeler. Well, maybe she could prove them all right. If she worked at it—and no one could say she wasn't determined—maybe she could make it happen. "And they get ice water in hell, too," she muttered under her breath.

Back home, Kathryn adjusted her attitude for her friends. She complimented them on the fire, on the way the little cottage had warmed up, and for frying extra bacon for Murphy, who sat next to the stove, where Alexis was scrambling eggs while Isabelle made thick slices of sourdough toast and spread them with butter and blackberry jam.

"Aah, a feast fit for three queens and one hungry dog." Kathryn laughed. "I cannot tell you how hungry I am."

"Well, eat up, girlfriend. I scrambled a dozen and a half eggs, knowing how Murphy loves them. I made hot chocolate instead of coffee."

"Same amount of caffeine," Isabelle said, giggling.

"Yes, but the coffee doesn't come with all these little marshmallows. Eat up, girls!"

And eat up they did. So did Murphy.

"So when are we going to tell Maggie?" Alexis asked.

"We probably should call her now, but I think we should wait till morning. It's late, and she might be sleeping. By the way, has anyone said how much money we pooled?" Isabelle asked.

Kathryn and Alexis shook their heads, meaning they had no clue.

"We're going to need to know that ASAP. Should we call a meeting out at the farm for tomorrow, or should we call Maggie first, then call the meeting?" Kathryn asked as the girls set about cleaning up the tiny kitchen.

"I think we should call Maggie as soon as we get up, and take her out to breakfast and tell her. At which point we'll call the others and head out to the farm. Maggie is so unhappy and miserable, I hate to keep her in suspense one minute longer than we need to. She is going to go over the moon," Isabelle said as she clapped her hands. "We did it! We found her old teacher. How cool is that? And all thanks go to Kathryn, with her phenomenal memory. Maggie will love you forever, Kathryn."

"I'm thinking there are going to be a lot of sourpusses tomorrow morning, when we deliver our news. You know how Abner, Jack, and the others like to think they are the be-all and end-all to every mission. No offense, Isabelle, in regard to Abner."

"None taken." Isabelle laughed. "I'm all for woman power. I don't know about the rest of you, but I'm ready for bed."

"It's the floor in the living room. All the blankets and pillows are in the hall closet. If we huddle, we'll stay warm as long as we keep the fire stoked," Kathryn said.

"Have you given any thought to maybe finding a bigger place? Don't you get tired of pulling out that sofa to sleep on?" Alexis asked.

"Nope. This is my place. I bought it for me and Murphy. No one else. At the time, it was all I could afford, and it was my first very own house. I own it free and clear. It's not like I spend a lot of time here. It's my home base. Everyone needs a home base, no matter what. It's where I come to enjoy my victories and where I come to nurse my miseries. It's my home."

"We hear you," Isabelle said as she spread out the blankets and pillows.

"You said you had some flannel nightgowns. Where are they?" Alexis asked.

"In the linen closet."

Ten minutes later, the girls were nestled in their blankets. One minute after that, they were all sleeping peacefully while Murphy prowled the cottage until he decided it was safe to go to sleep. He cuddled next to his mistress and licked at the lone tear at the corner of her eye.

Kathryn, Alexis, and Isabelle could barely contain themselves as they waited at the House of Pancakes for Maggie to appear. She was late, which was most unusual. The girls were all on their second cup of coffee and hadn't ordered yet.

Alexis waved away the waitress for another coffee refill when Maggie entered the restaurant and looked around. Kathryn waved, and Maggie literally sprinted to the far left and flopped down.

"I hope whatever this meeting is about is good, because it is cold out there. I hate going to breakfast at six thirty in the morning." She held up the empty cup at her place setting for the waitress who had just been waved away. The waitress hurried back to the table to fill Maggie's cup with coffee.

Even before Maggie could get the cup to her lips, Alexis said, "We found her, Maggie! We found Alma Roland! All thanks to Kathryn and her memory."

Isabelle took the lead. "We flew to North Carolina yesterday morning and went to where Kathryn thought Miss Roland might be, and she was right. We didn't see her in person, but we met her husband. He said his wife was home with bronchitis. Later on, he called her by name and told us how she appeared one day and never left. We found her, Maggie!"

Maggie started to shake, the coffee cup in her hand dropping to the floor. She barely noticed. Coffee splashed all over her shoes. She started to jabber and ended with, "Honest, you found her? You aren't making this up? Why didn't you call me right away?"

"It was late when we got back, and to be honest, Maggie, we wanted to tell you in person. Please don't fault us for that," Isabelle said.

"I won't, I won't. Tell me everything, and don't leave anything out. I want to hear all the little details." She looked around for her coffee cup in a daze. The waitress appeared with a frown and filled a fresh cup.

The girls obliged.

"Now we're going out to the farm. We called everyone. We need a plan. The good news is Miss Roland, now Mrs. Donald Tennyson, is safe and sound and not going anywhere. We have time to make plans and do whatever it is you want to do," Kathryn said.

"After all this time. I can't believe it. No wonder Abner couldn't find a trace of her. She got married. To a minister. I can see that. She walked in and just never left. Amazing, after all these years. We should tell Mrs. Ryder, her old neighbor. Maybe we could arrange a Christmas party for all their . . . um . . . flock. She could bring all of Miss Roland's Christmas decorations she said she saved. This is so wonderful, I want to cry. I don't know how to thank you girls."

"Hey, it was Kathryn and her memory. If it weren't for that, we'd all still be searching for your old teacher," Alexis said.

Maggie bolted off her chair and around the table, where she hugged Kathryn until Kathryn gasped for mercy. "You're welcome," she said hoarsely as she rubbed at her throat. "Glad to help. Now we need a plan, so let's eat up and head to the farm. Is it still snowing?"

"It is, but there is no accumulation. The temperature is really dropping, though," Isabelle said.

The girls finished off their pancakes in record time. When it was time to pay the bill, Maggie insisted she pay it. The girls didn't argue as they bundled up and headed for the entrance. There was a definite spring in everyone's step and a smile on their faces at the same time.

The girls were delighted to see and smell, as Alexis put it, Christmas. Beautiful balsam wreaths adorned all the doors and windows. The tree was up in the family room, and Charles was cooking something that smelled delicious, even though it was barely past breakfast, which pretty much guaranteed that whatever he was cooking would take a long time and would be mouthwatering in the end.

"Dining-room table, everyone!" Maggie shouted. "Hurry. Hurry. Take a seat. We have news. Well, Kathryn, Alexis, and Isabelle have news! Hit it, Kathryn."

"We found Alma Roland. She's married to a minister, and together they run a mission in Fayetteville, North Carolina, called the Guardian Angels Mission. They feed the homeless three times a day. It is so clean there. They never turn anyone away, and they exist on donations. The pastor invited us for lunch, and it was delicious. He serves hearty fare to his flock, as he calls them. They do such good work." Kathryn went on to describe their conversation with the pastor, the call to Alma, and the people who benefited from their kindness. "The bottom line is everything is worn-out, they don't have enough room, and they need money to keep doing what they're doing. So, everyone, let's run it up the flagpole and see what we can do for the Guardian Angels Mission."

"How much money did we collect?" Nikki asked.

"At last count, we had two hundred eleven thousand dollars. That includes Maggie's donation of her husband's insurance, which amounted to one hundred thousand dollars. That should buy a lot of new appliances. Myra and I can add whatever you need. And young Dennis will be willing to part with some of his recent inheritance, won't you, young man?" Annie said.

"Absolutely, and I know someone who owns an appliance store. I bet I can get us a nifty discount if we buy a lot of stuff. I assume we want the best of the best, because it will all get hard use."

The others agreed.

"I know a piano tuner," Ted said. "A couple of years ago we did a human interest story on him and his family. I'm sure if we paid him, he'd travel to Fayetteville to tune the mission's piano."

"Jack and I can get the blankets, pillows, cots, and crockery," Nikki said.

"I know a plumber I did some work for," Abner said. He's the king of plumbers. When he fixes something, it stays fixed. Like Ted's piano tuner, if we make it worth his while, he can put in the toilets and do all the plumbing. And if we use our own people, we are in control."

Kathryn fiddled with her iPhone. "This is a picture I took when we first got there. See those two little stores next to the mission? If we could relocate those two stores and cut through the walls, then Pastor Tennyson would gain about three thousand square feet. He did tell me the person who owns the building charges him only a thousand dollars a year, and some years he can't make the rent. Maybe we could find a way to buy the building using . . . ah . . . some of Angus Spyder's money. That would be the ideal solution."

"I'll check the real estate records," Maggie volunteered. "I think that's a great idea."

"Food," Myra said. "A guaranteed food supply. I'd like to work on that. Knowing they won't run short, will have enough to feed everyone who walks through their doors, will be a tremendous relief to the pastor and his wife. We'll fill the freezers at the outset, then arrange for food deliveries every two weeks."

"Do they have a chapel?" Espinosa asked.

The girls looked at one another and admitted they didn't know.

"Well, then, we'll make sure they have one," Espinosa said. "If you can secure the two side stores, we could use that space. I have some cousins who would be happy to do the construction work. Alexis and I can oversee the work."

"Can I arrange the Christmas party?" Isabelle asked. "That's what all this is leading up to, right? If so, I'd like to do it. I think in my other life I was a party planner."

"The job is yours, dear," Annie said. "That leaves me, Fergus, and Charles. What do you want us to do?"

"Coordinate and make sure it all runs smoothly. Schedule and oversee. If we don't have a system, none of this is going to work," Myra said.

Annie mulled all this over for a moment or two, then agreed. "Do we know if the good pastor has transportation?" she asked, addressing Kathryn.

Kathryn looked baffled as she gazed at Alexis and Isabelle, who just shrugged. "We don't know. But there was a rusty-looking van parked in front. It could belong to anyone, though."

"I'll order two vans, then. If we set up Pastor Tennyson to grow his mission, he might have to hire some people to help. From what you said, he's not a youngster, and Alma is about fifty. Working twenty-four/seven can't be that good for a person. Doesn't matter how dedicated you are. You still need some personal time. I say we help ourselves to a little more of Mr. Spyder's monies and set up a fund for hired help."

"That's a great idea, Annie," Abner said as he typed away. "I'm setting up an account right now, along with a business fund. Just tell me when you want to transfer the funds."

"No time like the present. Do it now, Abner," Annie said. "Then it's one less thing we have to worry about."

Charles raised his hand. "Should we give some thought to the pastor's flock? By that I mean warm clothing, boots, shoes, and the like."

"You're right, dear. We do need to think about that. The weatherpeople are promising a very cold, snowy winter. What do you all think?"

It was unanimous. Charles beamed and immediately appointed Fergus as his assistant.

Annie stood up and clapped her hands for attention. If there was a mist in her eyes, the others pretended not to notice. "This, boys and girls, is what giving is all about. Helping and giving to someone who can't do it alone but works tirelessly to make life better for others. The dream is for others, never for himself. Such selflessness should and will be rewarded."

The clapping and the hooting forced Annie to cover her ears. When it all died down, she whistled sharply. "Okay, we all have jobs to do, so let's do them."

"It's wonderful, isn't it, Annie?" Myra whispered.

"Yes, and we didn't even have to threaten anyone," Annie whispered in return.

"You know what, Annie? We can do so much more if we want to. No one needs to know. Anonymity is a wonderful thing. And as you always say, it's better to give than to receive."

Annie winked at her friend. "For starters, why don't you consider donating that messy five-mile-long scarf you've been knitting the past three years to someone?"

"And have my friend Claudeen laugh me out of the knitters' club? I don't think so."

"Whatever you say, Myra."

Chapter 9

The Sisters' plans in place, the days moved forward with lightning speed as the girls, as well as the boys, went at it with a vengeance. The days literally raced into one another, right through Nikki and Jack's Thanksgiving dinner, their only reprieve.

In shifts, they became commuters out of necessity as they flew back and forth between Washington and Fayetteville, North Carolina, courtesy of Annie's and Dennis's Gulfstreams, which were always at the ready.

It was the fifteenth of December, with just nine days to go until what the Sisters called Maggie's Magic Moment, when she would swoop into the Guardian Angels Mission and present herself to Alma Roland Tennyson.

They were meeting now at Pinewood for Sunday dinner and a break to discuss the progress they'd made to date and what was yet to be accomplished.

Pinewood was decorated from top to bottom; the scent of fresh balsam garlands and wreaths was everywhere. When that combined with the delectable smells coming from the kitchen, the group knew they were in for a wondrous dinner. Christmas music, thanks to Myra's surround-sound system, wafted through the old farmhouse. And the mood of the guests this Sunday evening was one of high excitement because they were, as Dennis put it, almost down to the finish line.

Dinner was Szechuan braised meatballs served over shredded Chinese cabbage. Charles's guests oohed and aahed over the delectable food, asking for leftovers to take home. The only problem was, there were no leftovers. Dessert was a mango-pear torte with a rich caramel-marshmallow topping. Before anyone could ask, Charles said there were no leftovers, because Jack and Ted had come back for seconds and Dennis for thirds.

Harry and Yoko, back from China, where they had eaten only fish and seeds, complimented Charles, and Yoko asked for the recipe. Charles preened at the request. If Harry and Yoko liked his meatballs, then he knew he'd succeeded in his culinary efforts.

Cleanup took the usual twelve minutes, and then the group was once again settled at the heirloom dining-room table with their after-dinner coffee. Folders, notebooks, pictures, and diagrams littered the table.

"Who wants to go first?" Myra asked.

Dennis raised his hand. "I was lucky at the appliance store. I bought two of everything, except the washers and dryers. I bought four of those. Viking. The best of the best. Delivery is scheduled for December twenty-third. Plumbers and electricians have to finish first. I'm on top of that, too." He looked down at his list. "Two industrial stoves with double ovens. Two deep freezers, two refrigerators, two dishwashers, and two of those big, as in really big, bread-making machines. I saved over five hundred dollars by buying so much. I shamed the guy into free delivery when I told him where all of it was going. That was another three hundred dollars saved." Everyone clapped as Dennis slid the order, marked PAID, to the center of the table.

Ted took the floor. "I got the old piano tuned, and the tuner turned me on to a church organ that was for sale. I snapped it up, and it's being delivered December nineteenth. I also got free delivery."

Nikki was next up. "Jack and I went to this woolen mill in Maryland and bought in bulk. We got blankets, sheets, pillows. Then we hit this discount mall and just about bought out their supply of heavy-duty crockery. It came yesterday by freight to our house. We couldn't work out any special deals, because we bought discounted merchandise to begin with, but we still did good. We have to figure out how to get it all to Fayetteville. Oh, Jack came across a place that sold us two hundred sturdy cots, because the place was going out of business. They're supposed to be delivered to our house tomorrow."

"That's fantastic," Charles said.

Kathryn pulled a sheaf of papers out of a canvas bag at her feet. "Mr. John Matlock agreed to sell the building to Pastor Tennyson at a truly remarkable price. He's a nice elderly man. He said he was relieved not to have to maintain the building any longer and to go on the books as having done a good deed, so that when he meets his Maker, he can look Him in the eye. Really sweet man, and he likes the pastor and his wife very much. Alexis did all the legal paperwork. Annie and Myra paid for the building, and we plan to gift the building to Pastor Tennyson on Christmas Eve."

"We also found—well, actually, Joseph found—new quarters for the two tenants on either side of the mission. They moved out last week, and he and Ted arranged for carpenters and plumbers to ready the building," Alexis said. "When it's finished, it will be one huge building. Everyone is working around the clock. They're even renovating the second floor, which was just used as storage, so that the Tennysons can move in there and out of the hovel where they now live. And they won't be paying rent any-more. The unit on the right is going to be the chapel, but we decided that Pastor Tennyson is in charge of that. The last time I spoke to him, he couldn't decide if he wanted folding chairs or pews. His wife convinced him to go with the pews. They're both overwhelmed. In a good way."

"I ordered two vans. Each seats twelve. They were deliv-ered this past Friday. Charles and Fergus took care of the in-surance, registration, and all that," Annie said. "They're white, in case anyone wants to know the color. Fergus vol-unteered to arrange the logos, or whatever you call them, on the side panels. They're flying down in the morning to do just that."

"If we all pitch in, we can get all the stuff from our house to the plane, and then the pastor can use his new ve-hicles to transport it to the mission. Win-win!" Jack said.

"Fergus and I hit the army-navy surplus stores in the area and bought up their supply of clothing. It was hit or miss on sizes, but I don't think anyone will care as long as they're warm. We literally bought them out," Charles said. "We need to load all of that in the plane, too."

They all clapped their hands in approval.

"Not so fast, everyone!" Isabelle shouted to be heard over the clapping. "Did you all forget that Abner and I are in charge of the Christmas party?"

"No, dear, we didn't forget. The party is the cherry on top. All this other stuff has to be done before we can have the party. Tell us what you have planned," Myra said.

"Abner said we ran out of money, so Dennis said he would pay for the party. We should all thank him."

They did. Dennis blushed at their thanks.

"The party goes hand in hand with Yoko and Harry's donating the live Christmas tree, the different wreaths, and all the poinsettias and greenery for the new chapel," Isabelle said. "As for the party, I am having it catered by a caterer in Fayetteville. No one is cooking this year. The pastor and his wife deserve a night to remember. It will be a buffet, of course, all you can eat of everything known to man. We also ordered presents by the hundreds. Abner's fingers are almost raw from wrapping. Poor thing can barely type these days."

The others hooted with laughter, knowing that would never happen. "And we called Mrs. Ryder, and she said she would do her best to make the party and bring along all of Alma's Christmas decorations that she left behind. She was truly excited when I told her what her old neighbor and friend has been doing all these years."

"What did you get in the way of gifts, dear?" Myra asked.

"TracFones, iPads, all that digital stuff that Abner loves so much. Pastor Tennyson will be in charge of the minute cards. He'll monitor them so there is no abuse. Abner also got three state-of-the-art computers, fax machines, and copiers for the mission."

"Did you get anything for the pastor and his wife?" Myra asked.

"We did, actually, but it isn't something that can be wrapped up. It was Dennis's idea, because on one of his trips to Fayetteville, Pastor Tennyson mentioned that his wife's dream was to someday open a medical clinic where the poor could go for help. Two blocks away from the mission was an empty building, and Dennis bought it. Renovations start after the first of the year. Maggie's teacher is going to get her dream. We'll wrap the deed to the medical clinic property in a box with a big red bow and leave it and the deeds to the other three properties under the Christmas tree, with instructions that both gifts are not to be opened till Christmas morning."

This time, the clapping was so loud, along with the cheers, that Dennis buried his face in his hands.

"Nice going, kid," Harry said. "You got heart. I like that."

Dennis thought he was going to fly to the moon with Harry's praise.

"It's nine o'clock now," Fergus said. "I think if we all put our shoulders to the wheel, we can transport all the merchandise from Jack and Nikki's, plus what Charles and I bought, to the plane by midnight. The cots that are being delivered tomorrow will have to go on the next flight out. We plan to leave by seven in the morning."

"Then let's get to it," Ted said as they all scrambled to their feet for their outerwear.

Annie looked at Myra, who said, "Do we belong to that group, or are they leaving us behind?"

"I think they think we're too old to do our share," Annie hissed in return. "I hate when they do that, so move your ass, Myra!"

Dennis poked his head in the door. "Aren't you coming? This is a team effort, you know. Everyone has to do their share. Shake it, ladies. I'm driving."

Annie hissed again. "I can't give that kid another raise. He's making too much money as it is. We have to do something nice for him. He's been in such a funk lately. You do know that new girlfriend of his dumped him, right?"

Myra stopped in her tracks. "No, I didn't know. What happened?"

"Okay, now, this is in confidence, Myra."

Myra nodded.

"Well, it seems Miss Mitzi Overton, UPS driver, playfully or maybe not so playfully asked young Dennis how much money he had in the bank, and he just as playfully said he was overdrawn. That was the end of that. It happened right before Thanksgiving. He came to me for advice, and I told him to forget he ever met her."

"Sound advice, Annie. How did he take it?"

"Pretty good, all things considered. He was going to buy her a cashmere scarf for Christmas. She would have dumped him for sure when she saw the scarf. Young women today want bling. Lots of bling. He's fine now, I think. He's caught up in this mission, which is a good thing. He'll find his princess when it's the right time and not one minute before. This is going to be such a great Christmas, isn't it, Myra?"

"The best, Annie. The best!"

A light snow was falling when the gang arrived at the airport in a caravan of vehicles. Jack looked at his watch. They were right on time. Annie's Gulfstream was sitting on the private runway, ready for boarding. The date was December 24, and the time was five minutes to noon. This time, there was no cargo, no overnight bags. Maggie was the only one who carried a bright red shopping bag with a huge silver bow on the crinkly handles. Her gift for her old teacher. Annie had the four property deeds wrapped and stuffed in her huge carryall. She was so excited, she stumbled twice going up the portable stairs.

They were airborne in less than fifteen minutes. The moment they were at cruising altitude, Isabelle swung into her party mode. Since there were no stewardesses, she popped champagne bottles and set out a wide array of canapés, which the gang devoured the moment they saw them. They toasted their mission, Maggie, and the Tennysons.

"And the game plan is to be back on board by nine this evening for our return to Pinewood, with one stop at St. Ann's for midnight services, where Lizzie and little Jack will be waiting for us. Then we will all spend the holidays together, and Charles promised us a Christmas goose for dinner," Nikki said, holding her champagne glass high in the air.

Maggie was on her feet in an instant. Tears rolled down her cheeks. "I don't know how to thank you all for . . ." She waved her arms about. "What started out as a mission to locate my old teacher turned into this . . . this . . . wonderful thing we're doing for so many people. And on top of all that, it's supposed to be a white Christmas. All I can say is thank you, thank you, thank you!"

"Believe it or not, my dear, we've enjoyed every minute of what we've been doing these past weeks. I think I speak for all of us when I say if we had to do it all over again, we wouldn't change a thing. The biggest reward is knowing we're helping others. In the end, isn't that what Christmas is all about?" Myra said.

Maggie nodded tearfully as Ted moved closer and hugged her tightly.

Dennis chirped up. "Did Abner tell you he opened bank accounts for the mission? Well, he did. Pastor Tennyson will never have another worry. He can tend to his flock, work on his mission to get the street people jobs and training. Annie, Myra, and I funded it, along with . . . um . . . a generous donation from Mr. Angus Spyder."

"Hear! Hear!" Kathryn shouted. She started to pour coffee into Annie's monogrammed cups. Isabelle was corking the champagne for the return flight.

The group made more toasts, one after the other, for every conceivable thing they could think of. The mood was bright and cheerful as they settled down for the remainder of the flight, which was over before they knew it.

When the gang deplaned, they saw at least an inch of snow on the ground. Everyone smiled as they waited for the two mission vans to come to a stop. Annie was the last to board the van because she was giving last-minute instructions to the pilot.

"We absolutely have to leave here this evening. You have my cell phone number. Give us time to get here if you think we need to leave ahead of schedule due to the weather or some unforeseen circumstance."

The pilot nodded. He wanted to be home for Christmas as badly as everyone else.

"Just make it happen, Anthony," Annie said, patting his arm before she sprinted for the van that was waiting for her.

Forty-five minutes later, Pastor Tennyson threw open the doors and welcomed his guests. Myra, Annie, and Maggie were the only ones who hadn't already seen the Guardian Angels Mission, and they complimented the pastor. Maggie looked around in awe at what she was seeing. How wonderful it all looked. And it smelled delicious, with the scent of fresh balsam and the food that was being prepared by Isabelle's caterer.

Long tables with real tablecloths in red and green graced the room. Every table had beautiful centerpieces of poinsettias and greenery. There were poinsettias everywhere, compliments of Yoko, who had flown down yesterday, the plane full from top to bottom. Kathryn said she didn't think there was a prettier sight anywhere.

Maggie looked around for a glimpse of her old teacher. When she didn't see her, she started to panic. The grip she had on her gift bag was fierce. "I don't see her. Where is she?" There was such panic in her voice, Harry put his arm around her shoulders to calm her. At his touch, Maggie calmed and smiled. Harry had that effect on people.

And then she had her answer. "I'm sorry my wife isn't here at the moment. I surprised her by giving her my present a little early. A new dress for the occasion. She went home to, as she put it, get dolled up. She'll be back shortly. So, until she gets here, why don't I give you all the dollar tour?"

The gang trooped along, offering compliments and smiling.

"We're a work in progress, but we're getting there," Pastor Tennyson told them. "In my wildest dreams, I never thought this was even a remote possibility, as much as I prayed for it to happen. There has been such a change in our people. Yes, they still come for meals, and yes, they still come to sleep, so they aren't on the streets at night, in the cold. They're asking to help. They're starting to see what we're trying to do, and they want to be part of it. I've been in touch with some of the smaller businesses in the area, and we're working on a jobs program. It's all like a miracle. Thanks seems so . . . lame, but it's all I can say."

"We were glad to help," Myra said. "Just so you know, while we are going to be leaving you to return home, that does not mean we are going away. We will always be just a phone call away. If you need *anything,* anything at all, or if you run into problems, just call us."

Pastor Tennyson raised his eyes and said so softly only Maggie heard him, "And the angels sing."

The tinkling bell over the door could be heard as members of the pastor's flock started to arrive. And then it was mild chaos as men, women, and a few small children wandered around. It was obvious to the gang that the flock had made a real effort to clean up and be at their best. It was so heartwarming, they all felt their eyes fill up.

Dennis, Mr. Social himself, decided to give tours and repeated almost word for word what the pastor had said when he'd done his own tour just minutes ago. He'd seen the look of panic on the gang's faces when they saw the children appear. He was glad now that he'd listened to his gut and bought toys on the off chance some children might appear. He'd gotten doll babies, doll buggies, trucks and cars, mittens and warm hats. And, of course, candy canes. He gave himself an imaginary pat on the back for having the foresight to snap up all the Christmas stockings in one of the Big Lots stores. The stockings came in different sizes. Those for children contained small toys, candies, and things like toothbrushes, bubbles, and individually wrapped soaps. In the adult stockings, there was deodorant, soap, toothbrushes, razors, wool socks, and warm gloves. He wasn't sure, but he thought there were over three hundred stockings. More than enough to go around.

It was coming up on five o'clock when Annie's phone rang. She moved off to take the call. It was the pilot.

"Ninety minutes, and we have to be wheels up, or we're here for the holidays. The snow is coming down heavy now," he said.

"Okay. We'll be on time."

Annie clapped her hands and whistled to get everyone's attention. She explained the situation.

"Well, then, we need to get this show on the road," Pastor Tennyson said cheerily. "I hear my wife's car in the back, so let me welcome her in her new finery so she doesn't get all flustered. She's supposed to be Mrs. Santa Claus. You all do what you need to do while I greet my wife."

Everyone fell to it, and within minutes, the pastor's flock was seated at the tables. The buffet was set up as everyone scurried to help. Except Maggie, who stood rooted to the spot where she was standing. She waited, her gift bag clutched firmly in her hands.

As Nikki whizzed by, she whispered, "I can hear the angels singing. Look alive, girl. This is what you've been waiting for. Smile. Please."

And Maggie smiled as Pastor Tennyson led his wife, who looked beautiful in a long red dress with white faux fur around the neck and sleeves. Her hair was all gray now, but she looked the same to Maggie, her smile just as beautiful as she remembered. Maggie stepped forward. "Hello, Miss Roland. Remember me?"

In that instant, the sudden silence was louder than thunder. It was as though the flock knew somehow that this was a momentous moment, and they honored it with silence.

"Margaret! Margaret Spritzer! Of course I remember you. You were my favorite student. How wonderful to see you after all these years! You are part of this! I should have known that. I cannot tell you how often I thought about you over the years and wondered how you were doing." She moved forward to take Maggie in her arms.

Maggie started to cry. Then everyone else started to cry. Pastor Tennyson rushed around to find tissues but ended up with rolls of toilet paper, which he unrolled and handed out. Which made Maggie laugh as she handed her gift bag to her old teacher.

Alma Roland Tennyson carefully picked at the tissue paper and withdrew ten-year-old Maggie's Christmas decoration, the toilet-roll Santa with the colored cotton balls.

"You saved this all these years!"

Maggie's head bobbed up and down as Alma swiped at her eyes.

"Ah, now I know why my husband said we weren't going to decorate the tree. This will do the job nicely. What a wonderful present. Come along. Let's hang this on the tree together."

"Isn't this the most wonderful thing you've ever seen, Annie?" Myra asked.

"I can hear the angels singing. Can you?" Annie beamed.

"Loud and clear, my friend, loud and clear."

"Did we do good or what?" Dennis said happily.

"It doesn't get any better than this, Dennis," Harry said.

His eye on the clock for the gang's benefit, Pastor Tennyson gave the signal that Christmas dinner was now being served.

Once everyone had been served and the blessing was over, Pastor Tennyson held up his glass of apple juice and said, "Merry Christmas, everyone!"

The return greeting could be heard a block away as the

flock and the gang shouted, "Merry Christmas to one and all!"

"I hear the angels singing," Harry whispered to Yoko.

"I hear them, too, Harry, and Lily is singing the loudest! And you know what else? I just heard Cooper bark."

"You heard that?" Harry asked in awe.

"I did, my husband. I did."

Naughty or Nice

Prologue

December 2015

Teresa Amelia Loudenberry—known as "Toots" to friends and family and "Nana Tootsie" to her precious grandchildren, twins Jonathan and Amy—stood in the center of the formal living room of the home she shared with her adored and adoring husband, Dr. Phillip Becker, inspecting the Christmas decor in order to make sure it was historically accurate, looking just as it had more than two hundred years ago. She and Phil, along with Sophie, Goebel, Abby, and Chris, had spent months researching and locating antique Christmas ornaments exclusive to the late eighteenth century, since they were all participating in the annual holiday showcase of historic homes.

Donations would be accepted but were not necessary. They had all agreed that whatever money was collected would be donated to the new organization Toots and Phil had recently started, Hope for Heroes. It was their hope to build as many homes as possible for those hundreds of war veterans returning from overseas. A new start, a small reward for their service. It was her latest endeavor, and she planned to make this as successful as her other charitable organizations. Maybe even more so, given the necessity. She focused her thoughts back on the present.

Strangers would be traipsing in and out of their home, and Toots knew that a few of her snooty South Carolina so-called friends would also take advantage of the opportunity to get a bird's-eye view of her Southern mansion. And knowing some of them, they wouldn't bother dropping one red cent into her latest and, to her, most important project to date. Knowing her critics, meaning those "so-called friends," who were really nothing more than a bunch of rich old women with nothing better to do, she realized that they would note every imperfection. Over the next four weeks, from six to eight in the evening, when her doors were open, Toots planned to disappoint them. She and Phil had hired a team of Charleston's hottest holiday designers, Blanche Harding and Associates.

Their charges were astronomical, but Toots didn't care. Some would have squawked at such a large sum, but she knew she would get her money's worth, and then some. Personally, she disliked Blanche intensely, but the woman's decorating eye was spot on, and her specialty was Southern plantation homes. If asked, neither Toots nor Phil could say anything nice about her other than that. They had both observed the way she treated her underlings on more than one occasion since she had been hired, and they most definitely did not like what they had observed. After the holidays, Toots planned to give the snooty, pumped-up harridan a piece of her mind.

She walked over to the fireplace and moved the exquisite crystal candleholders away from the edge. Now three years old, Jonathan and Amy were growing by leaps and bounds. She was sure that if either of them chose to, they could reach the delicate crystal and topple it over. Satisfied that the tapered red candles and holders wouldn't cause harm to her grandchildren, Toots stepped back to admire the decorators' work.

The fragrant evergreens flanking the floor-to-ceiling

windows filled the room with the sharp scent of pine. The sweet-smelling magnolia blooms, which she had personally picked from her trees, had been placed in exquisite vases throughout the main room. The hoity-toity Blanche had insisted that the main room was to be referred to as the "parlor." To Toots, it was simply a beautiful formal living area that in no way was off-limits to anyone, especially not her grandchildren. However, for the month of December, she would allow the fine citizens of Charleston to parade through her "parlor."

The focal point of her "parlor" was the twelve-foot Fraser fir in the corner, beside two large windows. Velvet red and green ribbons tied in large bows, hundreds of miniature white lights, and the many antique ornaments Toots had collected made her tree unique, one of a kind. Blanche Harding thought the lights too modern, but there was no way Toots was going to have a tree as gorgeous as this without Christmas lights. She knew candles were used back in the day, and she also knew many a home had been destroyed by fire. No, she'd stick to store-bought lights. Let someone else take a chance with the candles.

Christmas was her very favorite time of the year. The decorations, the sweet smell of baking, packages wrapped in bright, shiny colors, the added cheerfulness of store clerks, and most of all, the looks she was bound to see on Jonathan's and Amy's faces when they opened their present this year, or rather when they saw their present, as it was much too big to wrap. Last year they'd been excited, but as most toddlers did, when their presents were opened and tossed to the side, they had more fun playing with the ribbons and boxes. This year would be different. Both had a vocabulary that could rival that of a ten-year-old, and they knew all about Christmas. Abby and Chris had taught them the true meaning of the holiday, and every time Toots would ask the children what they wanted for

Christmas, both would respond with, "We want to sing 'Happy Birthday' to the baby Jesus first," and then they would recite a litany of the latest board games they wanted.

Toots was sure Abby was never this smart at such a young age, but she knew the times were much different. Jonathan and Amy each had their own iPad mini, and both were quite proficient as they navigated their way through the many apps that were for older children. Both knew how to write their name, they knew their address and phone number, and just in case that wasn't enough, they knew they were to call 911 in an emergency. They were still having a bit of trouble distinguishing what a true emergency was, but Toots had faith in Abby's and Chris's parenting skills.

She smiled when she thought of her daughter and how her life had changed. At one time, Abby had lived and breathed Hollywood gossip; she had spent several years working as a tabloid reporter. Of course, when Toots had learned that Abby might lose her job at *The Informer*, she had purchased the tabloid on the sly and had made Abby the editor in chief. This was all behind the scenes, but when Abby was kidnapped by the paper's former owner/editor and held for ransom, Toots had had no choice. She'd revealed that it was she who'd purchased the struggling tabloid.

Abby was appreciative, and never once had she accused Toots of trying to control her career. Abby thought it was a grand gesture to this very day, and even though Toots had given Abby the deed to *The Informer* on the day of her baby shower, and it now belonged exclusively to her, Abby had allowed Josh, a onetime cub reporter, to climb the ranks, and now the day-to-day duties were his alone. Abby had said she didn't have a reporter's instincts anymore, but Toots wasn't so sure about that. Once a reporter, always a reporter.

Abby's reporting instincts had simply been transferred to the twins. She investigated every source of food that went into their mouths; every toy they owned was checked and rechecked for safety and recalls, just in case; and last but not least, Abby refused to use any product of any kind that wasn't organic. Personally, Toots thought this was taking things a bit too far, but she kept those thoughts to herself. She respected Abby's decisions and always did as she asked. Well, almost always.

She remembered that just last week she'd brought home dozens of cookies from The Sweetest Things, the bakery she and Jamie owned in Charleston. She'd let both children have three cookies apiece. Abby was okay with one, because she knew the goodies at the bakery were made with top-quality ingredients, but sugar was sugar regardless. Sugar was something Toots would never give up, but she wouldn't even think about getting the grandkids addicted to the stuff. Nor would she smoke around them. She was down to just a couple of cigarettes a day, thanks to the new vapor smokes she'd started using. Her and Sophie's days as bona fide smokers were coming to an end. Maybe.

She swept another glance over the room, making sure everything was in its place. Tonight was the first night of the parade of homes, and if there were any last-minute details she needed to attend to, now was the time. She walked the length of the room, stopped to fluff several red velvet pillows on her emerald-green sofa, which she thought just happened to be a perfect match to her Christmas tree. She refolded a soft golden fleece throw that the decorators had casually placed over the arm of one of her newly reupholstered cherry-red, Queen Anne–style chairs facing the fireplace. The room was a bit too overdone with antiques, but for now, it was what it was. After the holidays were over, she would put the antiques she'd had Phil and Goebel bring downstairs back in their rightful places in the up-stairs guest bedrooms.

Seeing that everything was in perfect order, at least by her standards, Toots whirled out of the room like a tornado. She had a long to-do list to get through before six o'clock tonight, when she would officially open her home up for all of Charleston to see.

When Abby had approached her with the idea, she'd had doubts about opening her home to strangers, but Abby had convinced her to join in, and it'd been her idea to use this opportunity as a fund-raiser for Hope for Heroes. Abby and Chris had spent hours researching the Clay/Clayton Plantation, as their home was called in the late eighteenth and nineteenth centuries. Toots had become quite the expert on the old plantation's history, which reminded her that she'd promised to bring Abby that old leather-bound book entitled *The Book of Life and Death*. She had found it in a box filled with Garland's things and wanted to return it to its rightful owner, Chris, her stepson, her son-in-law, and Garland Clay's son by his first marriage.

Once they'd started planning, Toots and Phil had jumped right in feet first. Toots had convinced Sophie and Goebel to join in, too, since they'd just recently finished remodeling their new home.

Ida had purchased a beautiful home on the Battery, where she and her husband, Daniel Townsend, were living, and Toots had invited them to join in, but Ida was adamant. She was not letting strangers in their house. Period. End of story. Instead, she and Daniel had donated a large sum to HFH, and for that, Toots was very appreciative.

Mavis was staying with her while her husband of less than two years, Wade Powell, was away in connection with the funeral-parlor franchise operation they were setting up, and she'd been a godsend this past week. Toots was so lucky to have those she loved so close. Sophie, Ida, and Mavis, Abby's godmothers, whom Toots had known since they were all teenagers, were located in Charleston now.

Life was good and was about to get even better, when she revealed her secret surprise. Yes, this holiday promised to be one to go down in the record books—at least in her own.

Chapter 1

"No!" Abby shouted seconds before she caught the antique crystal vase that Amy was about to topple off the shelf. "This is not for little girls to play with. Remember what I said?"

Amy, at three years old, was the spitting image of Abby. Abby thought that her daughter, with her big blue eyes, blond ringlets, and rosy red lips shaped in a perfect little Cupid's bow, was quite exquisite. Ditto for Jonathan, though the feminine attributes looked anything but on Jonathan. He looked like a little man. Of the two, he was the more serious, just like his father. Amy, on the other hand—Abby was reluctant to voice these thoughts—was personality wise a miniature of her grandmother. Everything was funny to her. Only three, yet she could successfully tell jokes with a straight face, and most that she told were quite creative. Abby recalled last night's joke.

"Mommy," Amy had said while Abby helped her into her pajamas.

"Hmmm?"

"What do you give a piggy when it's sick?" Amy had asked.

Abby had grinned, knowing this was another one of her daughter's silly animal jokes. She'd been around Dogs Displaced by Disaster long enough to learn a few catch-phrases.

"I don't know. Why don't you tell me?"

Amy giggled, her little button nose scrunching up. "*Oink*ment!"

Abby laughed loudly. "That's very good, Amy! Did you make that up all by yourself?"

She shook her head up and down. "Daddy said it was the best oink-oink joke in the world. Nana Tootsie said I was a true comeatdone."

"A what?" Abby asked.

"A comeatdone."

"Ah, I think you mean a comedienne," she said, correcting Amy.

Her head bobbed up and down excitedly. "Yep, that's what I am."

Abby kissed her plump cheeks and agreed. She moved the vase to a high shelf.

Looking sheepish, Amy asked, "Am I in trouble?" Her blue eyes focused on the vase.

Abby gave her a giant hug. "No, sweetie, not this time. But remember what we talked about? Pretty things are sometimes very old, and just touching them even a tiny bit can hurt them."

"And they can't get fixed, either, right, Mommy?" Amy said, finishing for her.

"Not always, but we were lucky this time. Let's try to be very careful. Remember, we're going to have a big Christmas house this year, and we want everything to look pretty."

"And sparkly, too, right?" Amy added. She reminded Abby of herself when she was little. Anything sparkly and shiny was always the best.

"Lots and lots of sparkles. Now, I think it's time for a

break. What about you?" Abby asked as she scooped her daughter in her arms and twirled her around.

Amy giggled. "Can we have apples with raisins and peanut butter?"

"Absolutely," said Abby as they entered the kitchen, where she found Chris busy slicing apples and filling little bowls with peanut butter and raisins. They really had this schedule thing down to an art.

Jonathan was already seated at the table, waiting for his snack. Abby fluffed his blond curls, kissed his cheek, then placed Amy in the chair beside him.

"You okay with them for a while? Charlotte is coming over so we can check for any last-minute decorating issues," Abby said to Chris.

"Absolutely. Nothing I'd rather be doing. Well, almost," Chris said with a wink. "By the way, Sophie just called. Said she was stopping by to pick up whatever it was you ordered for her. She's on her way over now."

"Good. I was hoping she'd stop over. You and I will talk later," said Abby, returning the wink.

Abby kissed the twins, who were busy dipping apple slices in peanut butter, then carefully sticking their raisins to the golden goo. "Be good for Daddy, okay?" she called out. She didn't hear a response but wasn't expecting one. Snack time was a very big deal in the Clay household.

In the formal living room, she searched for the blown-glass candleholders she'd purchased for Sophie. Abby thought they would go perfectly with the silver theme Sophie had chosen this year. She found them tucked securely inside their box filled with protective bubble wrap, just as she'd left them when they were delivered. After discovering Amy's little hands reaching for her own delicate candleholders, Abby had wanted to make sure her prying little fingers didn't find their way inside this box. Amy was a very curious little girl. *Just like I was at that age,* Abby thought. *Maybe she'll be a reporter, a* serious *reporter.* Reporting real news, not Hollywood fluff, like she had. Distracted by her thoughts, Abby jumped when she turned around to see Sophie framing the doorway. She placed a hand over her heart. "You scared the bejesus out of me!"

"Sorry, Abs," Sophie said. "You looked like you were deep in thought. Didn't want to disturb you."

Abby gave her godmother the once-over. Dark jeans with a red silk blouse. With her chocolate-colored hair hanging loose, she could easily take ten years off her age and still be in her sixties. "You amaze me, but you know that," she said.

Sophie being Sophie, she rolled her eyes, but she grinned, showing her pearly whites. "Of course I know that. Remember, I'm psychic?"

How could she not? Abby thought. Her abilities as an up-and-coming world-renowned psychic had changed all their lives. And mostly for the best. She hugged Sophie, then stepped back. "How could I forget? Those abilities saved my life, or did you forget?" Sophie's skill as a psychic had led police to Abby's location when she'd been kidnapped by that sick puppy she'd worked for at *The Informer. Rag, aka Rodwell Archibald Godfrey. Idiot,* she thought but tucked the memory away for another time.

"My best work to date, if you want my opinion," Sophie stated matter-of-factly.

"Don't forget those two missing kids. I think that's your best work to date, if you want my opinion, and I know you don't, but you're getting it, anyway."

"You're starting to sound exactly like your mother," said Sophie.

Abby laughed. "I'm taking that as a compliment. Mom is good people."

Sophie nodded. "Toots is the best, no doubt about that, but if you tell her I said so, I'll have to kill you."

"I'm shaking in my shoes," Abby countered.

"I'm sure. Now, show me those candleholders before I have to cast an evil spell on you," Sophie teased.

"You wouldn't dare," Abby shot back.

"No, you're right. I wouldn't and can't, so you're safe," Sophie said.

Abby located the box and carefully removed the antique candleholders, then, with extra care, handed them to Sophie. "So, what are your thoughts?" she asked expectantly, an air of excitement in her voice. The candleholders were a *big* find.

Handblown in the early eighteenth century, the glass was delicate and light. Most likely crafted in Europe. The days of glassblowers of this caliber were long gone.

"Good grief, but these are fine-looking doodads! This must have cost you a small fortune! I've been doing my research," Sophie said in a serious tone. "This is too much, kiddo. You have to let me pay you for them." She carefully replaced the candleholders inside their protective wrapping.

Sophie remembered seeing candleholders similar to these at the Corning Museum of Glass in Corning, New York. The reason she had such a clear memory of her trip was that Walter had beaten the crap out of her, and she'd had to hide for a week before she was able to go back to work. A week upstate and her first venture crossing the border into Canada. *Bastard.* She hated him still to this very day. She felt sure he was providing enough fuel to keep hell aflame for many generations to come.

Abby shook her head, her blond curls falling out of her haphazardly twisted ponytail atop her head. "Ain't gonna happen, so just say thank you and be done with it. I've got tons of stuff to do before tonight. Plus, Charlotte is stopping over one last time to make sure everything is as it should be."

Sophie nodded. "I'll relent. For now, but only because it's Christmas."

Abby shook her head. She had known that Sophie would do something like this, and it was okay. However she chose to repay her, Abby would simply donate the funds to her mother's new project. "Whatever you say, Soph. When I saw these on eBay, I knew you'd love them. Hard to believe they're over two hundred years old, huh?"

Sophie peered inside the box she held. "It is, and it scares me, if you want to know the truth. Most of the stuff Goebel and I used to refurbish the old place is reproductions. Having the real deal means I have to be careful."

"And what's wrong with being careful? I've never known you to give a rat's ass about things. Is it you or Mom who always says, 'Things can always be replaced. People can't'?"

Sophie looked at her as though she'd lost her mind. "Your mother. And these are very special. They're a gift, and they're from *you*." Her brown eyes filled with tears. Careful not to let them spill over, she used the hem of her red silk blouse to blot her eyes.

"OMG! I can't believe you're getting all sentimental on me! Wait until I tell Mavis and Ida. They'll never believe me. Mom, too."

She sniffed, then darted a glance at her godchild. "Abby Clay, if you so much as mention my . . . my *softheartedness* to those old bats, I will . . . I will . . ."

"You'll what?" Abby interjected. "Send me to my room?"

They both burst out laughing.

Sophie swiped at her eyes while grabbing Abby in a hug. "This better stay between us, or I'll think of something to tattle to Chris. Or your mother. Remember, I managed to keep a few secrets from your mom when you were a teenager." Sophie and Abby were almost as close as mother and daughter. More than once, Abby had called Sophie for advice rather than going to her mother, simply because it'd been easier to tell her certain things she wasn't ready to reveal to her mother.

Abby had the grace to blush. "You promised, remember? And you also told me that you never break a promise."

"Yes, I recall promising you I would never tell 'certain things.' " Sophie made air quotes with her free hand. "My mistake," she added.

About to come back with a snide remark, Abby bit her tongue when she saw Charlotte walking through the entrance, where she bumped into Sophie.

"Excuse me. Is this a bad time?" Charlotte asked softly.

Abby shook her head. "Of course not! I was expecting you. Sophie, this is my decorator, Charlotte." She observed the young woman and her godmother and did not like what she saw.

"Charlotte, is something wrong?" Abby asked before Sophie could acknowledge the introduction. And from the look on Sophie's face, there was *definitely* something wrong with her. "What's going on?" Abby asked the pair. "Have you two met before?"

Of course they had. Charlotte worked for Blanche Harding, and Blanche Harding worked for Abby's mother and Phil, her latest stepfather. Sophie had probably encountered Charlotte during one of her many trips between Abby's house and her mother's. Charlotte Simonson was model material. Tall and willowy, she had creamy, latte-colored skin that glistened with a thin sheen of sweat. She wore her chocolate-brown hair in a loose braid that trailed down to her waist. Dressed in simple khaki slacks and a light blue blouse, she managed to look extremely professional, until one saw that her greenish gold eyes were watery with unshed tears.

Abby gave Sophie a sharp look. "What's going on here?"

Sophie continued to stare at Charlotte, while Charlotte appeared to be on the verge of some sort of emotional breakdown.

Sophie finally gathered herself. "I'm sorry, Abby. I just remembered something. I have to go." Clutching the box tightly against her chest, Sophie disappeared from the living room as fast as she'd entered.

Abby, in a mini-stupor, was at a loss for words. What the heck had she just witnessed? Yes, Sophie could be rude, but this was inexcusable. She hadn't even acknowledged her introduction, and if she'd met Charlotte previously, she hadn't acknowledged that, either.

"I'm sorry, Mrs. Clay. I didn't mean to run off your guest." Charlotte spoke softly.

"Of course you didn't. And that's Sophie. One of the three godmothers I told you about." During the time they'd spent together, Abby and Charlotte had become quite friendly. Abby guessed her to be in her late thirties. She had three young children and a husband stationed in Afghanistan. Though Abby had never met her family, Charlotte spoke of them often enough that Abby felt as though she knew them.

"Sophie acts strange sometimes," Abby said as a way to explain her godmother's weird behavior. That was putting it mildly, but she kept these thoughts to herself.

Chapter 2

Sophie stomped on the accelerator like she was at the starting line in a NASCAR race. Her hands were shaking and were slick with fear-induced sweat as she steered her way down the winding lane leading to the main road. A million thoughts swirled around in her head like a thick fog that hadn't decided exactly where to settle. She hadn't felt this way since discovering that the former mistress of the home that belonged to her and Goebel had been murdered. She remembered it as if it had happened only yesterday.

She'd woken up from a sound sleep, thinking she'd had a terrible nightmare, when further investigation proved she'd experienced another episode of *clairsentience,* which allowed her to see through the eyes of another by touching an item belonging exclusively to that person. Sophie had felt as though the woman in her dream had been trying to send a message. After many sleepless nights and a thorough investigation into the history of their home, she'd uncovered a murder that had taken place almost a century ago.

For the past two months, Sophie had been so involved in preparing for the start of the holiday parade of homes that she hadn't really focused on anything requiring her to use her psychic abilities. And for once, there had been no need, and of that she was glad. Her mind needed a rest. And now this. She entered through the new wrought-iron gates Goebel had installed last week, then parked in the front of the house. Clicking the key to the OFF position, Sophie leaned back in the seat, her head reclining against the headrest. Closing her eyes, she immediately captured the image of the woman Abby called Charlotte.

Sadness. Sorrow. Loneliness. Fear. All these emotions assaulted her at once. There was loss in the woman's life, a deep personal loss, though it wasn't recent. She tried to focus in order to determine exactly why this was coming to her as a personal loss, but nothing jarred her. Nothing to explain the sadness. Sophie took a deep breath and slowly released it. Sometimes when she had trouble focusing, deep breathing helped to stabilize her thought processes.

Closing her eyes, she tried to pull up an image of the girl as she had appeared in Abby's formal living room. Pretty. Upset. She'd been very sad, but try as she might, Sophie couldn't put her finger, or in this case, her brain, on exactly what was causing her to be so sad. Hating that the girl was sad during the holidays, worried that she might try to harm herself, as many did during the Christmas season, she decided that once she went inside, she would meditate in her special room. Sometimes she had to really work at this psychic stuff. And today, it seemed, was going to be one of those days.

With the utmost caution, she took the box containing the candleholders, grabbed her purse, and went inside.

"Hello," she called out. Having parked in the front of the house, she wasn't sure if Goebel was home. He always parked behind the house. "Goebel? You home?" she called, her words sounding empty and hollow in the big old house. When she didn't get a response, she walked to the back of the house and peered out the kitchen window. His car was gone. She was home alone. Not wanting to but not sure when she'd have another opportunity to be alone, she raced upstairs to her séance room, still clutching the box.

Carefully, she put the box on the shelf that held her candles, books, and all the other items connected to her psychic world. She closed the drapes, as she found the semidarkness much more conducive when trying to relax and put herself in a semi-trance. She sat in her usual chair at the wooden table, placed her hands on top, and closed her eyes. Inhaling, then exhaling, she slowly began to relax. Centering on the young woman, hoping to use her psychic energy to discern why the woman felt so lost and so sad, she took another deep breath, freeing herself from the daily details of her everyday life.

The image came so fast, it startled her. A large number five. In bright red font. Yes, it was font now. She remembered this from using the computers at Dogs Displaced by Disaster, the organization Abby and Chris had started a couple of years ago. The number grew smaller and smaller, then nothing. She tried calming herself by taking more deep breaths. Focusing on the number five, she visualized the number in the bright red lettering, but her mind was as empty as a paper bag. She tried once more and then again and came up with nothing.

She could only wonder what the number meant, assuming it meant anything at all. She had studied numerology, but only briefly. Glancing at the bookshelf, she saw that she had several books on the topic, most of them unread. Figuring she hadn't made a connection psychically, she would look at the numbers. Maybe the meaning of number five would jolt her subconscious.

Taking the first numerology book she saw off the shelf,

she thumbed through the pages until a paragraph caught her attention. *The number five indicates loss and conflict and, many times, instability. The number five also signifies change and challenges.* Sophie closed the book and placed it back on the shelf. While she wasn't going to place any bets that the girl suffered from any of these possible problems, she wouldn't rule them out, either, even though nothing indicated that anything significant would lead her in the direction in which she might come up with a specific reason for having experienced those jumbled feelings upon meeting the girl. Not that this was new to her—it had happened numerous times—but more often than not, her visions were followed by an answer.

"Sophie?"

"Upstairs," she yelled.

She heard a quick succession of thuds coming up the staircase. Walking across the room, she yanked the drapes open. The late afternoon sun dipped behind a scattering of alabaster clouds. The silky green leaves on the old Southern magnolia tree flittered in a breezy dance, and the grayish brown limbs, gnarled like old arthritic fingers, swayed back and forth. *A cold front is coming in,* she thought as she stepped into the hallway and closed the door behind her.

"Oh, crap," Sophie said, jumping away from the door.

"Did I catch you doing something you shouldn't?" Goebel asked before draping an arm loosely around her waist.

"If only. No, you just startled me. I heard you coming upstairs, but I wasn't really paying attention." *Lame but true,* she thought as her husband guided her downstairs.

"My feelings are hurt," Goebel teased. "I'm going to make a pot of that pumpkin-spice coffee you like so much. Then you can tell me what's wrong."

Damn, she thought! He knew her almost as well as she knew herself.

In the kitchen, Goebel pulled out her chair and motioned for her to sit while he made coffee. His moves were confident, efficient. A man who knew his way around a kitchen. Sophie smiled. She'd truly married a prince, but she'd keep these thoughts to herself. Couldn't risk spoiling him any more than he already was.

Wiping his hands on a kitchen towel, Goebel leaned against the counter while the coffee brewed. "I'm thinking about getting one of those newfangled coffee machines that make one cup at a time."

"What's wrong with the one we have?"

"Nothing. Just time for a change, is all. Now, before you distract me, tell me what's bugging you. You didn't look so hot coming out of your séance room."

The coffeemaker gurgled, gave a hiss of steam, then stopped. "Coffee first," she said, nodding toward the coffeemaker.

"You're a spoiled old girl, you know that?" Goebel asked as he filled two mugs with coffee. "You want regular half-and-half or that fake pumpkin creamer stuff?"

"Being that I'm just 'a spoiled old girl,' I want my coffee first with the fake pumpkin stuff."

He brought the steaming mugs to the table and sat down beside her. "Spit it out, sweetheart."

Sophie took a sip of coffee. "I hate to even voice these thoughts, especially now, you know, with the holidays and all. It doesn't seem right, but things like this never happen at the right time, and really, if you think about it, there's never a right time for things of this nature."

"You're stalling," Goebel stated.

"No, I'm not. I went to Abby's to pick up a gift. . . . Wait until you see what she gave us. There was a young girl there, very pretty. Tall, latte-colored skin. She works for that nasty old decorator that Toots hired. She bumped into me, accidentally, of course, but when she did, this onslaught of emotions hit me. It was damn near physically painful. A strong feeling of sadness, like she was lost. Fear, but not fear as in 'boo' fear, but rather the kind of fear when you know something is about to happen, and you don't know what it is." She stopped, remembering.

Goebel nodded. "Go on."

"I was so . . . awash in her emotions. It's hard even for me to explain, and we both know I'm rarely at a loss for words. I came home, thinking that I would meditate a bit, but all I saw was the number five in bright red letters. I'm not that well versed in numerology, but I did read that the number five is usually connected with loss. Poor girl," Sophie said. She took the last sip of coffee, got up, and poured herself another. "Want more?"

"Sure," Goebel said. "So what can you do for this girl?"

Sighing, she shook her head. "I can't do a darn thing. I guess I could warn her to be careful, but I'd probably come off sounding like a whack job. Besides, I wouldn't want to frighten her any more than she is already. Maybe I'll mention something to Abby. She might know if the girl has problems. For all I know, she could be upset over a breakup. Who knows?"

"You'll figure it out, Soph. You know that, right? I don't want you worrying over this. Check with Abby, but that's all I would do right now. We've got to get this old shack into tip-top shape for tonight. We don't want the neighbors thinking we're layabouts, now, do we?"

Sophie shook her head, rolling her eyes. "Absolutely not, and if you haven't noticed, we're all set for tonight. All that's left to do is light the candles. According to Toots, we should do this one hour before showtime." Sophie grinned. "Said this gives the scent time to work its way throughout the house."

"Yeah, and the last thing we want is a stinky house. Especially during the holidays," Goebel chimed in.

Sophie glanced at the clock on the stove. "We've got a couple of hours before we have to unlock the front door. Wanna play for a while?"

Goebel's eyes sparkled with mischief. "I'll race you upstairs."

Sophie grinned and chased him up the staircase.

Chapter 3

Toots located the old leather-bound book that she'd found among Garland's things and stored in her attic. Abby and Chris could add it to their collection of antiques, a collection that was growing daily. With the utmost care, she wrapped the book in tissue paper, then eased it inside a box. The pages were frail and had yellowed with age, but the childlike block lettering could still be seen clearly. She'd been too busy preparing for today to really peruse the contents of the old volume, but if there was anything worth knowing, Abby would be sure to share it with her.

A low growl from the dining room reminded her she'd promised Mavis she'd take Coco over to visit Chester, Abby's German shepherd. Coco the Chihuahua thought she was a giant, and of course, so, too, did Frankie, her and Phil's dachshund, which he had rescued from the place Wade and Robert had moved into three years ago. She remembered all too well when Phil and Frankie became best buds. It had been Toots and Phil's first date, and when Frankie was rescued, he had to have emergency back surgery. Phil had hired a private jet to return to South Carolina from Florida, then turn around and take Frankie to the surgeon in Florida, Dr. Carnes, who specialized in dachshund back injuries. Of course, Frankie had made it through the surgery with flying colors and now was as much a part of the family as Coco and Chester.

Toots had fallen in love a little bit that night, but no way would she have admitted it back then. Having gone through eight husbands and still swearing there would never be a number nine, after she met Phil, who had been Bernice's doctor when she had her heart attack, she had known that she would eat those words someday. And Teresa Loudenberry had done precisely that a few years ago, when she and Dr. Phillip Becker had participated in a quadruple wedding in which Mavis Hanover and Wade Powell; Ida McGullicutty and Daniel Townsend; and Bernice Hanover, Daniel's mother, and Robert Powell, Wade's brother, had all tied the knot on a glorious summer day.

And she had done so gladly, she thought as Barney and Betty, their adopted dachshunds from Dogs Displaced by Disaster, peeked around the corner. Betty, the black-and-brown dachshund, had the longest nose, while Barney's was quite small for a weenie. Toots's heart filled with a big surge of love every time she saw those two. She was fairly certain they were siblings, but she didn't care where they came from. They fit in with the rest of the canine kiddies as if they'd been here forever.

"I suppose you two want to come along, as well?"

"Woof!" from Betty.

"Woof, woof, woof!" from Barney, who always barked in threes.

"Then, let's go," Toots said.

As soon as they heard the word *go*, all four dogs ran to the back door, their tails wagging so fast, they created a strong gust of air. They thrived on these little excursions because they were going to spend the evening at Dogs Displaced by Disaster with Chester and the other rescued animals, while Dr. and Mrs. Phillip Becker hosted the parade of homes tonight. Besides, they loved seeing the new dogs and cats, an occasional pig, chickens, and sometimes cows and horses. Toots equated these visits to a giant playdate.

"Okay, gang, let's go see Chester."

As soon as she opened the back door, all four dogs ran to her Range Rover. Knowing that the dachshunds had a tendency for back trouble, as she'd learned firsthand with Frankie, she'd had a ramp built for them so they could get inside the car with ease. Yes, they were spoiled, and no, she didn't give a hoot. Coco climbed in first, since she was the queen, then Frankie, with Betty and Barney close behind. Toots replaced the ramp inside the garage, then climbed into the driver's seat. She'd ordered custom-made car-seat harnesses for their safety. She hoped they would arrive before the end of the year. She didn't like the lack of protection when she had them in the Range Rover.

"Sit," she said, cranking over the engine.

All four dogs obeyed immediately.

"Good pooches."

She was answered with a round of barks. Toots swore the dogs understood everything she said. They were all well behaved and rarely caused a problem. Other than Coco's believing she was royalty, she had the best of the best. Hell, she'd miss Coco when Wade returned, and Mavis took the little queen when she went home with her husband.

Having known that the separation was going to happen for a while before the big wedding, Toots and Mavis had come up with an arrangement for the dogs to be together from time to time.

A few minutes later, Toots pulled around to the back of Abby's house, knowing that Chester would most likely be waiting by the back door. Toots swore he knew when she was coming over. His nose must have been on high alert, because she saw him standing by the kitchen door. He knew not to jump out the doggie door when there was a car in the drive. Again, Toots was amazed at just how smart the dogs were. Smarter than some people she knew.

All four of the dogs piled on top of one another, waiting for her to help them out of the car. Coco raked her little paws on the window when she spied Chester. Toots laughed. "Okay, little Miss Royalty, out you go." She placed the dog on the ground, then scooped the three dachshunds in her arms and lifted them out of the car. Like little troopers, the four dogs marched up the steps, then waited for someone to open the door. Toots took the box containing the old book out of the car, then climbed up the steps and tapped on the back door.

"Be right there," said Abby.

Chester jumped up and down, his tail wagging ninety miles per hour. Abby grinned when she saw them. "Sorry, the door is locked. A precaution with the twins."

After Abby unlocked the door, Toots hugged her daughter. "Understood. Now, where are those perfect little humans? Nana Tootsie has missed them. Oh, here." She held the box out to her daughter. Abby tucked the box under her arm.

"Oh, Mom, Chris just put them down for a nap. They had their snack, and of course they plastered one another with peanut butter, so Chris bathed them and put them down for a while. Maybe they'll wake up while you're here."

"Nonsense! Never wake sleeping babies. I'll see them later. They need to rest when they can. Their little bodies tire out easily when they're that age."

"Tell me that at six in the morning, when they have enough energy to wear out a bear! Come on in. I want you to see the living room. Charlotte is here doing a little last-minute fluff. It really looks festive. I just love Christmas. I can't wait to see what kind of turnout we have."

Picking up on her daughter's excitement, Toots whispered, "Does Charlotte ask you to refer to this room as a parlor?"

Abby looked at her. "No, of course not! Why would you ask such a question?"

Whispering, Toots told her about Blanche. "She's so mean. I swear, when I'm finished with her services, I'm going to tell her what a bitch I think she is."

"Mother! It's Christmas! And remember those little pitchers have big ears."

"I thought you said they were sleeping."

"I did, but you never know. They could be awake. Shhh." Abby placed her index finger over her mouth.

Toots nodded, then followed Abby through the kitchen and dining room to the living room, which was not a parlor. She'd never get that word out of her head. *Damn that Blanche!* She gasped when she entered the main room. "Oh, Abby, this is even more beautiful than I imagined."

Evergreens draped the fireplace mantel. Candles of various heights in red and green had been placed strategically on the mantelpiece. Hard oak logs were stacked high inside the fireplace, waiting to be lit. In front of the fireplace were urns of deep red live poinsettias. On either side of the fireplace, two huge Douglas firs were decorated with colored ornaments in deep ruby red, with shimmering gold ribbons trailing the length of both trees. On closer inspection, Toots saw that many of the ornaments were handmade. Careful, so as not to knock the tree over, she touched a delicately crafted cardinal.

"Is this sweetgrass?" Toots asked Abby.

"Yep. I had a little lady from Mount Pleasant make them. They're dyed with crushed poinsettia leaves." Mount Pleasant was known for its sweetgrass basket making. It was one of the oldest crafts of African origin in America, and Toots had dozens of the baskets in her home. So well crafted, they were almost a luxury now, as many of the old basket makers had died, and many of them had not passed the art form down to the next generation.

Toots continued to admire the well-crafted birds. "How many of these do you have?" she asked.

Abby laughed. "Enough to decorate both trees." She fanned out her arms, pointing at the huge trees behind her.

"Next year, I'm going to do this." So engrossed in inspecting the tree's unique ornaments, Toots didn't pay much attention to the other details in the large room, until she heard someone clearing their throat. She turned around, expecting to see Chris. Instead, she saw a gorgeous, very tall woman with a smattering of gold ribbon trailing from her hands.

"You must be Charlotte," Toots said, extending her hand. "Your work is awesome. Better than Blanche's, to be honest."

Scrunching the bunch of gold ribbon next to her chest, Charlotte held a hand out. "Pleased to meet you, ma'am." Charlotte was so soft-spoken that had Toots not been standing directly in front of her, she wouldn't have heard what she said. She had tactfully avoided commenting on Toots's remark about Blanche. *Good manners*, Toots thought, then mentally chastised herself for having made the indiscreet remark aloud in the first place. She needed to brush up on her social manners. *Especially tonight*, she thought as she imagined Charleston's finest and nosiest as they paraded through her home.

Abby looked at the box still tucked under her arm. "Oh, this is something I thought you might want to see. Mother found it in a box of . . . my husband's father's things."

Toots raised her eyebrows at Abby's explanation. She

could've said, "Father-in-law" or "Stepfather," but hadn't. Too much to explain, what with Phil being Abby's latest stepfather, and truly, it didn't matter.

"Oh, well, of course I'll take a look," Charlotte replied, smiling. Her entire face lit up when she smiled.

Toots thought Ida might want to see this girl. She was stunning. Definitely worthy of a Seasons ad. Ida had taken the cosmetics line a step further when she'd introduced her skin-care products to the younger generation. Sales had skyrocketed, and Toots would bet the bank that those who used her products would age very nicely. She, Sophie, and Mavis had all started using the miracle cream. They could easily subtract eight to ten years from their age, which made them in their early to midsixties. Toots liked that very much. As did all their husbands.

Abby carefully removed the old book from the box. The leather was dry, and there were many cracks in the cover, but all things considered, it wasn't in too bad shape. Toots watched her daughter as she carefully turned the pages in the book.

"Mom, look at this! It's from"—Abby held the book up closer—"the eighteenth century! It says, *The Book of Life and Death*. Good grief, this is a fantastic find. Charlotte, have a look."

Abby gave Charlotte the old tome and watched as she turned the pages with the utmost care. She laid the ribbon on a chair cushion, then continued to skim the pages. Suddenly, she stopped, her face turning as pale as a whitewashed fence.

"Miss Abby, do you mind if I take a few minutes to read through some of this writing?"

Abby shrugged. "Sure. You're finished here. All I have left to do is turn on the lights on the Christmas tree, make sure the lights leading up to the house are on, then get ready. Take all the time you need."

"Thank you, Miss Abby. I'll try to hurry. I promised the kids we'd see about a tree tonight."

Abby had a lightbulb moment. "Charlotte, why don't you bring the kids here tonight? It's open to the public. Maybe you'd like to act like a fly on the wall and see what kind of reaction people have to your tremendous Christmas decor."

"Thank you, but I don't think so. I . . . I'm waiting to hear from Lamar. We've been expecting a Skype call the past week and haven't heard anything. I want to be home just in case he calls." She looked down at the book again. "The kids and I were hoping he'd call so he could watch us decorate the tree. It's been so long since we shared a Christmas together."

Toots sensed there was more Charlotte wasn't telling. It wasn't her place to ask, but she just had to know why the father wasn't home for Christmas. "Charlotte, tell me if I'm prying, and certainly you don't have to answer, but why isn't your husband home for Christmas?"

Charlotte looked at Toots, giving her a sad smile. "He's in the marines. He's been in Afghanistan for the past eighteen months."

Poor girl, Toots thought. "Charlotte, he must be a fine man you've married. So many of our servicemen are underappreciated these days. Did Abby tell you what we're doing with the funds we collect from the parade of homes?"

"No, ma'am," she said politely.

"Abby Clay, I can't believe you didn't tell your friend about our big venture."

Abby shot her mother a "Stop while you're ahead" look. "Charlotte has other things to deal with, Mother."

Okay, Abby calling her "Mother" meant she needed to shut her mouth. "Of course she does. I apologize. Now, I have a zillion and one things to do before tonight. I just wanted to drop the pooches off and bring the book. Are you going to dress the twins in the Christmas outfits I gave them?"

"Of course I am. Amy can't wait to wear her sparkly red shoes. Jonathan, on the other hand, I think he would be okay wearing his little Thomas the Tank Engine undies. He's obsessed with trains now."

Toots chuckled. "He's such a bright little guy, he'll be designing one of those high-speed trains in China."

"I think he's a bit young for that," Abby said. "I hear a dogapalooza in the kitchen. I'd best get those canines to Lacy. She promised she would keep them entertained for the evening." Lacy was studying veterinary medicine and spent as much time as possible volunteering at Dogs Displaced by Disaster.

"Then I will take my leave, even though I missed seeing those little stinkers. When they wake up from their nap, tell them Nana Tootsie will see them tonight."

"Will do, Mom. Don't mean to be rude, but those pooches are getting antsy. Coco is squealing."

Toots blew her daughter a kiss, then turned to Charlotte, who was still looking through the old book. "Charlotte, the invitation stands, if you change your mind."

She looked up and gave Toots a wan smile that didn't reach her eyes. "Yes, ma'am. I doubt that I can, but thank you again."

With nothing more to keep her, Toots left through the back door. Abby and the dogs were racing to the buildings where the Dogs Displaced by Disaster offices had been set up. They'd have a blast tonight.

Ten minutes later, Toots returned to find the entire gang, all but Sophie, Goebel, and Wade Powell, at the house she shared with Phil.

"Okay. What's up?" she asked her husband, who wore an ear-to-ear grin and stopped to give her a kiss.

"It's a surprise," Phil said.

"Mavis, Ida, Bernice, do you know anything about this? Robert? Daniel?"

Sure that they'd been instructed by Phil prior to her return, Toots observed as they all made a massive show of zipping their lips.

"We've been instructed to keep quiet, Toots. Something I know you find very hard to do, but I think you will find this surprise worth waiting for," Ida said with her usual air of cattiness.

"One of these days, I'm gonna smack the shit right out of you, Ida. Bernice, would you be so kind as to make us a pot of coffee? The doors open in an hour, and something tells me I'm going to need all the caffeine I can drink before they do. Mavis, please call Jamie and Lucy at the bakery. They're baking all kinds of desserts for tonight. Ask Jamie if she has extra pralines. My sugar is so low, I may faint, but first I have to smoke."

Toots found her smokes on the counter, where she'd left them. She would not smoke in front of her grandchildren and wouldn't even carry cigarettes with her when she planned to be around them, just in case they decided to pry in her purse, something she allowed that Abby didn't approve of. Chris encouraged them, telling them that whatever loose change Nana Tootsie had, it belonged to them. They all got quite a kick out of this, but still Toots didn't want the kids knowing she smoked. She'd cut down drastically, but she needed a hearty dose of nicotine right now, before the evening's festivities began.

Chapter 4

Charlotte stepped off the bus in front of the run-down apartments in North Charleston where she and her three children had lived for the past year. Even though it was still light out, she scanned the sidewalk to make sure no one had followed her. More than once she'd been harassed on her walk home from the bus stop, and so far she had managed to keep the thugs and drunks at bay. Base housing had a waiting list, and, sadly, they were at the bottom. Still.

With three kids, and drowning in medical bills from her mother's cancer treatment before she had been able to get insurance when the Affordable Care Act went into effect, Charlotte had been fortunate to find a decent job with Ms. Harding's interior designing firm as soon as they'd returned to Charleston, not long after her mother's death. She still missed her. Missed her stories. And Roxanna, her eldest, was still grieving. Even though it had been over a year, she still cried when they spoke of her. She'd been quite close to her gramma. Riley was five, and though he remembered Gramma, he hadn't been as close to her as his big sister had been. Rhonda was just a toddler when her grandmother died, and at three she really didn't remember too much about their life in Texas before moving back to South Carolina.

When Lamar was once again stationed in South Carolina, Charlotte had been thrilled. This was her birthplace, her mother's birthplace, and her grandmother's and great-grandmother's, too. The great-great-greats were from Charleston, too, but she'd never heard too many tales about their lives other than that two of them had actually been slaves. It blew her mind to think that any family member had endured such a life, but sadly, as her mother had explained to her, this was still accepted in the South less than two hundred years ago.

It didn't matter now, she thought as she opened the gate to the courtyard. What mattered most was her current circumstances. After she paid the rent, the electric bill, plus the water and gas, she had just enough money for groceries at the commissary. Lamar's checks had stopped coming two months ago, and it was getting harder to make ends meet. She'd contacted the human resources people at the base, filled out a dozen different forms, and been told to wait. Well, she was tired of waiting. And more than anything, she was so very worried about Lamar.

She hadn't told this to anyone, because she didn't have any real friends. Yes, she did. Miss Abby was sort of a friend. Treated her as though she was a good friend instead of an employee. Abby had asked few personal questions during the time they'd spent together. Charlotte had told her the generic version of her life, but that was it. Her mother had always said it was best to leave personal problems at home. Charlotte agreed. There wasn't any point in sharing too many details, as things were now.

Maybe when Lamar came home, she would allow their friendship to flourish.

She climbed the three flights of stairs to her apartment

and took her last twenty-dollar bill from her purse before stepping inside. Tracy, her sixteen-year-old neighbor, watched Roxanna and Riley when they came home from school. Rhonda stayed with another neighbor, Lucinda, who ran a day-care center from her apartment. It wasn't ideal—far from it—as there were six little ones crammed into the small apartment, but the kids were well taken care of, fed, and Rhonda was always clean and happy when Charlotte picked her up. When Lamar came home, things would be different.

If Lamar called her tonight, early morning his time, she would tell him that everything would be 100 percent perfect if he were there, and as always, she would assure him that they were getting along just fine. She stepped inside the apartment and pasted her happy grin on her face. Roxanna was playing checkers with Riley at the kitchen table. Tracy was talking ninety miles a minute on a hot pink cell phone. She waved at her.

"Momma, look at this," Riley said. "I'm winning. I have four kings, and Roxie has only one." Riley was the spitting image of his father. Big brown eyes, soft, curly hair, and at five, he was already taller than all the children in his kindergarten class.

"Well, I'd say your big sister taught you well." She dropped her purse on the counter and stood by the table, watching her kids battle it out. "You're both good. I don't think I'd have a chance with either of you."

"Mom, you know you can beat me. I know you let me win," Roxanna said. "I'm ten, remember?" Charlotte knew that Roxanna, who was tall and lanky, but shaped more like her, would grow into herself, and when she did, watch out. She was a beautiful child. Green eyes and light brown hair, she was the best of her and Lamar. Rhonda had the same green eyes, yet she was a petite little girl. Charlotte knew when these two matured, she'd have to be on high alert. The thought made her smile.

"Hey, I never let you win! You're just too good for me to beat you. And I do remember your telling me you were ten. I believe you reminded me again this morning, before school."

They laughed.

Tracy finished her phone call. "I'll see you guys tomorrow. I've got homework to do. They ate the mac and cheese I fixed, but I think they're still hungry."

Those words went through Charlotte's heart like a knife.

"I'll fix something else as soon as I get Rhonda. Thanks so much, Tracy. Don't know what I'd do without you." She placed the twenty-dollar bill in Tracy's hand. "I might run a bit late this week. I'm working on the plantation homes for the holiday parade this year. They're all decked out for Christmas. I have to make sure the flowers are fresh, and lots of other things, so if I am late, can you stay?" Charlotte wanted to ask how much more it would cost her, but she didn't.

"Sure, as long as I let Mom know. I can bring my homework with me. We're having finals now. It sucks bigtime."

Charlotte raised her brows at her language.

"Sorry. I forget they're little kids sometimes," Tracy said. "I'll meet you two at the bus stop tomorrow at three, okay?"

"Yeah!" both kids shouted.

"And bring that lipstick you told me about, too!" Roxanna exclaimed.

"Roxanna! You're too young for makeup!" Charlotte teased.

Tracy waved and left.

It was after six, and Charlotte needed to bring Rhonda home. "You two sit tight while I get Rhonda."

They nodded and went back to their game.

Charlotte calculated the time in Kabul. It was about three thirty in the morning there. If Lamar was planning on calling, it would be in the next couple of hours, as he always called her before starting his day. She didn't know how she was going to manage to find a Christmas tree, make something else for the kids' dinner, and keep acting as if everything were hunky-dory. Grateful the kids hadn't asked about the Christmas tree when she'd walked through the door, she thought about putting it off for another day or two, but then she had promised them, and she rarely broke her promises.

She hurried downstairs, hoping she'd get in and out quickly. Lucinda liked to chat, and sometimes it was hard to get away from her. Charlotte understood her need for adult conversation after ten to twelve hours with six children under three, but she could get extremely long-winded.

After tapping on the door, Charlotte heard Lucinda's "It's open," and hoped she didn't say this to strangers. Inside, it was a madhouse. Four three-year-olds, including Rhonda, were running through the small living room in the midst of a game of tattletale tag. She still wasn't quite sure what the game was all about, but the little ones seemed to be enjoying themselves.

"Hey, woman, you look like crap." Lucinda motioned for her to sit. "Take a load off."

"Thanks. I'd love to, but I promised the kids we'd get a tree tonight and decorate. They're antsy up there." She nodded toward the ceiling.

"Well, I can understand that." Lucinda's Southern drawl was almost comical. "I ain't too sure about putting a tree up this year." She looked at the kids, who hadn't stopped running through the living room. "Not sure how long it would last."

Charlotte nodded. "Might not be a bad idea. Maybe you could string some lights in the windows."

"Yeah, I'll probably do something. Can't have all these kiddies here during the holidays without something Christmassy. We're gonna make ornaments from macaroni this week. You okay with Rhonda using a bit of glue and glitter?"

"She'd love that. Sure. Okay, Rhonda." She raised her voice over the noise. "It's time to go home."

The little girl ran into the kitchen. "Mommy! I'm the biggest tattler!"

The two women laughed.

"That's a very good thing. Get your backpack now. Your brother and sister are anxious to see you." Charlotte said this almost every day. Her youngest never tired of hearing it.

"They are?" she asked, her big green eyes as round as marbles.

"You bet," Charlotte said while Rhonda found her backpack in a pile with several others.

"I'll bring her tomorrow, around eight, if that's all right. I need to get an early start."

Lucinda walked her to the door. "Of course it's all right. Heck, some of these kids are here at five. Anytime you need to bring her early, just come on up. No extra charge, either," she said.

"I appreciate that," Charlotte said. "Times are a bit tough, since Lamar's check seems to be lost in a pile of paperwork."

"Ain't that just like the U.S. government? Send our men into battle and don't give a good poop about the families waiting at home. You need to run a tab, no worries. I'm happy to take care of this little gal." She fluffed Rhonda's hair. "She minds better than any of the other kids."

"That's good to hear," Charlotte said, then added, "Speaking of kids, I'd best get back home. I've got two more waiting for their dinner."

"I'll see you in the morning," said Lucinda, waving, then closing the door behind her.

An hour later, Charlotte had made a quick supper of pancakes and scrambled eggs. The kids gobbled their food down quickly; then one by one they placed their plates in the sink, where Charlotte gave them a quick wash. With the last dish rinsed and dried, she tossed the dish towel on the counter. It was now or never.

"I think it's time for us to get the Christmas tree."

The words were barely out of her mouth before the three children started clapping and jumping up and down. Their excitement contagious, she found herself actually looking forward to shopping for their tree, even though she detested walking through the neighborhood at this hour, and especially with her children. Remembering her mother's favorite quote by Theodore Roosevelt, "Do what you can, with what you have, where you are," she decided to do just that. She just prayed she could find a tree that fit her reduced means.

"Jackets on first," she said. "It's going to be colder than a frog tonight."

"Momma, how can it be colder than a frog?" Rhonda asked. "I don't wanna touch one, either."

She laughed. "Oh, sweetie, that's just a silly old expression my mother used to use."

"Oh," Rhonda said, apparently accepting her explanation.

"We're ready," Roxanna said, holding their jackets. "I mean, we have to put these on, and then we're ready."

Charlotte smiled at her eldest daughter. She was growing up so fast. Sad that Lamar was missing so much of their children's lives, she pushed the thought aside. Tonight was not the time for regrets and what-ifs.

"I'll get my purse," she said. "Christmas tree, here we come!"

Chapter 5

Sophie inspected herself in the full-length mirror. The deep green Escada pants and matching jacket complemented her dark olive complexion. She wore the two-carat diamond studs Goebel had given her as a pre-Christmas gift.

"I like," Goebel said when he saw her.

"Really?" Sophie asked, twirling around for show.

"Really. It's going to be hard for the guests to take their eyes off you. I think all those decorations won't stand a chance."

Sophie laughed. "You sure know how to kiss ass, don't you?" She was joking, and they both knew it.

"I do, and I love every minute of it."

She stopped and really looked at her husband. Dressed in a black Armani suit and a claret-colored shirt, he looked every bit the man about town. "You know, you look sexy as hell. I think I just might jump your bones again. Soon as we close up shop." Sophie stepped into his embrace. She'd never felt so safe. So protected. So loved. Having this sweet, dear man was what she lived for.

And the gang, too. They'd started referring to everyone as the gang since the numbers seemed to keep increasing. Sophie relished each and every one of them. Well, maybe *relish* wasn't the word she would use to describe Ida, but still, if Ida were missing from their gang, she would be missed. No way in hell would she ever tell her that, of course, but she was willing to bet that the feelings were mutual. She and Ida had continued their love/hate friendship for a bit less than sixty years. Sophie didn't see it coming to an end just because Ida was a conceited old whore. Nope, she loved messing with her, calling her names and just being a general pain in the ass.

Goebel gazed into her eyes. "What's going on in that beautiful head of yours?"

She stepped away, returning to the mirror to add a deep red lipstick to complete her holiday attire. "You don't want to know," she said, rubbing her lips together. "It's not about you."

"Then my heart is broken. I want you thinking about me as much as I think about you. You know, dream, fantasize, all that fun stuff."

She grinned. "Oh, I do that most of the time."

"Good. Now, I think it's time we go downstairs, hit the lights, and see what kind of turnout we'll have."

"I'll allow you to escort me downstairs, Mr. Blevins."

"My pleasure, Mrs. Blevins."

Hand in hand, the two of them walked down the hall to the winding staircase, whose banister was entwined with fresh evergreens and twinkling white lights.

In the formal living room, to which they'd devoted most of their energies, Sophie squealed with delight when she saw that Goebel had turned on all the lights. The candles shimmered, bathing the room with just a light touch of vanilla.

Spying the box of candleholders Abby had given her earlier in the day, she carefully removed them and placed them in the center of the mantel above the main fireplace in the formal living room. She added a tapered silver candle to each, trimmed the wicks, then lit both candles. As an extra precaution, she repositioned the holders as far away from the edge of the mantel as possible. She couldn't have someone accidentally breaking them.

After taking a step back to admire the antique candle-holders, she closed her eyes for a moment, then opened them. What she saw was so unexpected that she screamed, "No!"

"Sophie, what's wrong?" Goebel asked, then wrapped her in his arms. "Are you all right?"

Trembling, Sophie shook her head. Her hands began to shake violently, and her knees weakened. "I need to sit down."

He guided her to the cream-colored sofa that faced the fireplace.

"No, not in here. The kitchen," she managed to say.

Goebel scooped her up in his arms and carried her to the kitchen, where he gently placed her in a kitchen chair. "Don't move." He grabbed a clean kitchen towel, then ran cold water over it.

"Here. Let me." He dabbed the damp towel over her face and neck. Sophie's eyes were closed. "Soph, you okay? You're starting to scare me."

Again, she nodded but kept her eyes closed. While Goebel dabbed at her with the towel, she forced herself to calm down. She began taking slow, deep breaths and exhaling, as she'd taught herself. In and out. Finally calm enough, she slowly opened her eyes. When she saw that she really was in the moment in her kitchen, she let out a deep sigh.

Neither spoke. Quietly, they remained seated at the table for the next five minutes. Goebel knew enough not to say anything until she gave the go-ahead. Though this was a bit odd, he trusted her to know what she needed to do.

"It's that girl I saw today. The one Abby hired to decorate."

"Okay." Goebel didn't want to say too much, didn't want to distract her from whatever it was she needed to say.

"I need to see her, Goebel. Tonight. I . . . I don't know exactly why, and it's scaring the hell out of me. I know I can't read her, but I should be able to. I just know something is going on with that girl. Maybe even right now. I have to get to her." Sophie raised her voice. "Let's forget this Christmas parade tonight. I have to get to Abby's right now."

"Meet me in the car in thirty seconds, Sophie." Though it was a bit of an understatement, Goebel knew time was not on their side now. He raced through the downstairs, turning off lights and blowing out candles. Sophie grabbed her purse and met him in the car.

He cranked the engine, stomped on the gas, and fishtailed out of the drive and onto the main road. Luckily, there wasn't much traffic, so he pushed the speed limit as much as he dared without endangering them or anyone else who just so happened to be driving on the road.

Five minutes later, Goebel pulled through the gates at Abby's old plantation house. The drive leading up to the house was lit up with colorful white lights. The oak trees above, decorated with more white lights, created a tunnel-like effect as they slowly followed several other vehicles.

"They must be here for the parade," Goebel said, stating the obvious.

"Stop! I can run faster than you can drive there. Meet me inside the house." Sophie tossed her heels on the floor, then jumped out of the car and started running. Goebel wanted to chase after her but realized he was being unreasonable. She knew what she needed to do, and he needed to listen to her.

Impatiently, he followed the cars to an area Abby had reserved for parking. Without bothering to remove the keys from the ignition, he jumped out of the car and ran around to the back of the house and entered through the kitchen.

"Chris, Abby?" he yelled, hoping he wasn't about to make a fool of himself.

A drone of "oohs" and "aahs" could be heard all the way in the kitchen. He hated to disrupt the holiday-house showing, so he casually, though not at all slowly, made his way to the main room. Several people were gathered about the room in small groups. Abby and Chris were acting as host and hostess, explaining a bit of their home's history to their visitors.

"And this was also discovered some time ago." Abby held out the old leather-bound book that Toots had brought over that afternoon.

Before she could explain its contents, Sophie emerged from behind a group. "Abby, I need to speak with you privately. Now." She turned around, saw Goebel, and motioned for him to follow.

Abby handed the book to Chris, making a hasty apology, then followed them to the kitchen.

"Sophie, this better be a matter of life and death! You just embarrassed the crap out of me in front of those people. I hope you have a good excuse." Abby was miffed, and that was putting it mildly.

"I'm sorry. There isn't a lot of time to explain. I need to know where that girl lives, the one that was here today, when I picked up the candleholders. It's urgent, Abby!" Sophie wasn't joking. She spoke fast, not caring if she'd embarrassed Abby or not. She would make it up to her later.

Astonished, Abby asked, "Are you serious?"

"Never been more so in my life. Now, Abby, I need to

know right now!" Sophie raised her voice to stress the urgency.

Abby looked dumbfounded. "I'm not sure. She never said, and I never had a reason to ask."

"Oh, crap! What about the woman she works for? That Blanche, whatever her last name is."

Taking a deep breath, Abby opened a drawer and took out her address book. "I have her number. I can call and ask, but other than that, I don't know what else I can do for you. Why? Is this one of your psychic visions?" She thumbed through the pages of her address book, stopping when she found Blanche's phone number. "Let me use your cell," she said. Sophie handed her the phone.

She punched in the number, and they all waited, each holding her or his breath. When Abby finally spoke, they all exhaled. "Blanche. Abby Clay. I hate to bother you, but we've had a bit of an emergency. I need to talk to Charlotte. Rather, I need her address. We've had a problem."

"No, no, nothing like that," Abby said. "Yes, her work is fabulous. Of course she agreed to come back tomorrow. Please, Blanche, just give me her address. This is very personal, nothing to do with Christmas decorations. Yes, I'll hold." Abby placed her hand over the microphone so as not to be heard, and said to Sophie and Goebel, "This woman is a true bitch. I'm never using her again."

"Yes, Blanche, I have a pen." Abby motioned for Sophie to hand her the pen and pad in the drawer. "Yes, I've got it. Thanks." She hit the END button, then tossed the phone to Sophie. "Here is the address. It's in North Charleston."

Sophie touched the address and closed her eyes. "Goebel, let's get over there as fast as we can. Abby, I want you to call Charlotte and tell her I'm coming over. Make up something, but just do it."

Sophie didn't wait for an answer. She raced out the door, with Goebel on her heels. In the car, she punched the address into the GPS while Goebel maneuvered through the parked cars. Once they'd made it out to the main road, Goebel put the pedal to the metal, again, trying to drive safely but fast.

"So, any clue what's going on?" he asked as he made a sharp left turn.

"A jumble of different images hit me when I lit those candles. A man. A little girl, and . . . some kind of metal. Maybe a garbage can or something. I don't know. At least that's what I think I saw. . . . I'm working on putting the pieces together. Just get me there, Goebel, before it's too late."

Chapter 6

The "parlor" looked like something out of *Architectural Digest*. Though Toots hated to admit it, Blanche Harding and her team had transformed the room into a historical-holiday dream room to be envied. At the last minute, she'd begged Toots to allow her to add real candles to the trees, but Toots had remained adamant. No fires on her tree. Take it or leave it. Blanche had acted as though Toots was ignorant of certain "historically accurate *thangs*," but not everyone could be expected to know as much as she did. Toots had wanted to smack her decorator, had wanted to tell her that the proper way to say "*thangs*" was "*things*," but had decided it wasn't the time for pettiness. Blanche had left after Toots refused to agree with her dangerous requests.

Phil looked as handsome as ever. He wore a dark gray suit, and his silver tie matched her dress. She'd never been one of those women who wanted "her man" to match, but the tie was perfect. Just the right amount of elegance to let everyone see that they were a married couple who shared similar tastes in clothing. Frankly, she didn't give a good rat's ass what anyone thought. She was happy; her marriage to Dr. Phillip Becker was as good as she had thought it would be; and her daughter and son-in-law, who was also her stepson, along with her adorable grandchildren, were all thriving. Life didn't get any better, she thought.

"So?" Toots said to Phil. "Think we'll have any crazies visiting our home tonight?"

He laughed. "Toots, if we didn't, the evening wouldn't be a success. Of course we will. All those gossipmongers you have been telling me about the past two years are sure to be here any minute." He looked at his watch. "And it's time to open the doors."

Taking a deep breath, Toots unlocked the heavy wooden doors and pulled them aside. A large crowd had gathered on her front steps. She looked at the small table she'd set up at the entry, and the book she'd arranged on top for guests to sign. At the end of the tour, she had an area set up where donations were being accepted. She and Phil had hired a team of waitpersons to keep the desserts that Jamie had made flowing, and to make sure the pralines were in abundance.

If all went according to plan during the month of December, Hope for Heroes would take in enough money to buy much-needed homes for the needy veterans. Since Bernice was such a coupon clipper these days, and Robert counted pennies as though his life depended on it, they'd volunteered to handle the donations. The finances of Toots's latest charitable effort were in good hands tonight.

The crowd formed a line. Some stopped to sign the guest book; others chose to race through the line to see the "parlor."

Toots heard bits of conversation as the fine folks of Charleston paraded through the room.

"I would never leave this room if it were mine!" said a young woman.

"Lovely!"

"What's that smell? It's divine," one woman remarked.

"Look at the size of those trees!"

"I bet this cost her a pretty penny," said another.

The group of Charleston's wealthiest women finally arrived right before eight o'clock, the hour to close up shop for the evening, just as Toots had known they would. They'd never be so gauche as to arrive on time or during an event. Toots tucked a stray hair in place as she prepared to greet the old hags.

"Mona Livingston, it's been what? At least thirty years and then some. You *are* Mona Livingston?" Toots added the last question just for meanness, knowing full well it was she, but wanting to get in the first dig.

Mona had not aged well. Too much time spent in her garden, tossing back vodka tonics, had taken a toll on her face, which was wrinkled as an old prune. If Toots were nice, she'd offer her some of Ida's special cream and tell her what a difference it would make. But she wouldn't, because she wanted the gossiping drunk to look as ugly on the outside as she was on the inside. Toots had heard that she was also mean to her gardener, and to his wife, who cleaned for her. Toots didn't like mean, not one little bit. Ornery, yes. But pure meanness, not even a smidgen.

"You know exactly who I am! I can see you're still as . . . unsophisticated as you were the day you arrived in Charleston," Mona huffed.

Toots wanted to rub her hands together in anticipation of a good verbal brawl, but instead, she simply smiled. "Oh, Mona, I can't believe you would even remember such an inconsequential day. I don't."

Toots walked away from Mona before she had a chance to reply. Phil had been standing to the side and a bit behind Toots. He winked at her, letting his wife know he'd heard their conversation. She blew him a kiss and hoped like hell Mona was watching.

Behind Mona came the self-appointed leader of what Toots thought of as the "old hags of Charleston," Bethany

Middleton-Spalling. Bethany could trace her ancestors back to the dinosaur age. Toots had had lunch with her once when she'd first moved to Charleston. All Mona had talked about were her family's lineage and how sinful she thought it was to marry outside one's station. She'd reminded Toots of a character in a Victoria Holt novel, minus the happy ending.

"Beth, how nice of you to come. I just knew you and the girls"—she nodded to the two other women who were official members of the "old hags of Charleston"—"would show up. Nothing better to do, I'm guessing?" Toots smiled, her eyes alight with mischief.

"In case you were unaware, I am currently the cochairwoman of Charleston's historical society. I'm here to check for accuracy, nothing more." Short and stocky, Beth, or Bethany, as she preferred, still wore the same short, blunt hairstyle she had sported when Toots had met her all those years ago and, for some reason, had tried to fit into all the right clubs. Fortunately, she'd learned very quickly that they weren't her idea of fun, but their members had never really forgotten her. At least twice a year, she was invited to join some new ladies' club, to attend some luncheon or other function, at which large donations were required. Toots donated to some of their causes but always anonymously. She had never needed or wanted their approval or their phony friendship.

"I wasn't aware of that. I would have thought by now you would've been made chairwoman, but I truly have been so busy traveling to and from California, I haven't had time to keep up with every single detail. Regardless, I'm glad you stopped by. You have a Merry Christmas, dear," Toots said, then walked away, not giving the cochairwoman a chance to make a riposte.

Beth's two puppets, who followed behind, didn't bother to acknowledge the exchange they'd just witnessed. Toots figured the second the four made their final exit, their jaws would be flapping so fast, they'd stir up hurricane-force winds. She giggled at the image.

Toots made her way to the main room, or rather the "parlor," and saw a few people still lingering, admiring the trees. She made small talk with one young couple. As she spoke, she led them to the door. Three others followed, with only one couple remaining.

Bernice pulled Toots aside before she had a chance to leave the room. "It's after eight o'clock. Isn't it time to shut down for the night? Robert's dying for a cup of coffee, and I have to pee. And we both want to go home."

"Go on. I'll see this couple to the door. And make a big pot of coffee. Phil and I will join you as soon as I lock the doors."

Twenty minutes later, Toots escorted the last couple out, then made sure that the front door was locked and the gates were closed for the night. Upstairs, in the room she shared with her husband, she traded her shimmery dress for a pair of jeans and a cherry-red T-shirt with a picture of a dachshund on the front.

Downstairs in the kitchen, where the gang congregated, Toots expected to see Sophie and Goebel, maybe Chris or Abby, but was surprised when it was just Bernice, Robert, Phil, and Mavis.

Rather than going upstairs to change, Phil had just removed his jacket and tie, tossing both over the back of his chair. He smiled when he saw her. "I love a redhead brave enough to wear red." He nodded at her shirt.

"It's my favorite color, as you well know, dear husband. I wouldn't dare to *not* wear red," Toots said. She reached for the pot in the middle of the table, poured herself a cup, then added five heaping spoons of sugar. Half-and-half, too. She took a sip and sighed. "Ahhh. I needed this."

"The sugar or the cream?" Bernice asked. "You don't have enough coffee in that mug for a pissant."

Toots flipped her off. "It's all good, Bernice. You, of all people, should know by now how much I like my coffee loaded."

"Between the sugar and the cigarettes, you're killing yourself," her husband chimed in, as he always did when her bad habits were being discussed.

She wanted to give him the finger, too, but decided not to, even though he'd watched her flip Bernice off. Another bad habit she was trying to work on. If Amy or Jonathan saw her do this, Abby would never forgive her.

Before she could respond, her cell phone rang. She looked at the caller ID and saw that it was Sophie.

But by the time she tried to answer, Sophie had hung up. Toots couldn't wait to hear about her first night in the parade of homes and figured she would call again later.

Chapter 7

The temperature was dropping faster than reported, and Charlotte wished she hadn't chosen tonight to buy their Christmas tree, but it was too late now. She shivered in her thin jacket as they walked, hunched close together, along the dark street. Streetlights loomed along their shadowy walk, minus the bright bulbs that would normally give one a sense of security. Along this stretch, someone had either shot the lights out with a gun or possibly thrown something heavy enough to break them. Whatever the reason for the missing bulbs, Charlotte hurried the kids along. Three more blocks to DiPalma's, a local mom-and-pop grocery store, where she'd spied several Christmas trees this morning, on her commute to work.

Roxanna held Riley's hand, and Charlotte had his and Rhonda's hands in a firm grip. Rhonda was at the age where she would up and disappear in seconds, and right now Charlotte didn't dare let go of her mitten-covered little hand.

"Momma, I need to go to the bathroom," Riley said, then began to hop up and down.

"We're almost there, sweetie. Just hang on," Charlotte said encouragingly. She shouldn't even be out this late with her kids, walking in this cruddy part of town. She picked up her pace, practically dragging the kids behind her.

"Mom!" Roxanna exclaimed. "We can't keep up with you."

Charlotte forced herself to slow down. They were fine. No one had bothered them or even paid any attention to them. She was making a bad situation much worse. Riley needed to get to the bathroom. That was the only immediate problem she had.

"Sorry, kids," she said.

"Momma, I can't wait!" Riley yelled. "I have to go now!"

"Roxanna, take your sister and follow me. Meet us in front of the store."

Without another word, she picked Riley up and ran the remaining block to DiPalma's. She blew through the door. "Where's the restroom?"

The young girl at the register pointed to the back of the store. Charlotte didn't waste another second getting Riley to the restroom. Inside, she helped him with his jeans and saw the relief on his little face. Poor Riley. He was at an age when having an accident was the worst thing he could imagine happening to him.

"See, Momma? I am big!" He held his long arms high in the air.

"Yes, you are. Now, wash up so we can pick out a tree."

Riley had to fiddle with the faucet to adjust the water temperature just right, and then he had to soap his hands more than necessary. Then he had to play with the automatic hand-towel dispenser.

"Riley, come along this minute. I think your hands are clean enough."

"But they're not dry," he whined as she led him out the door.

"Shhh," Charlotte admonished. "They're fine."

Hurrying now, as the girls were probably waiting, she

stepped outside with Riley. A crowd had gathered in front of the store, where several people were shouting obscenities. Hoisting Riley on her hip, she forced her way through the group.

"Roxanna! Rhonda!" She hollered loudly, her voice causing a few of those engaged in the verbal fight to stop for a brief second and look at her. Apparently, she didn't warrant their attention, because their shouting match resumed.

"Roxanna, Rhonda!" She pushed her way through a small group of teenagers. Cigarette smoke wafted in the cold night air. Riley coughed. Shouting her daughters' names over the group of hoodlums, Charlotte almost collapsed with relief when she saw the girls huddled against the side of the building.

"Momma, we were scared! Those boys called us a bad word," Roxanna said, tears streaming down her face. For once, Rhonda remained completely quiet.

Charlotte lowered Riley from her hip and grabbed her girls in a hug. "Oh, sweetie, I'm sorry. You did the right thing by staying here. You're safe now," Charlotte said. Anger soared through her. Her heart rate increased, and even though it was cold outside, she felt a gush of perspiration under her arms. Sweat dotted her hairline, and her hands began to tremble. She had to get the kids inside before the thugs' verbal warfare escalated into something worse.

Gathering Roxanna and Riley closer to her, she scooped Rhonda into her arms and raced inside the store. The young girl behind the register—she couldn't have been a day over eighteen—looked at the entrance and back at Charlotte as though she was asking her what to do.

Not wasting a minute, Charlotte said, "Call nine-one-one."

Nodding, the teenager picked up the receiver to an old-style wall-mounted phone with push buttons and punched in the three numbers. "This is DiPalma's Grocery. We . . .

uh, we seem to have a gang out front. I'm afraid they might . . ." She looked to Charlotte.

"Rob us," Charlotte said, feeding her the words, knowing that if she told the emergency operator that a group of punks was having a shouting match, they wouldn't consider this a true emergency. And who knew when they'd send an officer?

"Rob the store," the young girl said, nodding at Charlotte.

"Momma, what's wrong?" Roxanna said. "Those boys won't move away from the Christmas trees. What are we gonna do?"

It was times such as this that Charlotte hated Lamar for having joined the Marines. She needed him here to protect their children, not in some wild foreign country where politics and terrorist threats kept him from his family and where everything he was fighting for would go up in smoke the minute he and his fellow soldiers left.

"We are going to be the tough soldiers Daddy would want us to be. I want all three of you to be very quiet. Stay right where you are."

Their eyes were the size of quarters, and each child nodded solemnly. The cashier nodded, too.

Charlotte had a zillion and one thoughts running through her head. Lamar. Was he safe? Why hadn't he called? The alternative . . . Well, she wouldn't even go there. Servicemen and servicewomen experienced this all the time, she thought. Lamar had told her more than once that if she went a few weeks or months and didn't hear from him, she should not worry. He'd explained that there would be times when his location had to be kept secret. She had accepted that but truly hadn't expected it to be an issue. And now it was, and she was more than concerned. Just then, she wished for her mother. Her calm assurance was needed now more than ever. She gave up a prayer for both Lamar and her current situation.

The thought had barely entered her mind when she heard the high-pitched wail of sirens in the background. Breathing a sigh of relief, she said, "Help is on the way." This was more for the young girl than the kids. They were too young to realize the magnitude of what could happen. She glanced at the clock on the wall behind the register. It was after eight o'clock. If Lamar were to call, she'd have to race back to the apartment so as not to miss his call.

The ruckus in front of the store broke up, the teens escaping before the police could arrive. Charlotte hoped this was the end of whatever they were arguing about.

"I want you three to stay here. Don't move until I tell you it's okay," Charlotte said.

Again, the trio nodded, knowing now wasn't the time to question her instructions. The cashier peered around the counter as Charlotte made her way to the store's entrance. Thankful the doors weren't automatic, she pushed the door open, then stepped out into the brisk night. Cigarette smoke lingered in the air, footsteps could be heard pounding against the sidewalk, but she saw no sign of the former crowd of belligerent teenagers. As she was about to turn around and head inside, two police cars pulled alongside the curb.

"Are you the person who called?" asked a powerfully built officer as he exited his patrol car.

"No, but I told the girl inside to make the call," Charlotte said, her voice filled with relief. The other three officers didn't speak to her as they hurried inside.

Following them, she rushed over to the kids. "It's fine. The police are here, and those boys are gone."

Charlotte and the cashier were both questioned by one officer while his partner took notes, and the other two went outside to search the surrounding area, just to make sure there were no surprises. Apparently satisfied, they returned.

"All clear," one of them announced.

They took Charlotte's information and the cashier's, and told them to call again if the belligerent teens returned.

"Ma'am, I didn't see a vehicle out front," said the officer who had conducted the questioning.

Charlotte was a bit embarrassed when she answered. "No, there isn't one. We walked from Park River." She had given them the name of her apartment complex so they would know she wasn't *that* far away on a cold night like tonight, with three kids in tow.

"I wouldn't advise you to walk back to that area," said the officer who'd questioned her. "We can offer you a ride home."

More relieved than she wanted to admit, she nodded. "Thank you, Officer"—she read the silver-plated badge on his shirt—"Watkins."

By now, Roxanna, Riley, and Rhonda had calmed down enough to start getting antsy.

"What about our Christmas tree?" Riley asked. "You promised we'd get a tree."

Taking a deep breath, Charlotte nodded. "Yes, I did."

The cashier, who'd yet to speak directly to her, spoke up. "Pick out any tree you want. It's on the house. My parents own the place."

Charlotte smiled. "If you're sure? I'd be happy to pay you."

"Absolutely," the girl answered.

The young girl grinned, and then Charlotte looked at the officer who'd offered to take them home. "I can carry the tree back to the apartment," she said.

"I don't think that's a good idea. I can load the tree in the trunk."

"Are you sure? I don't want to be a nuisance."

"I'm sure," he replied. "Ensuring the safety of Charleston's citizens, especially the little ones, is never a nuisance."

Before she decided against taking the offer, she motioned to the kids. "Let's go pick out a Christmas tree. If we hurry, we can be home in time to Skype with your dad."

Charlotte crossed her fingers.

Hope.

Something she'd been short on of late.

Chapter 8

Goebel skidded to a stop in front of the run-down apartment complex. "Man, this doesn't look like the best area in town," he remarked, stating the obvious as he climbed out of the SUV.

Sophie, intent on the mission she still hadn't a clue about, jumped out of the SUV, scanning the numbers on the building. In the dark, she could hardly make out the numbers. "Goebel, shine that cell phone light you have on these buildings," she instructed as she weaved through the plain block structures.

He removed his iPhone from his pocket and clicked the app with the brightest light ever. Shining it back and forth in search of the correct building number, he followed Sophie as she continued to zigzag through the complex.

"Here," she shouted when she came to number 6378. "Upstairs." She hurried up the metal staircase to the third floor, in search of apartment 55-E.

As soon as she'd located the right apartment, Sophie banged on the door so loudly, Goebel's ears rang. When no one came to the door, she pounded even harder.

"Sophie!" Goebel whispered.

"I don't care," she shot back. "I need to make sure

they're all right." She banged on the door a third time. "If you're in there, open up! I'm a friend of Abby's."

Nothing but silence.

Sophie turned away from the door, unsure what to do next. She'd been led here by her psychic abilities, even though she'd yet to receive a message of any kind telling her just exactly what the problem was. Again, she wished Madam Butterfly, her old friend and a mentor of sorts, were still alive to give her guidance.

"Are you sure this is the right apartment?" Goebel asked.

Sophie took the slip of paper, on which Abby had written the address, from her pocket. "It's sixty-three seventy-eight, apartment fifty-five-E," she read aloud. At a loss, Sophie turned to her husband. "What now?"

He wrapped her in his arms. "I'm not sure, Soph. This is your show. Maybe you're just getting the wrong signal. Maybe it's another kind of . . ." Goebel searched for the right word for their current dilemma. "Situation."

Taking a deep breath, she nodded. "Okay. Then what next? Do I leave here, or do we hang out like some Peeping Toms or lurkers, waiting for her to come home? I can't figure out why I'm not getting any clear images. If this woman is in the kind of trouble I felt earlier, then she's toast." Sophie stepped out of her husband's embrace. "I don't like this, not one little bit."

"We can wait in the car if you want. Hang around, see if she comes home or anything else happens."

"Toots is going to slice my tits off for not hosting the Christmas house tonight. I did try to call, though."

Goebel gave a dry laugh. "I don't think Toots would object, especially if there's something going on with this woman. She'd be the first one to tell you to get your ass in gear and find out what's going on. You know better than that."

"I'm just making small talk. You're absolutely right."

"Let's wait in the car. It's colder than a well digger's ass out tonight," Goebel said.

"Okay, but I want you to move the car so I have a bird's-eye view of this apartment."

"I'll do my best," Goebel said. "Come on."

Inside the SUV, Goebel cranked up the heater and repositioned the car so they would be able to see if anyone entered apartment 55-E.

Sophie closed her eyes, took a deep breath, and tried to call up the emotions she'd felt earlier. The images. A man, a little girl, and something made from metal.

Metal. Why that? She thought of a Christmas ornament. Some were made of metal. Maybe that was it. *No, no, no,* she thought. There was something she wasn't getting, and it wasn't an ornament.

"I've got it!" Sophie shouted. "Kind of. Remember the number five in red letters I saw?"

"Go on," Goebel said encouragingly.

She held out the scrap of paper Abby had given her. "The address has two fives! That has to be of some significance."

"You're right. It does. But what?" he asked.

Sophie closed her eyes, took a deep breath, and tried to get to that place where only she and her subconscious existed. Try as she might, she couldn't elevate herself to that special place where she knew she needed to be. She turned to Goebel. "I haven't figured that out yet. I'm going to step out and take a puff. Don't say one word, either."

Not giving him a chance to respond, she opened the door and stepped outside. Glad for its warmth, she tightened the jacket she wore around her and pulled a cigarette from the pocket. She lit the cigarette and took a long drag. Centering on the number five, Sophie closed her eyes, challenging her subconscious to provide her with an answer.

Still nothing.

She pinched the lit tip off the end of her cigarette and stuck the butt back inside the cellophane wrapper. Then she climbed back inside the SUV.

Back in the car, Goebel scrunched up his nose. "That stinks to high heaven. I really wish you'd . . . never mind."

"When the time is right, I'll quit. It's not right yet, okay?" Sophie smarted. "I don't need this shit now."

Goebel reached across the seat for her hand. "Are we having our first argument?"

Sophie gave a halfhearted laugh. "I guess so. Sorry. I guess I'm just tense. I need to know why I'm here, and I can't seem to get to the place I need to be in order to figure out what I'm supposed to warn this woman about." She squeezed his hand. "I love you. You know that, don't you?"

He returned her squeeze. "I love you, too, old gal."

Sophie snickered. "You can lay off the 'old gal' crap."

They both laughed.

"You know I don't mean it like it sounds. Hell, you look younger than most fifty-year-olds."

Though Sophie knew that was pushing it, she thanked him, anyway.

"Let's go home. We're not serving any useful purpose here. And we can't just sit out here all night, waiting for her to come home. For all we know, the girl is out of town. It is Christmas. People travel during the holidays. I'm probably losing my gift."

The thought sickened her, but if it was meant to be, then she would have no other choice but to accept her fate.

"I don't think so. You've just hit a bump in the road. Let's get out of here. We'll think of something."

Those were absolutely the best words she'd heard all night.

Chapter 9

Abby had no more than put the twins down for the night when the phone rang. Alarmed because of the late hour, she picked up on the second ring. "Hello?"

"Abby, it's me," Sophie said. "Listen, I'm sorry for ruining your evening. I think I overreacted. We drove to the woman's apartment complex, but she wasn't home. I waited for a while, hoping I'd catch her, but nothing. Do you know if she had any plans to leave for the holidays? An evening out?"

Abby raked her hand through her stiff hair. She'd worn it on top of her head tonight and used hair spray. Now she remembered why she hated the stuff. "She didn't mention anything about going out of town to me. I'm pretty sure she didn't have plans. She's supposed to stop by every few days throughout the month to check on the flowers and all. I suppose she could've had an emergency. You're not getting bad vibes, are you?"

"That's just it. I'm not getting anything. I thought she was in trouble. Hell, I don't really know what I thought anymore. When she bumped into me at your place this morning, that's when I felt like I was being stampeded with emotions connected to her."

Chris came into the room and mouthed, "Who is on the phone?"

She mouthed back, "Sophie."

He nodded, then whispered, "I'm taking Chester out one last time."

She gave him a thumbs-up.

"This isn't unusual for you, Soph. You've been stumped before, haven't you?"

"To be sure, but usually I'm at least able to get some idea of where I need to go, what I need to focus on. Are you sure she didn't have travel plans? I'd feel a whole lot better if I knew where she was."

Abby didn't even want to think what Blanche's reaction would be if she called her this late, asking if she knew Charlotte's whereabouts. Her mother had said Blanche wasn't the nicest employer in the world. She didn't want to do anything that might jeopardize Charlotte's job, but what if Sophie was right? What if Charlotte and her kids were in danger of some sort? She'd never forgive herself if she didn't make the effort to find out if Charlotte had had any plans.

"It's late, but I'm going to call Blanche. I'll call you right back," Abby said, then clicked off. She raced downstairs to get Blanche's phone number and made the call from the kitchen phone.

"Hello," came a groggy voice after six rings.

Here goes, Abby thought. "Blanche, this is Abby Clay. I'm sorry to call so late, but there has been a bit of an emergency." She paused, giving the decorator a few seconds to wake up.

"Your flowers died?" Blanche said, her words sarcastic. "I can't imagine. I used only the finest growers in the country. I am very disappointed, Ms. Clay." She said her name like it put a bad taste in her mouth.

"Blanche, the flowers are fine and, frankly, the least of my concern. I'm calling because . . ." *One of my godmothers is psychic and believes Charlotte is in trouble. Yeah, right.* "I haven't heard from Charlotte. She told me she would call as soon as she got home. I thought maybe you might know if she had vacation plans." *Lie, lie, lie,* Abby thought, but at that moment she felt that she didn't have much choice.

"You're kidding. And this is supposed to concern me?" Blanche Harding said haughtily, making it clear by her tone that she could not care less about the welfare of one of her employees. "Ms. Clay, I will have you know that I do not socialize with my employees. I have no clue what they do during their time off. As long as they come to work and do their jobs, that's really all I care about. I can't imagine why you would think I'd keep track of . . . what's-her-name, anyway!"

This woman really is a bitch, Abby thought once again. And the bitch had really pissed her off.

"Her name is Charlotte. And in case you didn't know, she has three young children to support while her husband is overseas, protecting us! You know, as in 'we the people'?"

"Ms. Clay—" Blanche began.

"Ms. Harding, you need to listen up. First, I'm sure you know who my mother is. Teresa Loudenberry. She has clout and connections out the wazoo. I would hate to ask her to call in a few favors by having to tell all her social-climbing friends to blacklist Blanche Harding and Associates. She could ruin you." Abby delighted in those last words. She'd make sure to tell her mother about this conversation. Knowing her mother, she'd pull no stops.

Silence on the other end of the phone. *Good. Give the hateful woman a scare.*

"I don't like being threatened, Ms. Clay. For your information, I have quite a bit of clout in Charleston, too. I'm sure your mother knows this."

Abby was pissed. "It doesn't really matter how much *clout*"—she said the word sarcastically—"you might *think* you have. I'm asking you a question, and I'd like an answer. Do you know if Charlotte had plans to go out of town?"

"Why in the world you would think I know such nonsense amazes me. As I just explained to you, I do not keep tabs on my employees' social lives. So, to answer your question, Ms. Clay, no, I have no idea if Charlene had travel plans. If she did, then she can kiss her job good-bye. We don't take vacations this time of year."

Abby wanted to jump through the phone and smack the crap out of this woman! *What a snob.* She'd make sure to go out of her way to destroy this woman's reputation. As a matter of fact, she would enlist her mother and her godmothers. Something told her they would delight in doing so.

"For your information, her name happens to be *Charlotte. Charlotte Simonson.* And you have not heard the last of me, *Ms. Harding.*" Abby slammed the phone down before the old witch had a chance to reply.

Hands shaking, she dialed Sophie's number.

"So, is she out of town?" Sophie asked anxiously.

She repeated her conversation with Blanche.

"Are you kidding me? Why, that snooty bitch. I'll put a freaking hex on her!"

Abby laughed. "I don't know that I'd go that far, but she is definitely in need of a major attitude adjustment."

"And then some," Sophie said. "I just don't feel right shrugging this off. Something is going on with that poor woman."

Abby picked at a cuticle, then switched the phone to the other ear. "Sophie, you can't be responsible for the world. I'm sure Charlotte is fine. She's a very intelligent woman. Really has her act together. If she was in trouble, I'm sure she would call someone."

"What if she can't?" Sophie shot back. "I hate to say that, but it's a possibility."

Abby hadn't really put much credence in Sophie's vision, or whatever she'd had. But she knew better. Sophie was a real-deal, no-bullshit psychic.

"I'll get on the computer, see what I can find on her family. I still have contacts who have access to this kind of info."

"Good idea," Sophie agreed. "I'll get Goebel on it, too. What's her full name?"

"Charlotte Simonson. She's about thirty-eight or thirty-nine. Her husband's name is Lamar. He's in the Marines, stationed in Afghanistan, in Kabul. She has the three kids. Riley, Roxanna, and Rhonda. I know this because she talks about them all the time."

"Okay. If you hear something, let me know. I won't be able to sleep, thinking about Charlotte and those kids. Maybe you should call her real quick before we start a massive search."

"Good idea," Abby said. "I'll just put you on hold for a minute."

"Okay."

Abby clicked the flash button and dialed Charlotte's number. It rang seven times; then her voice mail picked up. She left a quick message for Charlotte, asking her to call her as soon as she got this message, no matter how late. She clicked over to Sophie.

"Not at home. I left a voice mail, but who knows? Now I'm worried. Charlotte wouldn't have her kids out this late, and especially in this cold weather. I'm going to call Josh at *The Informer*. If I learn anything, I'll call you back."

"I'll get Goebel on this, too. Same deal. I'll call if I hear any news."

Abby hung up the phone. Resigned to a night of digging into Charlotte's whereabouts, she made a pot of coffee.

Chris came in through the back door, with Chester prancing around, his toenails clicking against the hardwood floor. Abby gave him a piece of chicken from the refrigerator, then told Chris what was going on.

He rubbed his hands together. "Then what are we waiting for?"

Chapter 10

"Thirty-seven hundred dollars in cash, fourteen thousand in checks, and change. Not bad, if you ask me," Bernice said. She and Robert had delighted in counting tonight's donations before returning to their own home.

Toots shook her head. "It's not as much as I'd expected, but this is just the first night. Phil and I plan to match all the donations we take in."

"Absolutely," Phil said. "I like this project, Toots. It's important for our servicemen to have a place to come home to, especially those who are injured. I only wish more people would step forward and do what the government seems unable to do these days. I intend to spend more time on volunteer work from now on."

"What about all those TV interviews promoting your latest book? Not to mention book tours. Don't they take up a lot of your time?" Robert asked.

"Actually, my publisher agreed to cut back on the promotions since sales are going so well on the first two that the new one actually needs little or no promotion. I have an idea percolating for my next one, but for now I thought I would take a break from writing for a while. And getting involved in a hands-on manner with this latest charitable project sounds real good to me just now."

After Mavis returned to her guest room, and as Bernice and Robert got ready to return to the home Robert had shared with Wade, Bernice reminded everyone about the plans for the next day. "Remember, tomorrow we're baking all day. We're going to use that organic vanilla extract Robert told me about. Abby doesn't like the kids having anything nasty," Bernice said.

"You two are baking? What about Jamie?" Toots asked.

"She's busy, especially this time of year. Robert and I are having the little ones over. Abby promised she'd let them help out."

"That sounds like fun. Maybe Phil and I will join you," Toots suggested.

"I wouldn't trust you with a cookie sheet if my life depended on it," Bernice stated, staring at her former employer. "You can't cook shit, and you know it."

They all laughed.

"Then I'll wash the dishes."

"And pigs fly," Bernice added dryly.

"Oh, for Pete's sake! It's not like I'm without skills! I can do all sorts of stuff in the kitchen."

Robert stopped at the door and stared at her. As did Bernice. And Phil. Three pairs of eyes focused on her.

"What?"

"I won't waste my breath," Bernice said. "I'll tell you what you can do. You can stay the hell out of our way. Stay home and walk those mutts. Answer your phone. Call Ida dirty names. But the one thing you are not doing is working in my kitchen."

Toots laughed and held her hands out in front of her. "Any other time, I'd cuss your old ass out. But it's the holidays, so I'll be charitable and refrain. But you just wait until the New Year. I am going to chew your ass out like tobacco on a pitcher's mound."

"As I said, we had better skedaddle," Robert interjected. "Bernice and I need to get home and get our beauty sleep if we are going to keep up with those holy terrors tomorrow." He patted Bernice on the hand, and she followed him out the back door.

"Those two are priceless," Phil said. "I hope we're as perky when we're their age."

"Perky? Phil, we're not that much younger than they are. And if you hadn't performed open-heart surgery on Bernice, she wouldn't be with us today. Not that I'm not thrilled she's still with us, but I just don't think of those two as perky. More like ornery."

"Speaking of ornery, what's going on with Ida and Daniel? They're hardly around these days."

Toots refilled their coffee cups for the fifth time. It was a good thing that caffeine had no effect on either her or Phil; otherwise, they'd both be awake until they rang in the New Year. Though Phil hadn't always been so tolerant of the stuff. After hanging with her and the rest of the gang, he'd developed a tolerance, too.

"Ida's so busy with the Home Shopping Network and decorating their new home, she rarely has a minute to do anything else. At least according to her, she's getting laid on a daily basis, but who cares? Perpetual honeymoon, she calls it. Truly, I'm happy for the old slut, but don't tell her I said that, or I'll have to kill you. She's thriving. She loves being married to Daniel, even though Bernice detests the idea that Mavis is her daughter-in-law, which I am inclined to think is the funniest part of this whole marriage business."

"Bernice is too hard on both of them. They're happy. Their marriage is working out just as well as ours, as Bernice and Robert's, and Mavis and Wade's. Age doesn't make much difference these days."

Bernice's attitude toward Daniel and Ida's perpetual-honeymoon marriage was not the subject she'd hoped to be discussing or thinking about. All Toots really wanted to think about now was the holidays.

Amy and Jonathan were at the most adorable age, and she wanted to experience as much of their three-year-old Christmas as possible. Holidays at their age were memory makers. Anything else that needed to be discussed or thought about could wait until after the New Year.

She grinned. "I really want to spend as much time with the twins this holiday season as I can. They're only going to be three once. I remember what Abby was like at this age. It was the most exciting Christmas ever. That age, kids still believe in Santa, and they'll be old enough to appreciate that huge surprise we have for them this year.

"All I'm trying to tell you is, I want both of us to enjoy our grandkids, and yes, before you say anything, it is simply a given, since we got married and even before, that the kids, myself, Abby, and Chris all consider you to be the kids' grandfather. After all, you are the only grandfather Amy and Jonathan have ever known."

Phil grinned, his blue eyes twinkling like the Big Dipper. "Did Abby and Chris really say that to you?"

Toots widened her eyes. "Do you think that I would make up something as serious as this? Of course they said that. Amy and Jonathan call you Poppo, or did you forget?"

"No, I just want to make sure they want me in their lives as much as I want them in mine. As wonderful as these two years of marriage have been, and as much as I love those two kids just as if they were my own flesh and blood, I couldn't help but wonder if they feel the same. And, of course, I know of nothing they have done that should lead me to believe that they don't. But all the same . . ." His voice trailed off before he regained his composure, and then he said, "And I love you more than you can possibly imagine."

Without another word, Toots went around to where Phil was seated, sat on his lap, and pulled his mouth against her own. The kiss was sweet, passionate, and most of all, reflected the love she felt for him. Sparks of desire traveled throughout her, even at her age. "Does that tell you anything?" she asked.

Phil's breath was a bit unsteady. "It tells me it's time to go to bed."

"Then what are we waiting for? Let's call it a night, Dr. Becker, my dearest husband."

Chapter 11

It was two o'clock in the morning, and Josh had yet to return Abby's call. She'd asked him to pull out all the stops and see what, if anything, he could find out about Charlotte. She'd given him a brief rundown on their current situation. He was aware of Sophie's psychic abilities, so he hadn't questioned her request.

Chris and Chester had gone to bed an hour ago. He'd promised to let her sleep in tomorrow. He was taking the kids over to Bernice and Robert's so they could bake cookies with the two of them, and Mavis had promised to join them if Wade had not yet returned from his business trip. When the kids had learned of this, they were so excited. Having spent a lot of time at The Sweetest Things, they were always trying to help out. Now they'd get to play with cookie dough, and no one would worry about dirty hands or misshapen cookies.

Abby wanted to call Charlotte's place again, but it was really too late. If she'd gotten home late, most likely she hadn't listened to her voice mail. At least Abby hoped that was the case. Still, she couldn't dismiss Sophie's fears. Maybe Goebel would be able to track down a family member. His skills as a private investigator were renowned throughout the United States and abroad. He still got frequent calls from all over, asking him to come out of retirement and head up important investigations. And his contacts were legendary.

She decided to make another pot of coffee. She would need the caffeine in order to stay awake. She was as bad as her mother and godmothers in the caffeine department now. When she'd stopped nursing the twins, she'd found the extra jolt of caffeine got her through many late nights when Amy and Jonathan had colic.

Abby thought about her earlier conversation with Blanche Harding. First thing in the morning, at least when most normal people were up—and she knew her mother to be an early riser, but not quite this early—she planned to call and tell her what a witch Blanche was. Knowing her mother as she did, Amy was certain that Blanche wouldn't be working for many of the Charleston elite when Toots was through with her.

She smiled. By the time her mother was finished, Blanche would be lucky to have a job dusting at Rooms To Go, a big furniture chain in the South. It would serve her right for her cavalier, condescending attitude.

While Abby was waiting for Josh to get back to her, she wanted to peruse that old book her mother had found. She was really getting into the plantation's history, plus a bit of genealogy, and wanted to learn as much as possible about those who'd called the Clay/Clayton Plantation their home. This was part of Amy and Jonathan's history. She owed it to them to find out as much as possible about the origins of their family. Sad that Chris had no living family members, she'd wanted him to experience this search into the history of the plantation that bore his name. It had been in his family for several generations.

He had enjoyed restoring the plantation, was thrilled with Dogs Displaced by Disaster's progress, yet he still had time to volunteer his services at legal aid. Abby was very proud of her husband. She'd won the lottery big-time the day she had become his wife. And it was so nice to have her mother and all three of her godmothers married to the men they loved and living right here in Charleston. And then there were Bernice and Robert.

Holding the old leather-bound volume in hand, she carefully opened it. The pages were brittle and discolored with age, but the handwriting was still legible. It was written in block letters that looked like a child's scrawl, and she read through the first few pages. Mostly birth records, dates of marriages, and many deaths, so many that Abby found the contents a bit depressing.

She continued to skim through the yellowed pages. Nothing stood out to her except for the deaths of many young children and women. This was before modern medicine. Smallpox had taken the lives of many children. Abby knew from her research that smallpox had been treated by inoculation and isolation. Inoculation was very new in the late seventeenth century and was feared by many, as it involved injecting the infection into the patient. *Gross,* she thought, but then she remembered the flu shot, and inoculation didn't seem quite as barbaric. Yellow fever had killed thousands. With South Carolina's humidity, she could imagine all the mosquitoes that had carried the deadly disease. She carefully flipped through the pages. Many of those who'd died were children, some never making it past their teens.

Depressed, Abby closed the book and returned it to the formal living room, to be displayed again tomorrow night, during the parade of homes. Charlotte had thumbed through its pages. Abby wondered what her thoughts were, wondered if she'd ever be able to question her about them. She liked Charlotte, and were she not so reserved, Abby felt as though they could become close friends. But something held Charlotte back.

The phone rang, startling her. She grabbed the extension in the kitchen. "Hello."

"It's me. You have any news yet?" Sophie asked.

"Nothing. I was hoping to hear from Josh by now, but not a word so far. Goebel come up with anything?" Abby asked.

If anyone could, it was Goebel. A former New York City policeman who'd opened a private investigator's office soon after retirement, he was tops in his field and had connections all over the world. He'd proved himself to all when he'd investigated Ida's former husband's death, which originally was written off as simple food poisoning but in fact turned out to be a homicide. During the investigation, he'd uncovered a daughter Thomas had, unbeknownst to Ida, and that daughter had tried to lure Ida to her death in hopes of gaining Thomas and Ida's hefty fortune. If anyone could find information on Charlotte, Goebel could.

"Nothing yet. He's contacted a few people by e-mail, made some phone calls, but just like you, he's not coming up with a thing. He will, though," Sophie said.

"I should try her number again, but I'm almost afraid to. What if she's home, sound asleep? She'll think we're crazy."

"Better yet, we could drive back to her place. I can pick you up in fifteen minutes," Sophie suggested.

Abby considered it for a minute, then said, "Let's wait until it's light out."

"You're sure?"

"No, right now I'm not sure of anything, but I'm afraid if I don't do something, I'll regret it later. I'm going to e-mail Josh, see if he's come up with anything. Let's give it another couple of hours." Abby hoped she wasn't making a huge mistake. Sophie's instincts were usually right on the money, but even her godmother had her doubts.

"Okay, two hours. We'll contact one another if we hear anything before then." Sophie hung up, and Abby ran upstairs, checked on Amy and Jonathan, grabbed her laptop, and returned downstairs.

Quickly penning an e-mail to Josh, Abby knew he was right there at his computer, waiting for that generic voice to announce he had mail. He rarely left *The Informer*'s offices, as most of the communication between him and the team of reporters consisted of texts, tweets, and e-mails. Facebook and Instagram worked for most of the photos they took of whoever was lucky, or unlucky, enough, depending on the story, to have his or her face splashed across the tabloid's front page.

Only three minutes later, Abby got a ping, letting her know Josh had answered her e-mail. She clicked on the link and scanned his e-mail.

Nothing. Nada. When there was something to report, he'd let her know.

Abby sighed and exited her e-mail. From the looks of it, they were going nowhere. She would wait two more hours. If she or Sophie or Josh hadn't heard anything new, she was going to Charlotte's apartment. And she'd deal with whatever she needed to then.

Chapter 12

Bernice was up with the chickens, as was Toots. Robert and Phil had yet to make their early morning debuts, so the two women were sitting in Toots's kitchen, as they had for so many years before Bernice married Robert.

Each of them gulped down three cups of coffee before they spoke to one another.

"If you think I'm making you a bowl of Froot Loops, think again," Bernice said. "That ended when I got married and moved to Robert's house. So just forget I'm here, and keep serving yourself."

"Well, aren't we in a fine mood today? What's wrong? Robert run out of Viagra? You know, my husband is still a doctor and can still write prescriptions. And, for the record, I don't want Froot Loops for breakfast. I was going to sample your first batch of cookies. Remember, you're baking with the twins today?"

Bernice shot her the evil eye. "I'm not suffering from Alzheimer's yet. I assure you that I do remember. And no, you are not having my cookies for breakfast. Anyway, I am baking the cookies in my own kitchen, not yours. So find something else. Why don't you try your hand at toast?"

"Okay, Bernice, cut the shit. I've known you too long. What's going on? Did Robert screw up a recipe?"

Bernice took the carafe of coffee from the middle of the table and poured her fourth cup. "Why do you always think that whenever there's a problem, a man has to be involved? You're sounding more and more like your slut friend Ida, my dearest, darling, damned, demented daughter-in-law. You know that, right?"

Toots flipped her the bird. "Kiss my old ass. My slut friend just so happens to be boinking your son, her husband. Now, stop trying to avoid my question. What's wrong? You were fine last night, when you walked home with Robert."

Bernice rolled her eyes. "If I tell you, you have to promise to keep it to yourself until you hear it from someone else. Can you keep a secret?"

It depends, Toots thought, but she didn't say the words out loud. "If you ask me not to tell, you know I'll keep my word."

"Not even Phil?" Bernice asked.

"I won't tell a soul," she promised.

"If you do, I'll come over in the middle of the night and put Vaseline on all your windows. I know how much you like your sparkly windows."

Toots shook her head from side to side. "I'm not going to beg you. If you want to tell me, then do it." Bernice could be such a drama queen, but that was Bernice. Toots was grateful the old coot was still alive and kicking.

Bernice peeked over her shoulder, then looked around the kitchen. "Don't want anyone to hear this. Daniel called last night." Bernice did look worried.

"And?"

"He told me that he wanted to tell me first, before I found out from someone else." She paused. "He and Ida are thinking about adopting a baby. Well, not exactly a baby, but an orphaned eight-year-old. One of Daniel's clients, a single dad whose wife died while giving birth to their daughter, was killed in an automobile accident recently. There are no other relatives on either side. What do you think I should do? It's one thing to have Ida as my daughter-in-law. But they're too old to adopt an eight-year-old girl. We've got to stop this, Toots!"

This was the very last thing Toots had expected! She didn't blame Bernice for being upset, but as she always liked to say, "It is, what it is," and there wasn't jack shit she or Bernice could do to prevent Daniel and Ida from adopting an orphaned little girl.

"Well, aren't you going to say something?" Bernice whined. "Other than their getting married, this is the worst news I've had since my heart attack."

"I'm surprised. I knew their marriage was still in the honeymoon stage, even though they got married the same day you, Mavis, and I did. But I didn't realize there was any possibility of children. Did you tell Daniel how you feel about this? Did he actually say that he had started the steps to legally adopt this little girl? Will the state allow an adoption at their age?"

Toots felt terrible for her dear friend, but on the other side of the equation, Ida and Daniel were happy, and what was so terrible about having an eight-year-old child to raise? "I don't see this as the end of the world. So what? They adopt a child. They're both competent adults. They can afford plenty of help to assist them. And God knows their house is big enough to raise an entire kindergarten class. I would want Daniel to be happy if he were my son, and if adopting this child will contribute to his happiness, why not?" Toots wouldn't have chosen Ida as the mother of her grandchild, either, but it was almost comical, given the fact that Bernice and Ida had never been best buds.

"Don't make out like this is my fault! Of course I want Daniel to be happy. But will adopting a child work for this marriage, which I do not approve of, anyway? Will a child come between the two lovebirds?"

Toots couldn't help it; she burst out laughing. Her eyes filled with tears of pure silliness, and she laughed so hard that her stomach cramped.

"What? You think that's funny?"

Toots wiped her eyes on a napkin. "Bernice, first, you did everything you could to stop Ida and Daniel from getting married. Now you're worried about whether adopting a little girl will have an adverse effect on the same marriage you were so determined to keep from happening in the first place." Toots started laughing again. The thought of Bernice being worried about something going wrong in a marriage she was so against in the first place gave her another round of giggles.

Both women jumped when they heard Phil enter the kitchen. "What's so funny?" He sat next to Toots, gave her a kiss, then poured himself a cup of coffee.

Bernice's face was as red as the throw rugs on the shiny kitchen floor. "Nothing!"

"Okay, whatever you say." Phil raised his eyebrows at his wife, indicating he wasn't quite sure what to make of the two of them.

Bernice grabbed the coffeepot, filled it with water, added fresh coffee to the filter in the coffeemaker, dumped the water in the tank, then pressed the BREW button. Toots knew this was her way of saying she needed a few minutes. She gave Phil a slight nod.

When the coffee finished brewing, Bernice filled the carafe on the table, then brought out a fresh container of half-and-half and clean spoons for the bowl of sugar. She poured each of them another cup, then sat down. "Phil, I might as well tell you, too."

"Tell me what? You're feeling okay, aren't you? Your

last checkup was excellent, according to your new doctor. He called me."

"No, this is worse. Much worse, believe me." She took a deep breath, then said, "Daniel and Ida are thinking of adopting an eight-year-old orphaned girl. And I am concerned that it will cause problems in their marriage."

The words were hardly out of her mouth before Phil, too, started laughing. His laugh was hearty and rich, a man's laughter. He slapped his hand on his khaki-covered knee. "I think that's fantastic news!"

Bernice looked at him as if he'd lost his mind. "Tell me you're not serious. Phil, Ida is almost twenty years older than Daniel! She's old enough to be his mother, for crying out loud! And now they are going to adopt a child? Becoming a father in his fifties is bad enough. But Ida as a first-time mother in her seventies? It's unnatural!"

"Listen up, Bernice. I'm talking to you as a friend, not a doctor, okay?"

She nodded.

"In my line of work, I saw all kinds of people. Young people dying, old people wishing for one more day, family members wishing they'd taken the time to do all the things they had planned on doing later and didn't think about until it was too late. Look, what I'm trying to say is, let them spend their time together as they want to. Who cares about age these days, anyway? It's a number, nothing more. Having a child to raise could make their marriage even richer than it already is. What about you and Robert? Would a child in your lives be so terrible if it happened for some reason?"

Toots observed the two, but more than that, she really listened. Phil was right. No one knew when their last day was coming. Even Sophie, being psychic, couldn't predict the exact time a person would die. It wasn't like you were given a choice. Toots believed your destiny was determined at the moment of conception. Life was too short not to live it to the fullest. If Daniel and Ida's *fullest* was adopting a child, then why the hell not?

"He's right." Toots said this, knowing Bernice was giving serious thought to his words. She had that look she always got when she was serious. Her brows were scrunched in a frown; her bottom lip was sticking out more than normal.

She crossed her hands over her chest. "I don't suppose I could stop them from doing this. Hell, they're seniors. Daniel isn't yet, but he's getting there. Shit, piss, damn! I really don't have a say, do I?"

Toots and Phil said, "No!" at the same time.

Sighing, Bernice shook her head.

Chapter 13

Sophie picked Abby up as soon as the sky turned from a hazy bluish black to a pastel pink. The sun was just starting to show itself as Abby ran out the back door. Chester barked when he saw Sophie's car.

"Okay, I did get a tidbit of information from Josh," Abby said when she jumped in the car. "He called right before you got here. It seems that Lamar, Charlotte's husband, is more than just a jarhead. He's involved in a special mission, and according to Josh's source, it's top secret."

Sophie peeled out of the gate. "I don't know if that's really important just now. Okay, let's suppose that it is. Would this have anything to do with what I saw? Felt? Not to mention the fact that she's nowhere to be found."

"I agree, but he did find something. He's doing what I pay him to do."

"Good for him," Sophie said. "Let's just get to that apartment. We've waited long enough. I just hope that it isn't too long. I need to see for myself that the girl is at home, safe and sound."

Fifteen minutes later, Sophie pulled alongside the same curb where Goebel had parked just last night. The apartment complex looked even shabbier in the light of morning. It was made of red brick, and the mortar had turned black. Rickety metal stairs led to the second and third floors. The courtyard was covered with soda cans, and trash and cigarette butts dotted the dried-out ground like dirty polka dots.

They both stopped on the sidewalk, each lost in her own thoughts. *Shabby* didn't begin to describe the place.

"I had no idea Charlotte lived in such . . . squalor. Gosh, Sophie, have I been so wrapped up in my life that I just assumed everyone else has . . ." Abby raked a hand through her hair. "Let's go find Charlotte."

Sophie nodded, leading the way. "They're in fifty-five-E."

Weaving around the garbage, broken bicycles, and empty food cartons, they trod lightly when they found the metal steps leading to the third floor. At the top of the steps, Sophie said, "To the right."

When they reached apartment 55-E, Abby tapped on the door. Within seconds, the door opened. A little girl with big green eyes looked up at them. Abby's heart fell to her feet. She saw Sophie's eyes fill with tears.

"Rhonda! Don't ever open—" Charlotte stopped when she saw them.

"It's just me and my godmother, Sophie. The one you met yesterday."

Charlotte nodded. "I remember."

"You're okay? You haven't been hurt? The children?" Abby asked, almost dumbfounded.

Charlotte stepped out onto the balcony and closed the door. "Why would you think such a thing?"

Sophie cleared her throat. "I'm . . . I have . . . I see things."

Abby laughed. "Good grief, Sophie, Charlotte is going to think we've lost our minds." She looked to Charlotte, who didn't seem the least bit amused. "Sophie has visions. She's a psychic."

Charlotte's eyes went wide. "Okay."

"She isn't going to make this easy. Look—" Sophie placed her hand on Charlotte's arm. As Charlotte reached for her hand, Sophie went completely limp, crumpling in a heap on the small cement balcony.

Abby screamed, "Call nine-one-one!"

Charlotte hurried inside. "Of course."

Abby stooped down and lifted the top half of Sophie from the cement. Sophie moaned and tried to sit up.

"Please," she whispered, and Abby knew this was the psychic Sophie, not the crazy, oddball, lovable godmother she knew.

"Charlotte, hang up the phone! She's fine," Abby shouted.

Charlotte instantly appeared. "I called. They're on their way."

"I want you to call them back, tell them something, but we don't need their services. This is why we're here. Sophie had some sort of vision yesterday, and it was about you. She's in a trance state now."

Octavia pulled her hand away, frightened when she felt another gush of somethin' warm comin' from her woman parts. She clenched her teeth and felt a crampin' sensation in her belly. Then, as fast as the pain came, it stopped an' was just a dull ache, like she got when she ate too many peaches. Fearin' that Mr. Clayton an' the missus had heard her hollerin', she knew she had to act fast. Not wantin' to, but knowin' she had no other choice, she pushed herself up into a sittin' position. The thing was still attached to her, an' she remembered Momma sayin' somethin' 'bout this. She couldn't remember what her momma had called it, but she knew she had to cut the thing loose from her.

The kitchen was dark, but Octavia didn't mind;

she was glad for the darkness. She didn't wanna see that thing in the light. Workin' in the kitchen, she knew her way around with her eyes shut. She remembered usin' the butcher knife just this mornin', when she'd shown Telly how to cut up a chicken. Next to the pump on the choppin' block. All she had to do was slide across the pine floor with the thing stuck to her; then she could reach the knife.

Not knowin' how she was gonna get across the floor with that devil thing o' Mr. Clayton's crawlin' atop her, Octavia gathered the warm bundle in her skirt an' wrapped the thing up. It was whimperin', an' she felt sad, but she had to cut it away an' get to Momma's. With one hand holdin' the thing, she used the other to push across the floor.

"Sophie, can you hear me?" Abby shouted.

She felt another gush of hot liquid spill from her insides an' knew somethin' was wrong. When she reached the choppin' block, she used her free hand to feel for the butcher knife. Carefully, she ran her slim, honey-colored hand along the edge of the choppin' block, then felt the heavy wooden handle of the knife. With her fingers, she grabbed the knife an' held it tight in her shakin' hand. In the darkness, she could see the heavy steel blade glistening in the moonlight coming in through the big kitchen window. The thing made a sound again, an' Octavia thought it sounded like a wounded polecat.

Her hands were shakin' as she unfolded her bloodied dress. The missus would lash her, for sure, when she saw it. As her belly had grown, her house-dresses had squeezed her so tight, she was sure they'd strangle her. That was when the missus had given her that bolt of cloth, told her to sew a new dress. An' she had, an' now it was ruined.

Octavia smelled the coppery smell of her own blood, felt the stickiness thickenin' on her skin. The thing cried out again, only this time it wasn't a meow like a kitten made or a strange sound, like the ones she made when Mr. Clayton clamped his hand over her mouth when he crawled on top o' her. This was a real cry, like a baby's, like her little brother's, Abraham. She remembered her momma birthin' him. She had been scared for her momma when she'd heard her moanin' an' screamin'. Like her, she stopped, an' then the cryin' started. Now Octavia felt tired an' weak, like all she wanted to do was rest, jus' for a minute. She closed her eyes, driftin' off, remembering when she was a little girl. . . .

She jerked up, the knife still in her hand, the thing still nestled between her legs, on her bloody dress. Before she blacked out again, she touched the thing, found the shiny snakelike part that grew out of its tiny belly. Without another thought, she took hold of the sliminess an' quickly hacked through the piece of snake. Frightened, she dropped the knife on the floor, the noise soundin' like glass shatterin'. . . .

"Sophie, please listen to me!"

Moaning, Sophie pushed herself into a sitting position. "Where is Charlotte?"

"I'm right here, ma'am," Charlotte said in a soft voice.

"Abby, we need to get to your place, pronto. I need to see that book you had yesterday. Do you know what book I'm talking about?" Sophie said.

Puzzled, Abby nodded. "The one Mother gave me?"

"I don't know where it came from, but I need to see it."

Sophie looked at Charlotte. "Do you realize that you have a connection to all this?"

"No. I'm getting more confused by the minute. Come in. I have to get the kids ready for school, get their breakfast. We can talk inside."

Abby helped Sophie to her feet. Together, they entered the apartment.

"Have a seat in the kitchen," Charlotte told them.

They sat at an antique wooden table that seated four. Knowing antiques, Abby saw that this old table wasn't some flea-market find. Charlotte had good taste. The matching chairs were old oak but were polished to a high sheen. A pretty gold vase filled with evergreens and a poinsettia was positioned in the center of the table. Plastic place mats with colorful pictures of snowmen, Santas, and snowflakes circled the tabletop. The apartment building was shabby, but Charlotte's apartment, at least what she could see of it, was very well decorated and clean.

The three kids had remained silent, sitting in the living room, on the sofa, as their mother had requested. Abby fervently hoped that when Amy and Jonathan were a few years older, they were as well behaved as this adorable little trio.

Charlotte busied herself scrambling eggs and popping toast in the little toaster oven. "You all want juice or milk?"

"Juice," they all called out at once.

After plating the eggs and toast, Charlotte called the children to come into the kitchen. There, the kids waited for Sophie and Abby to get out of the chairs.

"You guys can take your plates into the living room, but let's eat as fast as you can. We don't have much time before the bus arrives and Rhonda goes to day care," Charlotte told them.

Sophie felt better than she had since she'd experienced

those emotions after bumping into Charlotte. Images from times past assaulted her, and she now knew why she'd been experiencing them.

Thirty minutes later, Abby drove Sophie and Charlotte back to her home. Sophie wasted no time at all in locating the book. She immediately closed her eyes and rubbed her hand on the worn leather, but now she was prepared to allow whatever or whoever she needed to contact to make contact with her.

Chris had taken Amy and Jonathan to Bernice and Robert's for the cookie bake off.

Once they'd arranged themselves in the formal living room, splendorous in all its Christmas glory, Sophie closed her eyes and began to meditate.

Her mother took a large leather volume an' opened it carefully. They was letters on the front of the book, but she didn't know what they say. Her momma took a piece of a bird feather an' a glass bottle of ink an' dipped the feather into the ink. "This is The Book of Life an' Death, Octavia. I been writin' in it all my life. I's learned to read an' write when old Mr. Clayton's missus was here. She teached me to read an' write. She tell me to always write down what was most sacred."

"What you sayin', Momma?"

"A minute, chile, an' I'll read it to you."

Her momma wrote in the big leather-bound book for a few more minutes. "I gots all the names wrote here, all them borned an' died. I write your son's day of birth an' day of death. I called him John Thomas Clayton, you Octavia Charlotte Clayton, an' Mr. Charles Garland Clayton.

"Now, you never speak this day again, you hear? The missus gone come fo' you soon, an' you jus' say

you scared 'cause your baby dead when he came out.
Missus don't want no one-armed baby to care fo'.
Now, you jus' rest until the missus gets here. This be
The Book of Life an' Death, Octavia. You must al-
ways take this wherever you be goin'.

Sophie knew what this meant. "Charlotte, I'm sure these
are your ancestors, too."

Abby thought for a moment. "Why would you say that?"

"Old Mr. Clayton fathered what I'm guessing was Charlotte's great-great-grandmother's firstborn."

Nothing more needed to be said.

Epilogue

Christmas morning

The twins hooted and hollered when they saw the custom-built playhouse Nana Tootsie and Poppo Phil had ordered from Santa. They ran in and out of the small rooms, laughing and sitting on the mini-beds, which fit them perfectly. A little table with four chairs would provide many hours of tea parties and a place for them to play the board games they loved so much.

"Mom, this is perfect. I never would have even thought of something like this. I can't wait until the summer so they can really enjoy it."

Toots and Phil were so excited at the kids' reaction that they couldn't keep their hands off one another. All morning, while they opened silver and gold packages with red ribbons, they'd acted like newlyweds. Toots gave Phil a first-print edition of Shakespeare. He gave her a locket with pictures of Amy and Jonathan inside.

Chris and Abby drank too much coffee, smiled too much, and couldn't stop thanking everyone for their gifts. Mavis and Wade, Bernice and Robert, Ida and Daniel, and Sophie and Goebel sat back and enjoyed opening their own gifts and watching the reactions everyone, especially the little ones, had to what was happening all around.

Then Phil took the floor and indicated that he was ready to announce the surprise that all the gang, except Toots, already knew about. "Toots, love of my life, when I was on the book tour, one stop was in Washington, D.C., where I had a discussion with a woman named Maggie Spritzer, the former editor in chief of the *Washington Post*. While we were talking, I happened to mention how you were starting Hope for Heroes and what it was about. She became very interested and said that she would really like to do an interview with you sometime after the New Year. She opined that a feature article in the *Washington Post* would probably help get the ball rolling big-time. What do you think?"

When Toots did not respond immediately, Phil asked, "Honey, is something wrong? Did I let the cat out of the bag when I shouldn't have?"

Toots ran over and gave Phil a big hug and a kiss. "No, honey, it's just that your surprise seems to explain my surprise. You see, a little while back, I remember now that it was after you returned from that book tour, I got a letter from the owner of the *Washington Post,* someone named Annie de Silva. It seems that she is a very wealthy woman who also happens to control a large pool of money, along with some other people, that they allocate to worthy causes in need of funding, and she wanted to speak to me about funding Hope for Heroes. I guess that this Maggie Spritzer must have said something to her about what you told her. How about that?"

Phil shook his head, looking puzzled. "What did you say the name of the *Post*'s owner was?"

"Annie de Silva. Why?"

"Because I'm sure I've heard that name before, and not because she owns the *Washington Post*. Now, where have I heard that name? Darn it. This is going to bother me until I figure it out."

"Annie de Silva? Does she live in Virginia?" Sophie asked.

"I think that's where she said she lived. In a farmhouse not too far from Washington. She asked if I and anyone I wanted to bring with me could come to visit her after the New Year to talk about Hope for Heroes. Why do you ask, Soph?"

"Because I know where Phil heard that name before. In fact, I am sure that we've all heard that name before, or at least heard about the group she belonged to. Do you remember reading about a group of women called the Vigilantes? They were pretty active until a few years ago, I think, and then they sort of disappeared."

"Yes," said Ida. "I always wondered what happened to them. And now that you mention it, I think someone named Annie de Silva was one of them. How about that?"

"Wow," said Toots. "So that's who asked to meet with me. Anyone want to join me on a trip to Virginia sometime next month?"

Everyone agreed that a trip to Virginia sounded like a splendid idea.

When the hoopla died down a bit, Chris surprised them when Charlotte and her three kids showed up for Christmas brunch. "Thanks to much research on my part and my wife's, and mostly to Sophie's psychic abilities and a rushed DNA test, I would like to introduce my very, very, very distant relatives, Charlotte Simonson and her three children," Chris announced, grinning from ear to ear.

No one said a word, but to all it made perfect sense. After learning of Sophie's vision, and to what lengths she had gone to find out exactly what it meant, Chris was thrilled to have the Clay/Clayton bloodline continue, even though he detested the circumstances of life on the plantation all those years ago.

Toots, always the ringleader, cleared her throat so loudly, they all turned their attention to her. "I would like to make a very important announcement." She winked at Phil. "Would you do the honors?"

"It would be a privilege." Phil ran upstairs, and when he came back down, he asked Charlotte and the kids to gather in the kitchen.

"I thought, what with all that has happened this month, you all might need a little something extra for Christmas this year."

Coming down the stairway was none other than Colonel Lamar Simonson.

Charlotte raced over to be with her husband, and they wrapped their arms around one another, the kids squealing in delight. After they'd calmed down, Toots, with Sophie and Abby at her side, made one more announcement.

"We collected enough money this season for Hope for Heroes. Charlotte, Lamar, you are now the proud owners of a brand-new plantation house."

More hugs and shrieks of joy.

"I think this is the best Christmas I've ever had," Charlotte said. "You're like family. I don't know how I'll ever repay you, but I love each and every one of you."

Everyone clapped, hugged, cried, and started speaking all at once.

Coco, Frankie, Chester, Betty, and Barney began running in circles as they, too, were caught up in the excitement. They barked and ran around the house like they understood what had taken place.

Of the many Christmases Toots had shared with friends and family over all the years, this was the best.

Life truly was a blessing.

"Girls, I think it's time to seal our good fortune and welcome our new, albeit distant, relatives," Toots said.

One by one they placed their hands on top of each other's, Abby and Charlotte, too.

"On the count of three, when you're good, you're good!" They tossed their hands high in the air.

And that was the godmothers' Christmas Day.

A Golden Tree

Chapter 1

Monday, November 30, 2015

"You can't just up and leave me like this!" Holly Simmons said into her cell phone. "It's Christmastime, or did you forget?" she asked, exasperated.

Ava, her assistant and best friend, giggled. "I'm pregnant with twins, my dear, or did you forget? The doctor has ordered complete bed rest for the next three months."

Holly looked at her computer screen, which showed just how overbooked the inn was this year. Holiday parties almost around the clock. The Grove Place Inn, owned and operated by the Simmons family for five generations, had just been asked to host the governor's annual family Christmas party again this year. And if that wasn't enough, several dignitaries from other countries were flying in simply to attend the governor's "family" party. The state's chief executive had reserved the entire third floor for his guests. Holly could only imagine what kind of party he'd throw for his friends if this was just "a little family gathering." His exact words. She recalled last year's party, the aftermath. It wasn't pretty, but the guests had said it was the best party they'd ever attended. The governor had promised to host his party at the inn for as long as he was able. Holly would assign even more extra staff to the event to prepare for the unexpected.

"Well, did you?" Ava persisted.

"What?"

"You did," Ava stated matter-of-factly.

Holly smiled. "How could I forget that my best friend since second grade is having twins?"

"I can tell by your voice, you're distracted and a bit overwhelmed. I knew you would be, so I took the liberty of narrowing the pile of applicants down to six. If someone is going to take over my job, I want to make sure that person is up to the task. Now, all you have to do is the final interview and choose the person you think will do the best job."

"Ava, you know as well as I do that no one can replace you. I realize you're about to have twins, but when they're older, you might want to return to work. I'm telling all the applicants this is only a temporary position."

"Of course you will. I might want to return to work . . . when they're in college. Yes, please make sure to tell them the job is only for . . . let me see . . . That would be eighteen years, minimum."

Both women laughed. Friends since elementary school, Holly and Ava did everything together. Holly had gone to the University of North Carolina at Asheville, where she'd earned her bachelor's degree in business, with Ava at her side, majoring in the same subject. When she graduated, just like family members before her, Holly started working at the inn the very next day, wanting to continue the family tradition, and so did Ava. All Simmonses had to start from the bottom and learn every single job at the inn. And all the Simmonses' best friends, no matter how cute they were, had to follow the exact same rules as the family. Holly remembered her father telling her this when she'd asked if Ava could work alongside her.

Of course, they all had known it was a given, as both Holly and her best friend had started working at the inn within days of turning sixteen, the minimum age at which they were legally allowed to become paid employees at the Grove Place Inn. They both had lived, eaten, and breathed their jobs. When it was time for college, they'd studied hard, both achieving 4.0 grade point averages and graduating at the top of their class. Wanting to take their education one step further, they'd agreed it would benefit them to earn master's degrees in finance, as well. They did so by juggling their careers at the inn with their master's studies, and in two years they both had advanced degrees in hand. They had returned to the Grove Place Inn and immediately started their careers.

That had been eight years ago. Both thirty-one years old, they were total opposites outside the inn. Ava had married just three years out of college, a year after getting her master's degree, while Holly had dated a lot but had had only one serious relationship. Sadly, Michael Strauss had been killed in a motorcycle accident right before she'd decided he was "the one." Since then, she had avoided serious relationships. They hurt too much.

"Holly, is something wrong?" Ava asked.

Ava's question jolted Holly back to the present, and she replied, "Yes. No. I'm just a bit overwhelmed right now. I'll be fine once I hire a *temporary* assistant."

Ava giggled, her high-pitched laughter sounding like a squeal over the phone. Holly held the phone away from her ear until her friend's laughter subsided.

"I'm serious, Ava. I am not going to replace you. Who

Fern Michaels

knows? When the babies are older, you might want to have an adult day. And if you do, your job will be waiting."

"You could be right. Though I won't know for a while."

"Somehow, I can't see you and Stephen confined at home together twenty-four/seven. I know how you like your space. Add in those two little bundles, and I can see you needing an adult day now and then."

More laughter. Holly rolled her eyes, for once glad Ava wasn't in the room. She'd changed since getting pregnant, becoming much more emotional. She either giggled all the time or cried. Holly would be glad when Ava returned to her former, even-keeled self.

"Stephen is converting that old junk room above the garage into his home office. That way, he won't have to go to Starbucks to meet clients. So, it will be as if he's gone, anyway. I like the arrangement. Gone, but close by if I should need him. Plus, he can invite clients over. I think it's the perfect arrangement for now."

Holly wondered how long that would last. Stephen was thrilled at the prospect of fatherhood. She doubted he would spend a minute more than necessary in the new office. She didn't tell that to Ava. She didn't want to ruin her friend's image of life after babies.

"I'm sure you two will figure things out."

"Holly, what's wrong? And don't say, 'Nothing,' because I can hear it in your voice."

Holly inhaled and raked a hand through her short brown hair. The holidays were going to be rough this year without her mother. She'd been dreading them since February, when her mother died unexpectedly of a massive heart attack. Why was it that those she loved had to be taken away from her too soon? If it weren't for her father, her grandfather, and the inn, Holly would've preferred to skip Christmas altogether this year. And the year after. It was just too sad.

Pushing her chair away from her massive walnut desk, Holly stood and walked over to the window, where she had an absolutely dazzling view of the Blue Ridge Mountains. Looking at the majestic sight always calmed her. The sheer beauty, the totality of the mountains' greatness, the vast array of trees—poplar, red maple, oak, and so many more. Holly couldn't name them all. They had all but denuded themselves of their jewel-toned leaves, except for an occasional single deep red or golden leaf free-falling, with the powder-blue sky as its background. She always felt a momentary bit of sadness when the trees were naked and bare.

Though western North Carolina didn't have the treacherous winters found in the Northeast and the Midwest, she hated to look out this very window and see the limbs stripped of their autumnal glory. That was how she always thought of them. Glorious. Colors no one could re-create, not even an artist as skilled as Stephen. Though his title was graphic artist, he also painted phenomenal landscapes, but even he had yet to match the perfection of the colors the trees displayed in autumn.

Holly finally spoke. "I feel like skipping the holidays this year. It just doesn't feel right without Mom." Tears blurred her vision, and the back of her throat tightened when she remembered the raw pain from the events earlier in the year.

"Oh, Holly, I know how you must feel. Violet was like a mother to me, too. She'd want you to make this holiday as special as all the others. You do realize that?"

Holly knuckled a single tear away before it could ruin her carefully applied makeup. "You're right. I'm just being a big baby. I just miss her so much. And Dad is simply lost without her."

"Then we should devote this holiday season to her memory. Make it the best ever. She'd like that."

Ava was right. Her mother was the most kindhearted, generous, and forgiving person she'd ever known. Next to her father, of course. It didn't matter what had been tossed her way, be it a personal issue or a crisis at the inn, she had always handled herself and any situation with the utmost grace and dignity. The employees loved her almost as much as the family did. A truly bright star was lost the day she left this world. Another gush of tears filled Holly's eyes, and this time she let them fall. Mom would understand her grief, of that she was 100 percent certain. And Ava was right. In her mother's memory, she would make this Christmas season one of the best ever. Both personally and professionally.

"I'm going to start interviewing for that personal assistant today. I'm going to need all the help I can get." That was an understatement, but she didn't want to upset Ava any more than she had already. *I can do this,* she decided.

"That's my girl. Now, remember, I picked the best of the lot, so make sure you're thorough when you interview them," Ava insisted.

"Are you trying to tell me you missed something? Should I be aware of any one applicant's qualifications over another?"

"No, no, not at all! I think they're all qualified for my job. Maybe more than I am, but you have to make sure you two fit. You know what I mean?"

Yes, she did. She needed to click with whomever she hired. They could be the best in the business, but if there was a personality conflict, all the skills in the world would be of no use to her or the applicant.

"I get where you're headed. Basically, I need to *like* them, too. Is that what you're trying to tell me?" Holly asked.

"More or less," Ava replied.

"Then, I'd best get busy. I'll let you know who the lucky girl is," Holly said. After a hasty good-bye to Ava, she wiped her eyes with her hand and cleared her throat.

It was now or never, she thought as she glanced at the small stack of applications that had been placed neatly in the center of her desk.

Chapter 2

Holly took a deep breath and quickly read through applicant number five's qualifications before she asked Marlene, her secretary, to send the woman in. If anything, this Terri Anne Phillips was *overqualified*. Ava was right when she'd said some of the applicants were better qualified than she was. With a master's in finance, an undergraduate major in business, and an undergraduate minor in math, Terri Anne just might be her new assistant. She liked the name. It sounded quite Southern.

She buzzed Marlene. "Have Ms. Phillips come in now."

"Right away," Marlene said. Her secretary had been working at the inn ever since Holly was in high school. Her mother had hired the woman, and the pair had become the best of friends. For now, Marlene was the person whom Holly thought of as a substitute mother. Holly would be devastated when Marlene retired.

Holly ran her hands through her short brown hair, quickly applied a touch of clear lip gloss, then smoothed her dark green skirt before standing up to greet her prospective new assistant.

Marlene opened the door to the office, then closed it immediately after announcing Ms. Phillips.

"I prefer to be addressed as Terri," the woman announced even before Holly had the opportunity to offer a greeting.

Holly nodded and motioned for the applicant with an attitude to sit in one of the plush wing chairs placed in front of her desk. "Please, sit down," Holly invited in her most professional voice.

Ms. Phillips—*Terri,* she silently corrected herself—stood at least five feet ten. Slender, with a model's figure, she was everything Holly was not. Sleek, elegant, with long blond hair hanging to her waist. Holly looked for a bit of frizz, a split end, something to show that the hair was less than perfect, but she saw nothing. Terri wore a rich brown pencil skirt with a matching jacket cinched at the waist just enough to show her curves. She wore four-inch heels, which Holly knew to be an on-the-job no-no, but at this early stage, it wasn't important.

Holly skimmed over the woman's résumé again and saw that she was not married and that there were no children. A dedicated career woman. She liked that.

Elbows on her desk, fingers steepled, Holly began her interview. "You certainly have the requirements I'm looking for in an assistant. Actually, you're overqualified." She paused, waiting for Terri to speak. When she said nothing, Holly continued. "Your last employer, the Davis House, says you left for personal reasons. Do you mind telling me what they were?" The last thing the inn needed was some crazed ex-boyfriend stalking an employee.

"Actually, I do mind. It states on my application that my reason for leaving is personal, and I prefer to keep it that way."

Holly's gut told her to end the interview immediately, but her keen sense of professionalism dictated that she see it through to the end.

"Of course. So . . ." Holly tried to gather herself. She hadn't been expecting such a blunt response from Terri.

"So, tell me, what about this position appeals to you?" Holly asked.

"It's a job," Terri replied. "Put simply, I am in need of a job, and when I heard you were looking for an assistant, I applied immediately."

Holly wondered if Terri Anne was purposely trying to see how far she could go before Holly told her the interview was over. Curious, Holly asked another question. "How well did you get on with your previous manager and coworkers?"

A shadow crossed Terri Anne's clear blue eyes. In a carefully controlled tone, she said, "What does that have to do with anything?"

Holly's eyes widened; then she took a deep breath. "Ms. Phillips, I think we're through here. I will keep your application on file, with your permission, of course, and if I foresee the need to have you come in for a second interview, I will call you."

Terri Anne stood up so quickly, she almost toppled over the heavy chair she'd been sitting in. "So, you're telling me, thanks but no thanks, is that it?"

"No, that's not what I'm saying. I have other applicants to consider. When I make a decision, I will call you." Holly stood, indicating that the interview was over. "One way or the other. Do you have a cell number?" She hadn't seen one on her application.

"It's five-five-five-seven-eight-five-two, for whatever good it will do." Terri turned around and headed for the door. "But I won't hold my breath," she tossed over her shoulder.

Holly wanted to shout back at her, tell her not to, but her lifelong sense of professionalism prevented her. She did think about it, though.

As soon as the door closed, she dropped into her chair. "What an angry woman," she said out loud. She grabbed the last applicant's file and skimmed through his qualifications. Looked good, but she totally disliked it when people had initials, or rather used initials in place of their given name.

The last applicant's name was G. W. Montgomery.

Taking a deep breath, she called Marlene. "Is G. W. ready? If so, wait five minutes, and then escort him inside the office. And, Marlene, could you bring me a bottle of water and two aspirins? Terri Anne Phillips has given me a headache."

"Sure thing, sweetie."

A minute later, Marlene, all four feet ten of her, whirled into Holly's office with an ice-cold bottle of spring water and a bottle of aspirins. Holly reached for the water, took the two aspirins Marlene held out for her, then chugged the water down. She laughed.

"Sorry, but that woman had such an attitude, she gave me an instant headache."

"Yes, she didn't appear to be very pleased when she stormed out of your office. I'm guessing she's not going to be your new assistant?" Marlene observed, putting a question mark at the end of the sentence, her warm brown eyes suggesting she knew the answer but wanted to tease Holly a bit.

"You would be guessing correctly. I wish Ava could work. I know she's having twins, but lots of pregnant women work until they deliver their baby. Do you think there is something seriously wrong with her, and she's not telling us?" Suddenly, Holly feared that Ava was suffering from some unknown pregnancy issue that she wasn't telling her about.

"Not at all. She's simply following the doctor's orders. Carrying twins is sometimes risky. We want her to deliver two healthy, full-term babies, so I am guessing this is why her doctor has asked that she devote the next three months to resting and letting those two little fellas grow plump and healthy."

"Of course you're right. I just don't know how I'm going to function without her help. She's really an equal partner, not an assistant."

"We all know that, Holly, but I'm sure you'll find someone to replace her. And who knows? You might like working with the new assistant even better. Now, sweet girl, are you ready for me to ask G. W. Montgomery to come in?"

"Sure. I just hope there are no surprises from this applicant. He is the last one from Ava's list of possibles."

"I'm sure you'll find this applicant . . . Well, let me get out of here and ask him to come in for his interview." Marlene flew out of the office before Holly had a chance to comment.

She didn't bother with applying more lip gloss or with running a comb through her hair. This was the last applicant from the six Ava had chosen, and she had to concentrate on the interview, not her appearance, though she had to admit to herself that she hoped G. W. wasn't as pulled together as Terri Anne had been.

Holly picked up the application, glanced over the places of employment, and was mildly surprised when she recognized that the applicant's last place of employment was Draper's Lodge, a locally owned, upscale inn and restaurant that was her biggest competitor. He had received his master's in business from Trinity College in Dublin. *Interesting,* she thought.

Why would someone leave such a thriving business, and right smack-dab at the beginning of the holiday season, which had always been the lodge's busiest time of year? She was already suspicious of this applicant when she looked up to see an extremely handsome man smiling at her. Coal-black hair, clear blue eyes, and that ever so sexy five o'clock shadow, which very few could pull off. His face was chiseled in all the right places, with sharp angles, and his features were quite perfect, as they were all so symmetrical. He wore designer jeans, with a white button-down shirt loosely tucked in. No belt, she noticed. She felt her face turn beet red when she realized what she was doing.

"You like?" came a sexy voice, with just a tinge of an Irish accent.

Oh, crap, she thought. *This is just a lovely way to start an interview.* "Uh, sorry. I . . . uh . . . You're G. W.?" she asked in a croaky voice. She cleared her throat and motioned for him to sit in the chair that Terri Anne had just vacated. "Please, have a seat. I'm Holly."

She needed a minute to gather herself, a minute to mentally kick herself for not reapplying her lip gloss or combing her hair. She always liked to keep things casual during an interview. She didn't give her last name, because once it was out, people's attitudes seemed to change as soon as they realized she was the owner's daughter, but she felt certain this G. W. Montgomery already knew that, having worked at Draper's Lodge.

He eased down into the chair, making it appear small. He had to be at least six feet three, she guessed. Two hundred twenty pounds, maybe. Thin waist, shoulders as wide as a double-door frame. And he looked familiar to her, but right this second she couldn't place where she'd seen him or determine if she knew him. Maybe Draper's. She, Ava, and Stephen often went there for dinner. Maybe he was one of their out-of-work waiters. She'd hired a couple of them for the holidays last year. The inn paid a decent wage, and most of the time, the tips were outrageous.

"So," she started and had to clear her throat again. "So, I see you worked at Draper's Lodge. Why did you leave?" Hopefully, it wasn't for personal reasons that he wouldn't discuss.

"I needed a change of scenery. I wanted to move on, and when I heard that the inn's manager was looking for an assistant, I decided it was time to get out of my comfort zone. Start anew. I gave my former employer a month's notice," he said and smiled.

And suddenly she felt like she'd been kicked in the stomach, in a good way, if there was such a thing. Butterflies. She actually had butterflies in her stomach! Good grief. She hadn't experienced this sort of giddiness since she had been in junior high. With Rob Hadley. Her first boyfriend. Her first kiss. That was so long ago. She smiled, remembering how flustered they'd been.

"Something about me strike you as humorous?" came the sexy voice.

She inhaled and released the air in her lungs slowly, a breathing exercise she'd learned in the weekly yoga class she attended here at the inn's spa, Tranquility. It was supposed to help one relax, but all it did this time was make her light-headed and a bit dizzy. She laid both palms on top of her desk to steady herself.

With as much grace as she could muster, she said, "No. I was just thinking about something that happened a long time ago."

He smiled, and she saw a dimple etched deeply in his right cheek. "Want to share?"

This was not going as expected. She was the one who was supposed to be asking the questions. "No, I don't. Now, you're here because you've expressed an interest in the position as an assistant. You're looking for something new, correct?" Good grief. She was stating the obvious. He probably thought she was as bright as a dark night. Something told her that Marlene had deliberately saved Mr. Montgomery for last. Sly little woman.

"Not necessarily different as far as what the job entails, but as I said, a change of scenery. As you'll note, I'm qualified in most areas of hotel management. I started at the bottom and worked my way up the ladder. Pretty quickly, I might add."

Holly skimmed the application where it read "Skills." It seemed he *had* done a bit of everything. *Like me,* she thought and wondered why he hadn't stayed at Draper's. Possibly, a management position would have been in his future had he stuck it out. She didn't say this to him, though. She was getting down to the wire. Ava was gone, the season was here, and she didn't see anything on his application that set off any warning bells, but she knew not to appear too eager.

"I'll check your references this afternoon." She scanned the application again, looking for a phone number. "I see you've listed a cell phone number. Are you okay using this as a contact number, should I need to call you later?" *Dumb, dumb, dumb!* Why wouldn't he be okay with this? He'd listed the number on the application.

"That's what it's there for," he said, and when he grinned, those little butterflies started swirling for a second time.

She stood, and he followed suit. She held out her hand, offering up a handshake across the large expanse of her desk. He took her hand in his, then placed his other hand over the top of hers, the gesture almost tender and certainly unexpected. Jolts of something she wasn't even going to put a name to shot through her, unlike any she'd experienced from a casual handshake. Or if she had, they were nothing more than a distant memory. Not wanting him to know how his simple gesture affected her, she carefully removed her hand from his.

"Thank you for coming in, Mr. Montgomery," she said, then walked to the door. "Marlene will see you out."

"No. Thank you, Holly. This has been a pleasure." With that, he turned, giving her an excellent view of a very well-defined ass.

She returned to her desk and immediately dialed Ava's home number. She answered on the first ring.

"I was waiting for your call," Ava said, her voice containing a hint of humor.

"I'm sure you were. Now, spit it out. Somehow I just know you've already decided who's going to replace you, but before I make my final decision, I want to hear it from you first."

"I narrowed thirty-four applicants down to six. It's up to you, Holly," Ava said in her most innocent, "I didn't do anything wrong" tone. The one she used not necessarily when she was caught in a lie, but when there was something more she wasn't telling.

"Bull. I know you. Have known you for more than two decades. Now, either you spit it out, or I'm coming over. I can tell when you're feeding me a line. So you'd best save me the trip. We're busy. I'm busy."

She heard Ava's deep sigh. "It isn't that Terri Anne, that's for sure, but she is qualified. Her résumé looked good, so I thought it only fair to include her."

"I have no intention of hiring her. Too snooty for me."

"I knew you would feel that way, but fair is fair," Ava said, then added, "The inn hires only the best of the best."

"If you weren't pregnant, I'd come over to your house and strangle you, but since you're having those boys, and they will need their mother, I won't. So, for the last time, who did you have in mind? Out of the six applicants."

"G. W. Montgomery, of course. Why do you think I put him last?"

Chapter 3

Gannon felt sure he'd aced the job interview, and was willing to bet that within the hour he would receive a call telling him the job was his. He knew he was the last applicant interviewed. Experience had shown him that if any of the other applicants had been worth hiring, the last candidate would be given an excuse and a promise of a phone call later in the week. He had practiced this himself. He checked his watch. It'd been exactly forty-five minutes since he left Ms. Simmons's office.

He returned to his Jeep and was digging in his hip pocket for the keys when his cell phone blasted his favorite holiday tune. "Jingle Bells." Smiling, he slid his index finger across the face of the phone. "Hello? This is . . ." He almost said, "Mr. Montgomery," out of habit but caught himself. "G. W. Uh . . . Gannon."

"Mr. Montgomery, this is Holly. From the inn."

He said nothing.

"The Grove Place Inn," she added.

He jostled the keys in his hand before inserting one of them in the lock, then replied, "Yes, I remember." No way would he tell her he was still in the parking lot.

"I've called two of your four references. They've both

given you glowing recommendations, so . . . if you're still interested, the position is yours."

Yes! Everything was going perfectly, just as planned. He'd instructed his general manager and his assistant to respond positively when and if they were called as references.

"Of course I'm still interested." He wanted to add more but decided against it. Her interviewing technique needed improvement, but that wasn't his end goal. Maybe she wasn't the person who usually conducted interviews. "When do I start?"

"Well . . ." He heard the hesitation in her voice. "Is tomorrow too soon?"

Not soon enough, but again, he'd keep that thought to himself. "Just tell me what time to report in, and I'm there."

"I'm usually in my office by seven. Is eight o'clock too early?"

Definitely needed to improve her interviewing skills. "I'll be there. Is there a particular dress code you adhere to?" At Draper's, he usually wore dress slacks and a jacket on ordinary days. On special occasions, he'd add a tie.

"Casual dressy," she replied, and he could swear he heard a bit of laughter in her voice.

For some strange reason, he wanted to keep her on the phone, so he asked, "What is your definition of 'casual dressy'?"

She exhaled, the sound forcing him to hold the cell phone away from his ear. He grinned. "Khakis and a chambray shirt?" he tossed out, knowing with certainty that this wasn't the type of dress she required.

He heard her clear her throat again. She seemed to do that a lot. "When you're in the office, and not dealing with the guests, I suppose that's acceptable. During the holiday season, I would prefer that you wear dress slacks and a jacket. And, of course, on special occasions, a tie. It just so happens the governor is hosting his annual family Christmas gathering here again this year, so I would suggest the dress slacks and tie."

Finally, he thought, *a show of authority.*

"Of course," he replied.

Right after Labor Day, there had been a rumor floating around that the governor was considering hosting his party at Draper's this year. Apparently, it had been just that. A rumor. And a major loss of potential revenue for the lodge.

"Then I will see you tomorrow morning, at eight o'clock," she said, and again, he could hear a trace of authority in her voice. Maybe he had underestimated her. *No matter,* he decided. He had to do what was best for his future.

"Until tomorrow," he replied in his best authoritative *Mr. Montgomery* voice, then disconnected the call. It was his practice in all business dealings always to have the last word. He saw no reason to stop now. This was all nothing more than another business venture for him.

Before he could think too hard about what he'd committed to, he backed out of his parking space and headed home. A pang of guilt gave him a moment of regret, but he couldn't stop now. The wheels were in motion. If he was successful, Draper's would knock the Grove Place Inn into second place next holiday season. Or maybe *this* season, if he played his cards right.

He frowned at the thought. His father, were he alive, would be doing the same thing. And his grandfather Monty, who'd just recently given up living on his own, having relocated to the Haven, a fancy assisted-living community for those who wanted to continue to live independently while having any special needs met and enjoying certain conveniences, would be proud to know he cared so much about the family business. They were getting deeper in debt, their old guests seemed to prefer the inn to the lodge, and right now he wasn't sure he'd be able to make the monthly payroll without dipping into his personal funds. He desperately needed to know what the inn had that Draper's didn't.

He tried to rationalize his actions by telling himself that he was doing what any smart businessman would do.

He would learn his competitor's best-kept secrets.

And then he would apply what he had learned to Draper's and would blow his competition out of the water, or over the mountains, or whatever.

Satisfied that he was on the right track, he parked his Jeep in the five-car garage and spent the next hour going over the lodge's books.

"Not good," he said out loud when he was finished.

They had just one Christmas party booked for the evening, and it consisted of only twelve people. Not giving up, he showered, shaved, and changed into his best Brooks Brothers suit. He'd make this small party the best his guests had ever attended.

Yes. He smiled in the mirror as he adjusted his bright red tie. He was going to turn things around.

And very quickly.

Chapter 4

"And they're arriving when?" Holly asked absently, her thoughts focused more on Mr. Montgomery's paperwork than on Marlene's updated guest list.

"Day after tomorrow. They're here for only two nights. She explained that they had their own Christmas events to attend. I think the one that Ms. de Silva referred to as Toots is currently involved in a show of historic homes in Charleston. The other, uh . . . upscale guest, Myra Rutledge"—Marlene glanced at her notepad—"owns a candy company."

Marlene looked at her notepad again. "Another woman is arriving to assist this Toots character. Her name is Sophia, and she's somewhat of a celebrity herself. Some sort of psychic who has apparently saved the lives of kidnap victims. Ms. de Silva insisted that while they are here, their presence is to be kept absolutely secret. She said something about being on a mission with a group of vigilantes, saying that she and her friends *were* the vigilantes. I do not know what that means, but I think that's how she put it. I'm not sure this is the kind of guest you want, but she did say that her name was Anna Ryland de Silva." Marlene paused.

"Vigilantes? I don't think so. The last thing the inn

needs during the holidays is a bunch of thugs frightening our guests. So, you'd best tell them we're all booked up," Holly said absently.

"I take it that you don't recognize that name," Marlene said, her voice rising a notch.

Holly shook her head, her short brown hair bouncing. She looked up from her desk. "No, I don't. Should I?"

Marlene dropped down in the chair across from Holly's desk. "Anna Ryland de Silva, it just so happens, is the *Countess* de Silva. Not only that, but she is widely reputed to be one of the wealthiest people in the world. I believe *Forbes* lists her as the wealthiest woman. In the world, Holly. This year. Not only does she own a casino in Las Vegas, but she is also the owner of the *Washington Post*."

Holly tossed her pen to the side and raked a hand through her cropped hair. "How is it that you know all this?"

"My position as your personal secretary dictates that I remain aware of who's who in the world of wealth and celebrity. I don't want to be caught with my . . . pants down, if you will." Marlene smiled.

Holly rolled her eyes and laughed out loud. "No, I can't see you in that position, either. So, you're saying we should let these women spend two nights here? Nothing more?"

"Yes, but Ms. de Silva asked for the presidential suite, and the governor has already booked that for himself and his wife, and the entire third floor for the rest of his guests. I am a bit at odds over what I should do."

"Who's to say that the second floor doesn't have a"— Holly made air quotes with her fingers—"presidential suite? We do have rooms that are virtually the same, except for the Jacuzzi in the master bath. Why don't you put Ms. de Silva and her friends in rooms twenty-one-oh-three and twenty-one-oh-four? And just in case she needs more room, keep twenty-one-oh-five available until they arrive. Those three rooms combined will sleep a minimum of eighteen people quite comfortably, unless something has changed since I last looked in on them. Each room is virtually a three-bedroom apartment. With all the extras, I think this should satisfy Her Highness."

"The countess," Marlene said, correcting her.

"Of course," Holly said, her brows rising slightly.

"Then I will call her back immediately and tell her we would be honored to have her and her friends as our guests."

"Good. Now, I have to get the paperwork on Mr. Montgomery to the personnel office so we can get him on this month's payroll. I'm taking it there myself. Text me if you need me."

"Of course I will," Marlene added before scurrying out the door. Holly laughed, because Marlene really *did* scurry when she was in a rush.

Fortunate to have her, Holly thought how blessed she was as she took the elevator to the basement floor, which housed the personnel office. She wanted to tell Nancy, their accountant, to make sure Mr. Montgomery's salary wasn't held back the usual two weeks. She was sure he was in need of a paycheck immediately but was most likely too prideful to reveal that. He didn't even have a belt, for crying out loud! She'd save him the embarrassment. He would receive his first paycheck at the end of the week. *Funny,* she thought. She didn't recall his asking what the salary would be. Well, there again, he might be too prideful to ask. Pride wasn't always a good thing, she decided as she tapped on Nancy's door.

After a cheery "Come in" from Nancy, Holly entered and placed Mr. Montgomery's file on her desk. "I know this isn't the usual way of doing things, but I've just hired a new assistant. You know that Ava had to go and get pregnant with twins. Not sure I'll forgive her for dropping out during the Christmas season, but as you know, I was in the market for a new assistant. Well, I hired one today. I might be jumping to conclusions, but I think he's somewhat pressed for money. I want to make sure that Mr. Montgomery is paid this week. Don't prorate the salary, either."

Nancy looked away from her computer, where she'd continued to click away as Holly explained her current needs. "Hmm. *Mr. Montgomery?* This is not like you. What's the real story?"

Holly paced the small office. "I'm not sure. I just got the impression he needed a paycheck. He seemed overly nice and, well, a bit flirty. He is incredibly good-looking, too."

Shit! Had she really just said that? Yes, she had.

"Okay, you've hired a sexy new assistant who needs money." Nancy gave a female version of a wolf whistle. "So, other than being good-looking, what are his qualifications?"

"Do you really think I would hire someone based solely on his looks?" Holly asked, ticked off that Nancy would even think such a thing.

Nancy stood up and crossed the room to where Holly stood. "Hey, kiddo, I didn't mean that the way it came out. I know you better than that."

Holly nodded. "I thought so. How many years has it been now?"

"Your father hired me three days after I graduated from NC State. I really don't want to put a number to the years, but I knew you before you started elementary school. So, if you really want a number . . . ?"

Holly held out her hand, palm forward. "No, no. I know. We don't need to know these things. None of us are getting any younger, and before you ask, no, I am not dating anyone."

Nancy almost always made a habit of asking her if there was anyone special in her life. And each time, she told her no. Since Michael, she hadn't wanted anyone special in her life. She had good friends, her father, her grandfather, and her employees at the inn. And until earlier this year, her mother, of course. They were her life, and she was quite content.

"I'm not thinking about your lack of dates, kiddo. I'm bombarded with tax stuff for the New Year. So, you want this new guy's salary to start ASAP. I can do that. Anything else?" Nancy asked.

"Thanks. I can't think of anything, but if I do, I'll let you know," Holly tossed over her shoulder as she made her way to the door.

"Good thinking," Nancy called out.

Holly waved, then stepped back into the elevator and punched L for the lobby. There were a few issues she needed to clear up with the front-desk manager, plus she wanted to see exactly how many extra rooms they would have, if any, should there be a need.

The elevator doors swished open at the main lobby, or the grand hall, as they referred to this giant span of space. Holly never tired of seeing the room, and certainly it was extra special when all decked out in its best holiday finery.

The oak floors were polished to a golden shine, and the floor-to-ceiling stone fireplace, made from rocks found on the property more than a hundred years ago, still took her breath away every time she saw it. Throughout the years, there had been many changes, new furniture in the suites, updates from general wear and tear, and her mother had added the Tranquility spa when Holly started high school. It was the most luxurious spa in Asheville, or so she was told by her guests. Massages, facials, and a mineral-spring pool were just a few of the spa's amenities. Throughout the years, her family had continued to maintain the inn's rustic yet luxurious atmosphere. If reservations were an indication of success, then they were the cream of the crop.

Holly took another minute to soak up the newly decorated grand hall. Fragrant evergreens had been placed atop the main fireplace mantel, with red and gold ribbons draped strategically throughout the greenery. The evergreens would be discreetly replaced weekly to keep the appearance, as well as the fragrance, fresh.

The grand hall took up the entire ground floor. At every turn, guests were greeted by a variety of Christmas trees. Fraser firs, blue spruce, and white pines were decorated in an assortment of themes exclusive to the inn. In the grand hall, the main tree, a twenty-foot-tall blue spruce, dominated the entrance. Miniature handcrafted replicas of the exterior and interior of the inn hung from the giant tree, along with mini-replicas of each of their suites, of which there were twenty different designs. Thousands of tiny lights made the tree appear golden. *A golden tree,* she thought. To this very day, the beauty of the inn in all its finery managed to take her breath away. She never tired of the festivities during the holidays, but this year was sure to be the saddest on record, since her mother wouldn't be here to oversee them.

In the past, several of the employees' children had sung Christmas carols in the grand hall nightly, beginning one week before Christmas, and this had been organized by her mother. She had had hot chocolate–making contests, cookie cutter–design days, and most of all, she had made the guests and the employees feel as though the inn was truly a magical place. *It really is magical,* Holly thought as she made her way to the front desk.

Yes, the inn was lit up as bright as the North Star this time of year. The only thing lacking was her mother, but in her heart, Holly knew she was with them in spirit. She spied their front-desk manager, Mr. Haynes, with a guest, and as always, he was smiling from ear to ear. He'd been working for her family when her grandfather was still at the helm. He had to be close to seventy-five, but one would never know that, as he kept himself in very good shape. It was said he ran ten miles before work, he never touched a piece of red meat, and sugar was his worst enemy.

"Mr. Haynes," Holly said as she entered the suite of offices behind the main registration area.

"Why, Miss Holly, you look just as pretty as ever. What can I do for you today?" he asked in his soft formal voice.

She wanted to giggle but stopped herself. Mr. Haynes was always so formal. When she'd asked him to call her just by her given name, he'd said it was disrespectful. So to Mr. Haynes, she was Miss Holly, not plain old *Holly,* as most of the staff referred to her.

"I've just learned we're having a group of"—she almost said, "Vigilantes," but caught herself—"women, a countess and a few of her friends, as special guests. I've asked that rooms twenty-one-oh-three and twenty-one-oh-four be kept available. Also twenty-one-oh-five, in case there are more than expected. They're due to arrive the day after tomorrow."

Always the consummate professional, Mr. Haynes nodded, then said, "I will make sure each suite receives the royal welcome package."

Holly laughed. "We are really having a *royal* guest, so of course, please do what you must. I'm sure the countess and her friends will be quite pleased with the accommodations." She wasn't sure of this at all, but Mr. Haynes didn't need to know of her uncertainty.

"Should we contact Omar and let him know we're welcoming royalty?" Mr. Haynes asked in his most proper way.

"Absolutely," Holly said.

Omar was the head chef over all the restaurants at the inn. Guests could choose to eat at the Blue Sky, their most elegant dining choice; Vittles, where one could choose from a variety of locally grown foods prepared Southern-style; or Rustic, where beer and burgers were devoured heartily. Lastly, there was Chubs, a hip dining experience that catered to the younger set. Omar's expertise did not allow for mistakes in any of the restaurants, not even this most casual of eateries.

Holly did enjoy the occasional meal at Chubs, which had actually been named after her. When guests asked about the origin of the name, most were delighted when they learned it was the nickname given to Holly by her grandfather. Apparently, she'd had very chubby cheeks as a little girl, so Pops had given her the name Chubs, and it had stuck. She had asked the older staff to stop calling her that when she'd taken over as manager, and had insisted that they just call her by her given name.

However, Pops, who had just recently relocated to the Haven, an upscale assisted-living community, had insisted that this latest dining alternative at the inn be named after his one and only granddaughter. Holly didn't mind, though she felt that, at thirty-one, she'd outgrown the name. Hence, she'd asked the employees to call her Holly. And, of course, at this particular time of year, Holly was the perfect name to which to add all sorts of Christmas tags. "Holly Jolly," "Holly Berry," and "Holly Night" were just a few of the tags added to her name. It was all in fun, she knew, but she still wanted to maintain somewhat of a professional image for the guests and employees who didn't know her as "Chubs."

"I will make sure he prepares a fresh local dish upon their arrival," Mr. Haynes said. As always, he stood perfectly erect, his hands carefully looped behind his back, as if at parade rest, while he awaited further instructions.

"I'm sure they will be delighted with whatever we have. We do have one of the South's best chefs." Holly smiled and gave Mr. Haynes a friendly squeeze on the shoulder. "I'll keep you informed of their arrival, as well as that of the governor and his family." Holly made air quotes when she said the word *family*.

Mr. Haynes smiled. "Yes, he does have quite a large . . . uh, crew. I have the presidential suite ready and, of course, the entire third floor, as requested."

"If the governor has any last-minute arrangements, either Marlene or I will update you."

The governor and his "crew" were notorious for making last-minute changes, and a few of his "family members" had become quite rowdy at last year's gathering.

"As you wish, Miss Holly."

She gave him a huge grin and went back to her office.

Chapter 5

"The countess's Gulfstream just swooped down like a giant bird," Marlene relayed to Holly. "Then the four of them piled out of that jet as if they were *all* royalty."

Holly smiled. Marlene was always amazed by their guests' modes of transport. The arrival of the countess had obviously made more of an impression on her than usual.

"I appreciate your driving the inn's limo to pick them up. Sebastian and George had their hands full with the governor's guests. They're early, so we had to do a bit of rerouting. Plus, I know how much you love to drive that limo."

Marlene grinned. "I do. I never cared that much for driving until your mother and I . . . well, that time Sebastian and George had one too many drinks while we were in Asheville, attending that meeting with the heads of the chamber of commerce. I had no choice but to drive. Your mother had left without her contacts and was as blind as a bat without them. No way was I going to allow her to take the wheel."

Holly produced a halfhearted grin. "And thank goodness she didn't. Mom was a terrible driver *with* her glasses on or contacts in."

Marlene shook her head, dabbed at her eyes with a tissue, then threw her shoulders back as though she were standing at attention. "The ladies asked not to be disturbed this afternoon. They're planning something, I know, but I didn't have the courage to ask them about it. The countess, Annie—she insisted I call her that, though it felt terribly disrespectful—asked if we could send up sandwiches and coffee promptly at six o'clock."

"And you've relayed this to Omar?" Holly asked as she thumbed through a pile of papers on her desk.

"Yes. He seemed very excited and said he would prepare the sandwiches himself."

Holly looked up from her paperwork. "Really? Well, that's a first. I thought sandwiches were beneath him."

"Apparently, not when they're being served to a countess."

A tap on her office door discouraged further conversation.

"Come in," Holly said, once again directing her attention back to her paperwork.

Taking a deep breath, she knew, without bothering to look up, who had entered her office. Though he had been working at the inn for only two days, she already knew his scent. Of course, the cologne was a bit overpowering, in kind of a good way, though. *Gawd!* She didn't dare ask what he wore, but would bet anything it was that Old Spice Pops and her father wore. And here she thought it an old man's cologne. *Not!*

"Holly."

She cleared her throat and met his clear blue gaze. Hearing that one word, *her name,* for crying out loud, and she could barely lift her voice above a whisper. She glanced around her desk for a bottle of water. Seeing none, she reached for that morning's cup of cold coffee. She took a swig and began to cough as she peered into the cup and saw a ring of mold at the top of the brown liquid. Apparently, this particular cup had been on her desk way too long. Grabbing a wad of tissues from the box on the corner of her desk, she tried to discreetly spit out the brown muck.

She could feel two sets of eyes on her as she spat into the tissue. "Good grief, Marlene! How long has that cup of . . . never mind," she rasped, and again, she had to clear her throat. "Gannon, what can I do for you?"

He smiled, and that damned dimple sent her squirming.

She spied Marlene out of the corner of her eye. "Marlene, I'd like a fresh bottle of spring water. And some mints. Now." She glanced at her. "Please," she added, knowing that if she didn't, she would be in big trouble later.

"Of course, Ms. Simmons. Right away." Marlene shot her a "We'll talk about this later" look and hurried out of the office.

In her most professional voice, Holly said, "What can I do for you, Gannon?"

Immediately seeing the humorous glint in those stark blue eyes, Holly wished she'd phrased her question differently. But, damn him, she was not going to ask again. No way would she risk another chance for internal embarrassment.

"Do you mind?" He motioned to the club chair in front of her desk.

"By all means," she said, then gestured to the chair he'd sat in only two days ago, during his very brief and somewhat awkward interview.

He eased down into the chair as though he belonged there. "I know this isn't the best time to ask, given the fact that this is only my second day on the job, but something has come up, and I need to take the afternoon off."

Holly couldn't have been more surprised if he'd jumped out of a cake. She blew out a lengthy breath. There were a zillion reasons for her to say no, but she found that she couldn't. Plus, she was beyond curious as to why he needed the afternoon off. Even though she'd known Gannon Montgomery for only two days, she knew he wasn't the kind who would ask to leave his job unless it was truly important.

"Of course. I can have Marlene cover for you for the rest of the afternoon. We're in the 'lull before the storm' moment, anyway."

He nodded, then leaned forward in the chair, dropping his arms to his knees. "You're sure?" he asked.

"Of course. Whatever it is, I hope it turns out for the best," she said as a sneaky way of giving him an opening, if he wanted to share his reason for needing the afternoon off.

For the first time since she'd met him, he looked worried. Shadows clouded his indigo eyes, and his smile, which had been given so readily before, was gone. "It's my granda. Seems he's having a bit of trouble."

"I'm sorry," she replied, and she was. "My grandfather just relocated to an assisted-living community. I worry about him daily. So, do what you need to do." Ticked at herself for offering this unasked-for bit of personal information about herself, she was surprised when he nodded.

Then he said, "Mine as well. Though it's supposed to be one of the better facilities in Asheville, one never knows about those places." He paused, then asked, "Have you heard of the Haven?"

Holly felt like she'd been sucker punched. Was he serious? Did he know more about her private life than she thought?

Instantly on high alert, Holly replied, "Yes, I am quite familiar with the place. It's top of the line." *Crap!* She'd done it again. Given out too much personal information about herself without being asked.

Gannon finally stood up and walked to the door. "Good. I'm glad to hear that. I wasn't too keen on Granda's move, but he insisted it was time. He said I should have the family home to . . . Well, he thought I needed"—he gave a half-hearted laugh—"some alone time."

Holly laughed, too. For once, he'd revealed something about *his* personal life. Before she could stop herself, she blurted out, "My grandfather, Pops, lives at the Haven, too. He loves it there."

"Really?" he asked, his accent a tad stronger. "So your . . . pops is happy and safe there?"

"Didn't you check the place out before your . . . granda moved in?" He couldn't be that ignorant! Though he was quite a hottie, when she'd reviewed his credentials, she had learned that he held a master's degree in business. She knew there was more to this man than his fine body and handsome face. Surely, he wasn't naive enough to allow his grandfather to up and move without looking into the living and health-care conditions at the Haven first?

He looked at her as if he thought she'd lost her mind. "Of course I did. No way would I ever let Granda make such a move without first checking the place out. I didn't want him to move there in the first place. He insisted. Said it was time for me to settle down, start a family."

A family? She couldn't even go there. Ava had also decided it was time to start a family—in her case, it had turned out, with twin boys—and it'd already messed up Holly's nice, orderly life, hence the need to hire a new assistant.

"I see," she said but didn't.

He folded his hands, then nervously twisted them around. "It's not the Haven. Granda says he's been feeling worse since he moved in. He's diabetic. Told me he swore they were diluting his insulin, but I'm sure he's forgetting to take it. He swears this isn't the case, and asked that I check into the pharmacy. I know they deliver his meds for the day every morning. It's up to him to take them, so"—he held both hands out as if in his defense—"I wanted to spend the afternoon with him. Check up on him, just to make sure he's taking his medication properly."

Heart flip! Compassionate, too. Damn that Ava. She might have had more up her sleeve than a simple replacement, temporary or not. After the twins were born, Holly planned to choke her, BFF or not.

"Of course, I would do the same, but so far, Pops is in pretty good health and takes nothing more than a handful of vitamins. So, go ahead." Here she went again. "Let me know how this turns out. With Pops there, I wouldn't want him to stay if there's a risk of . . . well, you know. So, I guess I'll see you tomorrow morning?" she said, sounding like she was confirming a date. A *real* date. She gave herself another mental kick.

"Eight o'clock prompt," Gannon answered. "Thanks for this, Holly. I know it's a lot to ask given the fact I've been here only a couple of days. I'll make it up, I promise."

She nodded, wishing he would *leave!* Holly felt like a gaggle of geese had taken up residence in her chest, her heart rate was so erratic.

Once he left, she plopped down in her chair and blew out a lengthy breath, and it wasn't pretty. Her thoughts were everywhere, yet the only words she could actually focus in on were, "I'll make it up, I promise." What did *that* mean? Had he meant he would make it up to her personally, or was he telling her that he would make up the time taken away from his work? Either way, she knew this guy was going to be trouble.

Not in the typical way, either.

Chapter 6

Upon hearing a knock on her door, Annie de Silva shouted, "Come in." Without bothering to see who had entered her suite, she continued to speak to her guests. Her best friend, Myra Rutledge, sat quietly on the plush sofa beside her. "You can never speak of this. Never, not even to your husbands," Annie said, focusing her gaze on Sophia Manchester. "As much as you may want to confide in them after a romp in the hay, don't. I promise you there will be consequences if you do. Am I right, Myra?"

"Of course you are, dear," Myra replied kindly, then added, "Secrecy has always been of the utmost importance among the Sisters."

"This trial mission is no different. You got it?" Annie demanded. She wasn't going to take any shit off these *wannabe* Vigilantes. "Now, where are those sandwiches I ordered?"

Myra turned to see a tall older man standing behind a white tablecloth. "You've brought the food," she said, stating the obvious for Annie's benefit.

"Yes, ma'am. May I begin to serve?" Mr. Haynes asked in his most dignified tone.

Annie hopped off the sofa. "Nope, you can't. This is a very private meeting, mister. Now take this"—she reached in her jeans pocket for a wad of cash—"and make sure no one, and I mean no one, as in not a single living soul, disturbs us." She tucked the cash in his shirt pocket. "Now, skedaddle."

Without another word, Mr. Haynes flew out of the room and didn't look back when Myra slammed the door and clicked the dead bolt in place.

Sophie and Toots, for once, didn't mutter a single word. All they managed to do was nod in unison.

"You two hungry?" Annie asked before picking up a sandwich. "Tuna on rye, just as I asked."

Toots, dressed casually in navy slacks and a cream sweater, stood up and poked Sophie in the arm. "When have we ever passed up the chance to eat?"

Sophie, who was wearing dark blue Levi's with a red sweatshirt, blurted out, "Want me to name them all, or is this one of those casual comments you make when you don't really have anything of importance to say?" Sophie's grin was a mile wide and lit up her face.

They all burst out laughing.

"Yep, this is one of those times. So we've been there, done that. Now, let's eat before getting down to business."

For the next ten minutes, they picked and prodded, and consumed the elegantly displayed array of sandwiches Omar had prepared. Two pots of coffee later, they were all comfortable enough with each other to speak their minds.

"So, how is it you know this?" Toots asked after Myra and Annie had given them a rundown on their first mission.

"That's for me to know and you to find out. But, if you must know, I have a friend who called me and told me his suspicions. I trust him," Annie answered. "And if I trust him, you should, too. Am I always right on this stuff or what, Myra?" Annie asked.

"Always. Well, there was this one time," Myra began, laughter brimming in her eyes.

"Enough!" Annie shouted. "I say it's time we retire to our rooms. You two might as well suck up this luxury while you can."

"Annie, Toots and Sophie are quite used to living a luxurious lifestyle. At least this is what they stated on the questionnaires I asked them to fill out when I first asked them about the possibility of joining us. Am I correct?" Myra looked at the two seated across from her, her brow raised.

"If you call living in a newly remodeled home with every gadget known to man, a shitload of money to do whatever you want, vacations whenever the urge hits, and so on and so forth, I guess you might call that a luxurious lifestyle. But we don't have any royal bloodlines, so if that's a prerequisite, we're screwed," Sophie spouted in the smart-ass way she usually acted when she felt that she was being put on the defensive.

Annie clapped her hands and laughed loudly. "Myra, I think we've found the perfect additions to our little . . . group."

Both Toots and Sophie sighed at once.

"So, I need you both to state verbally that you understand and agree to the conditions we discussed on the flight here. I also need you both to acknowledge that you will not speak of this among yourselves when you leave this room, or at any other time. Do you both understand and agree to these terms?" Annie asked them one more time, just to make sure.

Toots spoke first. "I do."

Sophie rolled her big brown eyes. "Should we raise our right hand and swear to tell the whole truth and nothing but the truth? I feel like we're being treated like recruits into the Girl Scouts or sorority pledges being initiated. Maybe we need to add our own special handshake. We just happen to have one of these handshakes, in our godmother moments. It goes like this." She placed one hand on top of the other, then motioned for Toots to follow her lead. Without any indication to do so, Myra and Annie placed their hands on top of Sophie's and Toots's.

"Okay, on the count of three. One. Two. Three. When you're good, you're good," Sophie shouted, then pushed the others' hands high in the air.

Annie laughed and winked at Myra. "I think I could get used to this, but I still have to have your verbal agreement."

"Okay, I'm in," Sophie stated.

All four women swore to keep the mission they were about to undertake a secret.

No matter what.

Chapter 7

The Haven wasn't at all typical of most assisted-living communities. It was more like a small city within a city. It had individual residences for those who still wanted to continue living their life in private, with the latest in health care and other facilities a mere breath away. The assisted-living area housed almost a thousand residents and appeared more like an upscale condo/gated community with age restrictions.

The amenities were extensive. There were three churches, an eighteen-hole golf course, and a full-size concert hall. Four outdoor swimming pools were on the premises, and two indoor pools with three heated therapy pools. The library rivaled most to be found in small towns, and the movie theater presented all the latest Hollywood hits. There were four five-star restaurants, as well as shops for everything from groceries to the latest designer handbags.

The Haven offered classes on almost anything one could imagine. There were computer courses, photography classes, lessons in glassblowing, and even an aviation ground school for those who wanted to acquire a private pilot's license. To top it off, they even offered voice lessons for those who were brave enough to dare to try their hand at singing. The Haven's motto—"You asked for it, we've got it, and if we don't, we'll get it"—attracted seniors from all across the country. This was not at all a place that catered to the locals. Its clientele came from all fifty states and thirteen foreign countries.

Angus Montgomery, "Monty" to his friends, couldn't have been happier with his decision to move out of the family residence. Last year he'd decided to retire, and three months ago, when he made the Haven his permanent home, he knew he'd made the right decision. He had new friends, and every minute of his days and nights was accounted for. Not to mention he felt it was time for Gannon to settle down, get married, and start a family of his own. He spent way too much time at Draper's, the lodge that had been in the Montgomery family for more years than he cared to remember. He'd raised his family there, as had his father and his grandfather before him.

His great-grandfather had come to America from Ireland before the turn of the last century. He'd worked in what was once a boardinghouse, where he met and married the owner's daughter. They had three sons, who in turn worked at the family's thriving boardinghouse, where they also raised their families. By the time Monty's father was ready to take over the robust family business, boardinghouses were no longer in high demand. It was at this time that Draper's Lodge was born, the name originating from the original owners of the boardinghouse. Renovations and additions throughout the years made Draper's, as most of those who knew of it called it, one of the most exclusive resorts in the state.

Of course, there were many other successful inns and lodges. The Grove Place Inn had always been Draper's biggest competitor, and he knew for a fact that his family lodge was tough competition for the inn. He'd always been on good terms with the Simmons family, and this relationship had been even better since he'd moved to the Haven.

It was quite a coincidence that Rex Simmons lived in the condo next door. Not only had sharing their common background given them a source for lively debates, but they'd also become the best of friends. Each morning, promptly at seven o'clock, they met for coffee and a home-made biscuit at Ruby's, a diner that served residents but was also open to the public, at least to those who could obtain entry at the gate.

Two weeks ago, however, Monty had begun to feel terrible. He had become light-headed and weak. He had rarely had a sick day, despite his well-controlled diabetes, but suddenly he had found himself having more bad days than good. Last Monday, before heading to Ruby's to meet Rex, he'd measured his dose of morning insulin, just as he'd done for the past four years. Checked the syringe to make sure he was getting the exact amount of insulin, administered the shot in his upper belly, then almost immediately developed blurred vision and began to feel incredibly fatigued. When he could see straight, he checked his blood sugar, and it was dangerously high. He lay down, drank three glasses of water, and took some of the pills his doctor had prescribed before the diabetes required him to take insulin on a regular basis.

As an afterthought, he checked the bottle to make sure he was taking the right medication and also checked to make sure it hadn't been tampered with. Sweat beaded on his forehead and upper lip when he saw that the silver ring around the top of the bottle appeared as though it had been pried apart, then carefully repositioned. He took the bottle outside on the veranda, in the sunlight, so he could see clearly. Yes, this particular bottle had either been tampered with, dropped, or who knew what. Monty had immediately called Annie.

And today he'd called his grandson. He would be there later in the afternoon. *Odd*, he thought, because Gannon was always so concerned about his grandfather's health and well-being that he usually jumped like a fish out of water at the first indication that something could be wrong. Must be something going on at the lodge to keep him from rushing over.

As was becoming normal, the minute the nausea passed, he grabbed a light jacket and headed out to meet Rex. He told himself he was probably imagining things, acting like an old man, but he knew what he'd seen. Unless his eyes were playing tricks on him, meddling hands were hard at work. To what end, he didn't know, but with Annie and her friends here to assist him, he had no doubt they would track down the person or persons who'd messed with his meds, and when Annie found them, there would be hell to pay.

His only son, William, along with his daughter-in-law, Evelyn, God rest their souls, had been killed in a bombing in a café in Paris while celebrating their tenth wedding anniversary almost twenty-five years ago. He'd been shaken to the core with grief, but a brokenhearted grandson, Gannon, had needed him more than ever. Acting as both father, mother, and grandfather, Monty had had no choice but to grieve in silence while he saw to it that Gannon had as normal a childhood as humanly possible, given the tragedy he'd suffered at such a tender age. It was during the bombing investigation that he had met Annie, as she, too, had been at the café where the bombing took place, only she had escaped unscathed. They'd been friends ever since.

Though Monty suspected Annie of being more than a mere billionaire countess, he credited her friendship and loyalty for helping him through a parent's worst nightmare. They'd stayed in touch over the years—Christmas cards, the occasional phone call, and once, she had come for a surprise visit and had stayed at the lodge, where they'd become even closer. There were those who thought his relationship with Annie was a bit more than friendly, but that wasn't the case. He was older, and he'd really never gotten over the loss of his wife, Lily, who, strangely and tragically, had died of pneumonia just days after being diagnosed before Gannon's first birthday.

Monty had experienced his share of tragedies, yet he had managed to live a full and happy life. He'd dedicated his life to working hard and raising Gannon, who had surprised him all those years ago when he told him he'd applied to go to college at the University of Dublin. For six years, Monty had been lost without his grandson, but he'd managed to get by, and now, after all the tragedy he'd had in his life, when he'd retired, leaving the family business in Gannon's most reliable hands, he had yet another possible catastrophe to deal with, and at Christmastime no less. His favorite holiday of all. He planned to chop down his own tree this year, straight from the tree farm. In the past, he had hired interior designers to dress up the lodge during the holidays. Now, for the first time since he was a child, he was going to decorate his very own Christmas tree.

If he didn't die first.

Chapter 8

Gannon hated asking for time off so soon, but he didn't really have a choice. Granda needed him, and he would crawl through barbed wire for the man. He loved him like a father, worried about him constantly since he'd up and moved out.

Deep down inside, he knew the choice to infiltrate the inn surreptitiously was his and his alone. If Granda was ill, he would abandon his plans to find out exactly why the inn continued to be so successful and would spend the time to take care of him. He'd simply have to rethink his strategy, maybe hire a marketing firm to relaunch Draper's. He would have to use his own funds to do this, but if that was what it took to keep the family business running, then that was exactly what he would do.

Playing the role of a double agent, so to speak, working in enemy territory, wasn't nearly as easy as he'd originally thought. His plan was to work at the inn during the day and continue at night to carry out his duties at the lodge. However, he was no longer so sure he could manage to do both without being discovered. Just this morning, he had seen one of the lodge's regular patrons, who'd dined there two nights ago. While Draper's didn't have a five-star restaurant, Chloe's held its own as one of the finest dining spots in

Asheville. He'd seen Holly and some friends dining there on more than one occasion.

Had she been there to spy? And if so, why hadn't he noticed? Why hadn't he noticed how gorgeous she was? He had sneaked a look at her ring finger and had seen neither a wedding band nor an engagement ring. Didn't mean much these days, but if he ever chose to tie the knot, he would most certainly want his fiancée to wear his ring. Maybe he was a bit old-fashioned at thirty-five, but he still believed in courting a woman, as his granda had taught him.

Holly a spy? It certainly wasn't out of the question. He'd never thought of it before, but now he didn't know. Maybe *she* was trying to beat him at his own game.

But to what end? The inn was extremely popular with locals, as well as with guests from around the world. She didn't need to snoop into the way his family ran the business.

"Stupid," he said out loud, glad he was alone in the Jeep. Not every person he came in contact with in his line of business was a snoop.

Shamed by what he was doing, he put it out of his mind as soon as he pulled up to the gatehouse at the Haven.

"You have a pass?" an elderly man wearing a dark blue uniform asked from his post, a brick structure that was the size of a small house.

All family members of the residents had been given permanent guest passes. Gannon reached for his, which he kept in the center console, then held it out the window to be scanned. This was the Haven's way of keeping track of everyone who came and went. He found that he actually liked the idea. As Granda had said, "It keeps out the riffraff."

When the gate opened, he wound his way through the maze of what he thought of as a small city.

The windows of the various buildings throughout the

community were decked out with giant green wreaths with red bows. The buildings had brightly colored lights wrapped around the lampposts. He drove past a house that displayed a giant Santa with his team of reindeer; the scene covered the entire front lawn. One house was preparing for a live nativity scene, according to the signs posted. A crew of several men on a cherry picker were placing giant stars on the rooftops. Seeing all this, Gannon couldn't help but get into the holiday spirit. When he saw Grandpa's condo, he slid the Jeep into one of the guest parking slips. He then exited the Jeep and walked to the entrance to the building.

As soon as he stepped inside the reception area, he was hit with the strong scent of pine. He took a deep breath, laughed, and shook his head as he rode the elevator to Granda's third-floor condo. They certainly had the holiday spirit here.

Granda's condo was down a long hallway, several yards away from the elevators. *Smart,* Gannon thought. He'd stayed in hotels where his room had been close to the elevators, and it had made for lousy sleep. Granda had picked his particular condo for two reasons. No one was above him, and it faced the golf course. *Smart man,* he thought as he rang the doorbell.

Before he could raise his hand to tap on the door, it swung open.

"Granda!" Gannon exclaimed. "What the hell is going on?" Shocked at his grandfather's appearance, he mentally kicked himself for not having paid closer attention to his needs. "Are you sick? Should I take you to the hospital?"

Granda, tall and thin, with chipper blue eyes and a head full of silver hair, suddenly appeared old and fragile to him.

"No, no, and no. Now, young man, sit." He nodded toward the small table that just barely fit into the condo's kitchen. Granda liked an eat-in kitchen, said it reminded him of when he was a boy. Gannon thought the kitchen too small, but it was just for his grandfather. It was enough for one person.

He sat down, waiting to hear what was troubling his grandfather.

"You're not gonna like this, kid, but I think my insulin is being tampered with." He told him about finding the seal broken on a bottle and about how he'd felt after his morning injection.

"Did the pharmacy bring you a new bottle of insulin?" Gannon asked, shocked at his grandfather's claim.

"Nope, and I don't want any. I'm not taking this stuff anymore. It's no good. Just like all those commercials you see on TV these days. After they tell you the side effects, the damned disease is a joke."

"Granda, you have to take your insulin. It's life threatening if you don't. You could go into a diabetic coma! You're coming home with me." Gannon felt like he was the father and Granda the child. He was imagining things. No one would tamper with his medication. Just the suggestion was ludicrous.

"No, I am not. Look, I'm not crazy. I know what I saw. Here." He went to the refrigerator and removed a bottle of insulin, then set it in the center of the table. "Now, look at this." He used his index finger to point to the metal band. "See? It's been pried open."

Gannon checked the seal, and it had certainly been opened, but he was sure it was his grandfather himself who had done the opening. He'd taken the medication!

"I see, but you have to open it to use it," Gannon tried explaining, and felt bad, but it was what it was.

"I don't break *that* seal, Gannon. That's what I'm trying to tell you. The way you take insulin is to shake the stuff up a bit, then stick the syringe in here." He pointed to the top of the bottle. It reminded Gannon of a wine cork. "You draw the insulin out into the syringe. There is never a need to break that seal. It says so right here." He pointed to the label.

Gannon squinted to read the small print. When he looked at Granda, he didn't see an aging old man. He saw a man who was sick because he wasn't taking his insulin. And maybe there was something wrong with the stuff. People messed with medications all the time, but it didn't necessarily mean the pharmacy was responsible. There had to be a rational explanation. But it would keep. Now he had to get his grandfather to a doctor; he needed his insulin.

"Okay, so I'm wrong, and you're right. It doesn't matter now. What matters is you. You look bad, Granda. I hate to say it, but you do. Let's get you to the doctor before they close for the day." He'd wanted to say, "Before it was too late," but he'd caught himself.

"On one condition."

"Granda, we need to take care of your health right now. Anything else will have to keep."

"I'll go, but we have to take Rex with us. He's my neighbor and friend. I want him to go. He's next door. I'll call him and have him meet us downstairs." Without waiting for Gannon to reply, Monty pulled his cell phone from his hip pocket and dialed.

"I need to go to the doctor. My grandson is here to drive me. You want to ride along? Sure. Yes. Meet us downstairs, in the guest parking." He ended the call.

"He's coming along. I knew he wouldn't want to stay here. We were supposed to see that new Jason Statham movie tonight."

Gannon shook his head. "Sure. Let's just get out of here and find a fresh batch of insulin."

Fifteen minutes later, Gannon, his grandfather, and his

grandfather's new best friend, Rex, who just so happened to be Holly's grandfather, headed for the closest urgent-care center.

Leave it to good old Granda to make best friends with the person Gannon now thought of as the enemy.

Chapter 9

"Do you think we can pull this off?" Toots asked Sophie.

"Us? Please. You're kidding me, right? Compared to some of the other things we've had to do, this should be a breeze."

"We're with those Vigilantes, the ones from the news. What if we're caught and go to jail? Can't you just see the headlines? WIFE OF LATEST BEST-SELLING AUTHOR AND PSYCHIC SIDEKICK ARRESTED. I didn't really think about that when I filled out that questionnaire. Maybe we should back out before it's too late. If Phil and Goebel knew what we were up to, they would kill us. We wouldn't have to worry about getting caught and going to prison. I'm not so sure they fell for the story we told them."

Sophie leaned over from her position on the sofa. "What do you mean? Of course they believe us. We're going to spend two nights at the spa Tranquility. It's our pre-Christmas gift to ourselves, remember? At least that's what I told Goebel."

"I told Phil the same thing. But I'm not very happy about lying to him."

"Me either. So, let's call them and tell them the truth.

We'll clear our consciences, then continue with the plan. What are they going to say?"

Toots looked around the luxury suite. It was beautifully decorated and even had a ten-foot Christmas tree, which filled the rooms with its fragrant scent. She'd stayed in places just as nice as this and some even nicer, but this was homey. A nice mini-retreat. Yes, they'd walked away from their duties as hostesses in the holiday parade of homes. She and Sophie had agreed it would be good for both Phil and Goebel to have the experience of acting as hosts for two nights. Their adoring husbands had agreed, and now here they were, feeling guilty.

"You really think we should tell them the truth?" Toots asked, her tone not quite as commanding as normal.

"I think when we return to Charleston, we could tell them, just to see if Annie's true to her word. Something tells me that when Annie said we weren't to discuss this, she meant it. Look at us now. We're doing exactly what she asked us not to do. If we want to be a part of this group in the future, we need to start by following the rules we swore we'd follow," Sophie said. "If you can't handle the deception, we need to back out now. These people are counting on us to do the job we signed on for."

"You're right. I'm just having a bout of the guilts. Plus, I want to smoke. I forgot to bring my electronic cigarette," Toots whined. "It's such a nasty habit, but I swear, I'd give a thousand bucks for a smoke right now. A real one."

Sophie got up and went to the kitchen. "I'm making coffee. Annie said we weren't allowed to call room service. Come in here and look for the cream and sugar. It'll take your mind off smoking."

"Thanks for the reminder," Toots said but headed to the kitchen. Sophie was right, though she wouldn't tell her so.

As usual, Sophie loved being right, but when you told her this, she never let you forget it.

Sophie found a variety of different blends of coffee for the Keurig coffeemaker. Bold, sweet vanilla cream and pumpkin spice were among the more interesting ones. She took two servings of the pumpkin spice. It was her absolute favorite. Did Annie know this about her, too, or was it merely a coincidence? She supposed that everyone drank pumpkin spice coffee this time of year.

Toots found half-and-half and sugar in the well-stocked refrigerator. "You think Annie had this room stocked, or is it one of the perks?"

Sophie held out the box of pumpkin spice coffee. "You tell me."

Toots raised her eyebrows and put a finger to her lips. She ran out of the room and was back with the pad and pen provided by the inn. She quickly scrawled out the words, "*This place could be bugged!!!*"

Sophie rolled her eyes and yanked the pad and pen from her. "*Ya think???*"

Toots grabbed the paper and pen from her and wrote as fast as she could. "*Then we are screwed, because we've been discussing this case!!! Let's talk about something else now???*"

Sophie nodded and filled the machine with bottled water. "So, what did you get me for Christmas this year?" she asked, a big grin on her face.

Toots shook her head, her auburn hair falling out of her topknot. "You're really crude. You have no manners or etiquette. You know that, right?"

"So you say," Sophie quipped and handed Toots a mug of coffee. "I've been telling Goebel I want one of these fancy coffeemakers. Wonder if he'll get me one? Of course,

we can afford it, since we're used to living such *luxurious*"—she dragged out the last word—"lifestyles."

Toots flipped her off. She filled her mug with lots of
cream and sugar. Bad for her, but apart from smoking, it
was her biggest vice, and she didn't see it ending anytime
in the near future. Of course, if their plans were to go
awry, there wouldn't be a future.

What in the world had she been thinking when she'd
filled out that questionnaire at the countess's invitation?
That was just it. She hadn't been thinking at all. At least
not like a grown woman. She'd been thinking of the thrill
and the excitement of it all. Maybe she'd settled down too
soon? She and Abby's godmothers had been riding high
for the past few years. Toots wasn't so sure that settling
down was the right choice for her. She'd been searching for
something, again, and this time, there could be no going
back.

"What are you doing?" Sophie asked. She carried her
mug to the living room area and sat back on the sofa.
Toots followed her.

Using her hand to mimic a slicing motion to her throat,
Toots shook her head from left to right.

"What?" Sophie asked in that fake-innocent way she had.

"You tell me. It's your specialty. Seriously. I am not joking. Do you *see* any trouble? With this?" She waved her
hand across the room as if she were about to open a cur-
tain to reveal a prize.

"Aha! Okay, I get it, and the answer is nada. Trust me, I
did a lot of . . . stuff beforehand." She placed an index finger over her lips.

"That's a relief," Toots said, sighing. "Though I don't
know why I never thought about asking this before we
left."

"Toots, listen and listen good. I want to enjoy this cup of
coffee. I want to enjoy these two nights as spies or under-

cover agents or whatever we are. And more than anything, I want you to stop worrying so much. We're going to be just fine. Trust me." Sophie spoke in a tone that left no room for doubt.

Toots nodded and took a sip of her coffee.

What, she wondered, had she gotten them into now?

Chapter 10

Holly arrived at the inn at six thirty, hoping to get a head start on her day. She hadn't been able to sleep last night. With the holidays here, she really needed to sleep, because her days were going to be really long. She'd tossed and turned all night, questioning her decision to hire Gannon Montgomery. Two days, barely, and he needed time off. Had he been telling the truth when he'd told her the story about his grandfather? Though she couldn't think of a reason why he would lie, still, there was something about him that didn't ring true. And right now she didn't have time to worry about it. If he didn't work out, she would manage. Tears filled her eyes when she realized her thoughts were exactly like those of her mother. Her mother had always told her she could manage anything in the world. She smiled at the memory.

This was the first night of the planned activities for the guests. She had arranged for a local craft store to set up shop in the Autumn Room, where the guests, both young and old, would make holiday wreaths. It sounded boring and old-fashioned, but they'd had a blast last year. She would need Gannon to stay late tonight. She hoped it wouldn't be a problem.

Glad to be alone in the office, she would make it a priority to come in early during the holidays. Marlene didn't arrive until seven thirty. The quiet was nice. She made a pot of coffee, turned on her computer, and printed out the week's work schedule for the personnel office. She scanned the sheet, making sure the inn was fully staffed. Temporary workers were a must if she wanted to pull off a successful season. She should've had this out of the way, but Ava had had to leave, and she hadn't gotten around to it. Ava usually did all the interviewing. She would miss her more than she could imagine, but she'd manage that, too.

She took a sip of her coffee and made a face. "Ugh," she said out loud. No wonder Marlene always insisted on making the coffee.

"Holly?" Gannon called her name from the door, which she had left open, then entered her office.

She whirled around, almost knocking her cup of coffee over. "Gannon, you scared me. Don't you know how to knock?" *Damn this man!* He was irritating her.

"I did, but you were busy making faces." He offered up a slight smile. "Sorry."

Holly felt like she was twelve again. What was he doing here so early, and why was he sneaking up on her like some thief in the night?

"Well, then, I suppose I owe you an apology. I'm sorry. I wasn't expecting anyone. You startled me." Once again, she was explaining herself to this . . . this man who was her employee! He should be the one doing the explaining.

"I thought I could get an early start today," he explained. "If you'd rather I come back . . . ?"

"No, no. Please have a seat." She motioned for him to sit in the chair, the one she was starting to think of as "his" chair. "Would you like some coffee?" she asked, then felt like slapping herself. She was the boss. He should be asking *her* if she wanted coffee.

No, no, no! This wasn't the way she normally acted.

Why, her thoughts were downright mean. And she did not like mean. Though she did *not* like the effect Gannon Montgomery's presence had on her, either.

"Yeah, a cup of coffee would be great. I had a late night," Gannon said as he accepted Holly's invitation to be seated.

Why was he telling her *that?* Did he want her to ask why he'd had a late night? It sure seemed like it. She tried to focus on pouring a cup of coffee. Nothing more. This was nothing. She filled the cup too full, spilling coffee all over the box of filters. She grabbed two packs of sugar and a handful of cream mini-cups and put them on her desk.

"Here. Drink this," she insisted. Realizing she sounded incredibly rude, she softened her voice. "I wasn't sure how you took your coffee." She pointed to the cream and sugar.

"Black. It's better that way," he said, then took a sip. "Sometimes." The look on his face spoke volumes.

Holly's eyes widened; then she burst out laughing. "I do make the most hideous coffee, don't I?"

"It's . . . bold," he said in tactful agreement.

"Strong. Yes, I have yet to learn the fine art of coffee making. Marlene usually handles that task. I couldn't sleep, so I came in early. We've got a full schedule planned tonight. The craft store is setting up in the Autumn Room. I'm guessing we'll have a turnout of at least a hundred. Maybe more." *Nothing like rattling on,* she thought, but the awkward moment had passed. It was time to get down to business.

"I don't understand."

Holly looked at him in amused wonder. "We're making wreaths tonight. It was quite successful last year. Didn't you do this at Draper's?" she asked.

Gannon looked as though he'd been sucker punched. His eyes glazed over, and lines of what appeared to be intense concentration deepened along his brows and under

his eyes. He met her gaze. "Crafts? Is that what you're saying? You're having a crafts class tonight?"

"Don't look so surprised. Surely you worked a holiday
function once or twice when you were at Draper's?"

He shook his head and took a sip of the horrible coffee.
Holly didn't know what she'd said to upset him, but she
knew a deer-in-headlights moment when she observed one.

"You know what, Holly? I didn't. Not one time in all
the years I've . . . worked for the Drapers, not once have I
worked a holiday function. They don't have holiday functions." He said the last words as if he'd suddenly been
struck in the head by a bolt of lightning. "And you do this
every year?"

"We have all sorts of functions, activities, contests, out-
ings, whatever you want to call them. That's why we hire
extra help for the season. There is so much going on, it
takes about a hundred extra employees to make it happen.
When my mother was alive, this is what she enjoyed most.
I . . ." Tears pooled, and Holly quickly knuckled her eyes.
"I lost her in February. This is my first Christmas season
without her. Dad is acting brave, but I know he's dying inside."

She stopped to collect herself. "Look, I'm sorry. I shouldn't
have dumped that on you. I'm fine. Really, just a bit overwhelmed this year. From the looks of the reservations, it's
just starting to hit me. The work and all. I think this is
going to be the busiest year we've ever had."

Gannon nodded. "And to what do you attribute this . . .
this sudden rush?" He moved to the edge of his chair, placing his elbows on the edge of her desk.

"You really want to know?" she asked.

"Yes, I really do," he answered quickly. "It's . . . fasci-
nating. The business end."

"First, we always want our guests to feel as if this is
their home away from home. We do whatever we can to

make the rooms homey and inviting. I'm sure you know this, but we try to go the extra mile. That was Mom's specialty. She started this way before I was old enough to work here. She had a bit of success with her parties, all the little extras during the Christmas season. Word got around. Within three years, we were taking reservations two years in advance. With the economy the way it is, that is no longer true. But we are usually full up by the time the season is in full swing.

"The guests loved the planned activities during the holidays, the contests, and so on. Mom loved Christmas, and it showed in everything she planned. This year and next year, we are as booked as we allow because of this. Of course, we have to leave room for things like the governor's family affair or visits from royalty. After that, I don't know if I'll have quite the success my mom did, but I will give it my best shot."

Gannon shook his head. "It's really that simple," he said, more to himself than to her.

"Not really, but business-wise, it's a simple move. Make the guests happy. And who isn't happy during the holidays?" Holly asked, then remembered she wasn't all that happy, but she truly didn't sound *unhappy*. She enjoyed sharing her mother's ideas with Gannon, and he appeared to listen with an avid interest.

"Yes, the holidays are happy times," he said, not sounding happy at all.

Holly suddenly remembered he'd come to her office early, so there must be a problem. "Gannon, you're not here to listen to me rattle on about the inn. Is there a problem you wanted to discuss?"

He leaned back in the chair, leaving the half-full cup on her desk. "I wanted to explain what happened yesterday with my grandfather."

Concern etched on her face, she asked, "Is he ill?"

Gannon smirked. "The old guy is ill, but not terribly so. He had some issues with his insulin yesterday. I had to take him to urgent care, but he's fine. He really had me scared at first, but the doctor assured me he was going to be just fine if he takes his medication. He's diabetic and hadn't been taking his insulin. Granda thought someone in the pharmacy at the Haven might've tampered with his bottle of insulin.

"I don't think there's anything to be worried over, but I didn't admit this to him. He's now the proud owner of one of those insulin pens that you can carry in your pocket. He told me when I left him last night that he and his neighbor were on a secret mission, and he'd been sworn to secrecy. I'm not sure what to make of his comments. Just getting old, I guess."

"As long as he's feeling better, that's what matters."

"Yes, he'll be okay, but I want to warn you ahead of time. His neighbor and new best friend, the man who's involved in this secret mission, is none other than your grandfather. Rex, right?"

Holly looked at Gannon, bewildered. "You're serious, aren't you?"

"I certainly am."

She raked a hand through her hair. "I'll talk to Dad. Pops will listen to him. You don't think they're really involved in some crazy . . . mission?"

"I haven't a clue. What I do know is that Granda's faculties are intact, he's reasonably healthy, and he wouldn't allow anyone to take advantage of him, so who's to say what they're up to? He's not that old!" Gannon threw back his head and laughed. "That old coot mentioned something about a bunch of vigilante women, and told me that I'd better not repeat it or there'd be trouble. I think he and Rex are trying to make it with the ladies at their condo. I'm sure I'll hear all about it."

Temporarily taken aback by Gannon's words, Holly stood up and walked around her desk. She sat in the chair next to Gannon.

"Did I hear you correctly? Did you say vigilantes?" She spoke so fast, she feared he couldn't understand her.

He grinned. "Crazy, huh?"

She nodded. "That's putting it mildly."

Chapter 11

"Sophia, you will act as the whiny, nagging sister-in-law, worried he's not taking his meds. Let me see you cry," Annie demanded.

Sophie wasn't one to caterwaul, but she could bring up the tears when she had to. Closing her eyes, she thought of Walter, her former husband. Dead as a doornail. No, thinking about that wife-beating son of a bitch would only make her laugh. She mentally erased the image of his drunken face. Clearing her head, she focused on bringing real tears to her eyes. As soon as she felt a backwash fill her eyes, she opened them and let the tears drip onto her white silk blouse. Her nose always stopped up when she did this. She grabbed the tissue box from the end table and blew her nose, making a loud snorting sound so that the other women stared at her.

"Sorry. I was trying to make it real."

Toots was having trouble keeping her laughter to herself. Sophie looked at her and winked.

"Now, Toots. You are going to pose as the new wannabe girlfriend. You'll have to slobber a bit and act like you're about to fall madly in love with this guy, Norton Baumgardner. Can you do this and make it believable? You'll need to keep him away from the pharmacy for a few hours. I believe he'll take the employee Christmas party as an opportunity to be by himself in the pharmacy and do his deed. If it turns out that that's what he is planning, you'll need to do whatever it takes to keep him by your side."

Toots almost choked. Annie had to know she had quite a lengthy list when it came to deceased husbands. Phil was husband number nine. Could she act like she was madly in love? Of course she could. When she'd married her eighth husband, Leland, that awful cheapskate, she had pretended daily that she loved him. She could do this. "I think we both know I'm quite capable of making a man feel loved. Though I have to admit, falling in love on a first date, if you want to call this 'meet up' a first date, I will have to force myself."

"Does she have to sleep with him?" Sophie asked.

Annie and Myra looked at Sophie.

"Absolutely not! What do you think we're doing? Running a prostitution ring? This is the mission you all signed up for. You can't back out now even if you want to. I've made all the necessary arrangements, and tonight you will begin your mission." Annie never lost her cool.

"I knew that. I just wanted to see your reaction," Sophie said snidely.

"We are professionals, Sophia. Surely you know this. You've had time to study the cases Myra and I have allowed you to examine. This isn't Hollywood or some psychic fair we're planning. This is serious stuff. Most likely, people are going to get hurt, not physically, but lives will change when we have completed this mission. I imagine those responsible will be facing lengthy prison sentences. This is serious, not a game."

"Are you insinuating anything, Annie? Because if you are, you can kiss my rear end. I'm pretty well respected in my field, too. I am quite accomplished. If I thought there was any risk in this assignment, I would never have volunteered my services. Are you getting this?" Sophie was ticked. "I know what we're about to undertake."

Annie glanced at Myra. "Then, we're all set. Now, let's get back to our rooms and prepare for the evening ahead."

Sophie and Toots left Annie's suite of rooms so fast, they created a breeze when they walked past them.

Once they were safely ensconced in their own suite, Sophie spoke up. "That woman doesn't trust me."

"No, Sophie, you're wrong about that. She does trust you. And that's the problem. She is frightened of your abilities. She has to know of your successes. They've been in newspapers across the country. I think our Annie is a bit intimidated by you. And Myra is loving every minute of the two of you badgering one another."

Sophie plopped down on the sofa. "You really believe that?"

"Yes, I do. Aren't you getting any kind of vibes from Annie?" Toots asked.

"Not a thing, but I do know that our little mission is going to go off as planned. If we follow the rules."

"And what happens if we decide we don't want to follow the rules?" Toots singsonged.

"Whatever you do, Toots, follow the rules. I don't want you to challenge this, okay? You have to trust me on this."

"I would trust you with my life, Soph. You, of all people, should know that. Look at all the garbage we've been through. You and I, we're two birds of a feather."

"That we are. But, Toots, I want you to promise me, no matter what happens, you will stick to Annie's plans. I know we're not very fond of her right now, but she and Myra know exactly what they're up against. Now, promise me."

Toots rolled her eyes. "Okay. I promise."

"To follow Annie and Myra's rules, no matter what. I want to hear you say it," Sophie demanded.

"Good grief, Sophie. You're acting as if I were a child. I

know you won't stop until I say this, so here goes. I promise to follow Annie and Myra's rules, no matter what. Now, are you satisfied?"

Sophie took a deep breath. "I am."

"Are you sure you're telling me everything? I have the feeling you know more about this mission than you're telling me."

"Toots, we signed up for this. It was your idea, remember? We're gonna be just fine. I promise."

"You're one hundred percent sure?" Toots asked.

"I am never one hundred percent sure of anything, Toots."

Chapter 12

"I can't do one single thing, Holly. However, I can sit in a chair, a comfortable one, of course, and observe. Make sure everything is organized. Sort of like an eye in the sky. I will need an assistant, too."

Holly rolled her eyes. "Of course you will, and before you ask, no, you can't have Marlene. She already has her hands full. She's taking on Mom's duties tonight." Which they both knew was hostess with more than the mostest.

In desperation, Holly had called to ask Ava to come in this evening to help with the wreath party, promising her she wouldn't have to lift a finger. She'd hated to ask, but Gannon had absolutely no experience with this type of gathering, or so he'd said. She still found it hard to believe that Draper's didn't have planned holiday functions for their guests. To her it sounded like a very poor business practice, but she'd kept that thought to herself.

"Then who?" Ava asked.

"I suppose I could offer up Gannon, despite the fact that he has absolutely no experience, though I'd planned to use him elsewhere," Holly told Ava. "He does a very nice job of adding something to the scenery. I'll have to give him that."

"I knew it," Ava teased. "I was right about suggesting him."

Holly raked a hand through her hair, a bad habit, as it ruined her early morning blow out. "What are you talking about?"

"You think he's hot, right?" Ava said encouragingly.

Holly took a deep breath, a yoga breath, and slowly exhaled. "His looks have absolutely nothing to do with his capabilities to act as my assistant. So far, he's been useless."

She realized that it was true. This was day three, and he really hadn't assisted her with anything. She'd gone over a few duties with him, and, of course, this morning she'd explained the inn's holiday activities. He'd appeared shocked that such events took place. She'd even gone as far as to ask him if Draper's offered any type of organized Christmas-themed activity, and he'd said no. Maybe he just hadn't participated, and so he wasn't aware of this, but he'd been adamant when she'd repeated her question. Again, she felt this was bad for business, but Draper's was not her concern.

"Then why did you hire him?"

"Ava, need I remind you that you were the one who narrowed the applicants down to six? Need I remind you that you told me that G. W. Montgomery was *your* pick of the list?"

"But *you* hired him, my dear, I didn't," Ava stated quite bluntly.

"Yeah, I did. And there isn't a thing I can do about it now. After the holidays, I will have to reconsider my decision, but for now, he is all I have. Unless you have another suggestion?"

"Terri Anne Phillips?"

"You're lucky I am having this conversation with you on the phone and am not sitting next to you. Doubly lucky you've got a couple of buns in the oven. Otherwise, I'd have to choke you." Holly had always threatened to choke, strangle, or throttle Ava since they were old enough to understand what those things meant. They knew it was all in fun.

"Yeah, whatever. So, you want me to call her? I'll call Marlene and have her give me her number. If I recall, she did have an excellent résumé."

Holly shook her head and laughed. Ava delighted in teasing her.

"You're laughing, aren't you?" Ava questioned. "And at such a critical time, too."

"Ava, shut up! It's not that bad. Frankly, I'm a bit lost without Mom, and you. I feel like I'm the captain of a sinking ship right now. Yes, yes, I know what to do, but I also have a zillion other responsibilities to consider. So, let's just cut to the chase. Do you have anyone in mind? To be your assistant?" Holly needed to know. As she'd said, she had a zillion other responsibilities to contend with.

"What about Mr. Haynes?" Ava asked. "He's one of our best employees, if you want my opinion. He knows everyone's job right down to the last detail. You can have Brenda work in registration. She knows her stuff."

Brenda had worked as Mr. Haynes's right hand for as long as Holly could remember.

"No, he won't want to relinquish his duties. He takes them quite seriously, as he should. I'll ask Brenda if she's up for a craft party."

"Oh, I don't want *her!* She's too formal for my tastes."

Getting more infuriated by the moment, Holly asked, "And Mr. Haynes isn't?"

"He's a lot of fun when he wants to be. Of course, you wouldn't know that, being at the top of the pecking order. Us peons do have a lighter side when we're away from our boss lady."

Both women giggled, as they knew this wasn't true, but

it was funny. "Let's stop playing around, Ava. I really am swamped. What about Dad?" Why hadn't she thought of him before?

"Beau?" Ava questioned. "Isn't he needed elsewhere? Isn't he supposed to be overseeing the Christmas parties this year? I was sure that was on my list."

"Yes, and yes. He owns the place, Ava. If he's needed in another capacity, he'll jump on it."

And he would. For years, Holly had seen both of her parents perform duties that weren't generally considered among those to be fulfilled by owners. But she had to remind herself that her parents weren't like the owners of other inns or hotels. They truly cared about the guests and their employees. They were not like the "bottom line is all that counts" owners found in so many places. Whether it meant washing dishes or having a glass of champagne with the governor, both were always prepared to do what needed to be done.

"I know that, but I think I'd rather have Gannon. Maybe I can teach him a thing or two. That's if you're sure you won't need him."

Again, Holly wanted to strangle her best friend. She wasn't making a simple decision very easy. Had to be the pregnancy hormones. It was unlike Ava to be so wishy-washy where decision making was concerned.

Exasperated, Holly spoke a bit louder than normal. "Then he's all yours, okay?"

"Okay, okay. You don't have to get all stuffy about it. I'll take him under my wing, show him the ropes. Maybe he'll work out, after all."

"Then it's settled. Gannon will act as your assistant tonight. And, Ava, if you so much as breathe a word to him about me, I promise you, as soon as you deliver those boys, I will personally strangle you with their umbilical cords."

"Holly! That's terrible. I can't believe you'd even say

such a thing. I'll never have a normal thought about their umbilical cord again. Shame on you!"

"Ava, calm down. You're overreacting. I'm kidding, okay? Your hormones are definitely out of whack."

"I suppose, but still, that's not a very nice thing to say, especially at Christmastime."

"I'm sorry, okay?" Holly said sweetly.

"I accept your apology. Now, make sure Gannon wears his black suit and the red tie. It will be perfect."

"Okay," Holly said, then hung up. This conversation had taken up way too much time already.

Only after she had started on the next item on her agenda did Holly wonder how Ava knew that Gannon owned a black suit and a red tie.

Chapter 13

"It seems like it's been forever," Monty said, giving Annie a big hug.

"It's been too long, that's for sure," Annie replied. "I'm glad you called me. I was getting bored, and so was Myra. You remember my telling you about Myra?"

"I do, but you failed to mention what a beauty she is." Monty took Myra's outstretched hand, then placed a light kiss on top of it.

"Pleased to meet you, Monty. Annie's talked of you often through the years." Myra winked at him. "She certainly didn't tell me how debonair you are, either. Shame on you, Annie."

"Enough of this sappy stuff. We've got a job to do."

Leave it to Annie to cut straight through the fat and aim right for the bone.

Sophie and Toots stood around and waited to be introduced. When Annie and Myra failed to take charge of introductions, Sophie stepped into the small space in which Annie and Monty were standing.

"I'm Sophia Manchester, and this"—she motioned to Toots—"is Teresa Loudenberry. We're here to find out what's going on in the pharmacy and who's been tampering with your meds."

Sophie's introduction went unnoticed.

"Annie, I thought you said you were taking care of this yourself? I'm not so sure this is such a good idea."

"Hello. We've gone to a lot of trouble for this assignment, Mr. Monty. Teresa and I could be home right now, showing off our homes to hordes of admiring Charlestonians, rather than leaving that oh-so-pleasant chore up to our long-suffering husbands, so I'm not sure what Annie's told you, but *she* is not going undercover. Nor is Myra. *We* are." Sophie pointed a finger at her chest, then at Toots. "And who are you?" she asked the man standing silently in a corner of Monty's living room.

"This is Rex. He's Monty's best friend. His son, Beau Simmons, owns the inn where you gals are staying," Annie said in a friendly voice. "Come over here, Rex, and make yourself known."

Rex joined the group clustered around the large coffee table. "Pleased to meet you, ladies."

"Okay, now that the introductions are out of the way, I say it's time to talk business. Monty, you know Myra and I can't directly involve ourselves in this mission. We've been in enough trouble over the years. And our pardons do not cover future misbehavior. However, Miss Toots and her partner, Sophia Manchester, were invited to apply to our group for a temporary assignment. They've more than passed muster. I have complete confidence that they will be able to uncover whatever underhanded shenanigans are taking place at the pharmacy. Toots and Sophia will act as guests tonight at the Christmas party for the pharmacy and its clients. I've explained to them in detail what's required of them in order for us to consider this mission successful. I assure you, these two are up to the task."

"It would've been nice if you'd told us that. You led us to believe you viewed us as two old women with nothing better to do," Sophie said in a none-too-friendly tone.

"The least you could have done was tell us this to *our faces*."

"She's right, Annie," Myra agreed. "We've kept them in the dark. I, for one, apologize." Turning to Sophie and Toots, Myra continued, "You wouldn't even be considered for the assignment had we not believed in your ability to complete the mission. It's rather small compared to those we've undertaken in the past, but one can never make any mission out to be less than it is."

Turning once again to face Annie, Myra said, "I think you need to tell these women you're sorry." Myra said this while staring Annie directly in the face.

"Oh, crap. I'm sorry, okay? I didn't want you two getting too full of yourselves, that's all," Annie explained somewhat reluctantly. "Does that make you feel better now?"

"It's a bit on the crude side, but yes, it will do," Myra replied. "Now, let's get this show on the road. The party is scheduled to begin at four. Cocktails first, then dinner. Toots, you will want to make sure Mr. Baumgardner drinks a lot. I heard he likes his booze, so that shouldn't be a problem.

"Sophia, you're going to moan and whine about your brother here, Monty, complain that he's not dealing with a full deck, and mention that he keeps forgetting to take his meds. Again, let's stick to the instructions to the letter, and we shouldn't have a problem. Are we all clear about what's expected? Rex, you're too quiet. Have you anything to offer?" Myra asked.

"I don't like deceiving Beau, if that counts as anything. Normally, I would tell him when I'm . . . up to something, so if that counts, it's all I have to offer."

"Of course it counts. Right, Annie?" Myra said. "Think about it this way. You're not really going to *lie* to your son. Beau, is it? He knows you're attending this party tonight, rather than being at that craft gig going on at the inn. You're here for Monty because he invited you. If your son questions you later, you can explain that there were a couple of ladies you two had taken an interest in. And there are Sophia and Toots. So, in the strictest terms, you're really not lying to your son."

"Myra, you should have been an attorney," Sophie said. "You lie quite convincingly."

"I'll take that as a compliment, dear. But, really, it's not that far off from the truth. Think about it," Myra concluded.

"Beau won't ask, really," Rex added. "As long as I'm enjoying myself. I just wanted you all to know that concealing things from Beau isn't something I'm comfortable doing."

"You need to hang around with Toots for a while. She'll have you behaving like a habitual liar in no time at all," Sophie teased.

"Sophia! How dare you?" Toots shouted, no longer caring that they were in the company of strangers. "Why on earth would you say that? I am not a liar!"

"I was kidding, okay? But you did lie about owning *The Informer* for years, remember?"

"That was different, and you know it. Now is not the time to bring up our personal lives, Sophia. You have no class whatsoever." Toots shook her head. "Beau, I would never want you to become the prevaricator that my dear friend Sophia is turning into."

"It's fine, really. I know this is just a bunch of malarkey."

"Enough!" Annie shouted, then clapped her hands to get their attention. "The party starts in two hours. Let's get out of here so we can all get ready. There is no dress rehearsal, kiddos. This is it. Opening and closing night at the same performance. The real deal. Now hustle."

"Yes, ma'am," Sophie said, giving a crisp salute.

"I'm leaving now," Toots said, "but I don't need two hours to prepare for a party. I can get ready in less than ten minutes." She glanced at Sophie. "Unlike some women I know."

"Out, out, out!" Annie ordered. "I don't want to see you or hear another word out of any of you until this mission is accomplished!"

Chapter 14

Holly spent the afternoon going over the event schedule for December. Her mother had thought of everything, except the extra employees required to make it all flow as smoothly as possible. Taking care of that was Holly's job, and she'd been putting off hiring holiday help. Without Ava, she wasn't going to have the time to conduct interviews, so she contacted a temp service agency they'd used in the past and arranged for them to supply the extra help they needed. If they did a good enough job, she would consider using their services in the future, which would make things a lot easier at holiday time.

That taken care of, she could turn her attention to the first guest event of the season, and with luck, she might even enjoy herself. With a few minutes unscheduled, she called her father to catch up.

"Hey, Dad. What's up?"

"I just talked to Pops. He's not coming tonight."

Odd, Holly thought. Pops was usually at his best during the social events. Before retiring, he'd worked tirelessly alongside her mother to make sure each event was a bigger success than it had been the year before.

"Did he tell you why?" Holly asked.

"He said he had made plans with Monty. They're going to a Christmas party of some kind at the Haven. I guess he's really enjoying his retirement."

"Dad, did Marlene tell you about the countess and her friends?" Holly asked.

A seed of an idea had been forming, yet what it was precisely she couldn't quite put her finger on. All she knew was that it had been planted this morning, when Gannon told her that his grandfather had mentioned something about vigilantes. Instinct told her she needed to be on high alert. Though exactly what she needed to be alerted to, she wasn't sure. She knew those women were up to something, and it might involve Monty, and maybe even Pops.

"They arrived yesterday, of course. Marlene said they asked not to be disturbed. I respect that."

"Of course, and I do, as well. But there is something off. I can't put my finger on it. This morning I came to the office early. Thought I'd get a head start on my day. The new guy I hired, Gannon Montgomery, to replace Ava showed up unannounced. He'd taken the previous afternoon off. His grandfather was having some problems. Dad, you're not going to believe this, but his grandfather is Pops's neighbor and new best friend."

"Is that what he wanted to tell you?" her father asked.

"No." Holly thought about it. What exactly *had* Gannon wanted to tell her? "No, he just wanted to let me know his grandfather was okay. I'd asked to be informed. But he did mention that his grandfather had been talking about a group of women. He said that they were vigilantes, and that if this was repeated, there would be trouble. I'm not sure what to make of it all." Glad to get that off her chest, she went on. "Do you know anything about the countess and her friends?"

"Other than that they're our guests, no. Why? Is there more I should know?"

"I'm not sure. As soon as Marlene comes in, I'm going to speak to her. I need to clear something up. If I have any news, I'll call you. You're going to the wreath-making party tonight?" she asked.

"I wouldn't miss it. I'm just sad your mother isn't here to share it with. Knowing she planned this helps, though." Her Dad's normally smooth tone had become gruff. She knew he was tearing up.

"I miss her, too, like you can't imagine."

"I feel . . . angry. She was fifty-eight years old, and I thought she was in excellent health. I get so frustrated when I think of the effort she put into eating healthy and keeping herself fit and trim. She spent every single morning in the spa, exercising and doing laps in the pool. It just angers me that she was taken from me."

"I'm angry, too, but not in a normal way. Not at Mom. Like you said, she did all the right things, at least all the proper moves one makes to stave off a heart attack. I still don't understand it," Holly said.

"My only comfort is knowing your mother is in heaven, looking down on us. And if I know her, she's going to make sure this little craft thing tonight goes off without a hitch."

Holly laughed, though her eyes were filled with unshed tears. "She'd hate having you refer to it as a 'little craft thing.' She worked hard to make her Christmas events—I think that's what she always called them—as exciting as she could. Dad . . ." Holly had wanted to ask her father this for a while, but the timing had never been right. It seemed right now. "Did Mom ever locate her biological family? I know she spent a lot of time researching right before she died."

Her mother had been adopted, yet both adoptive parents had died when Holly was still in elementary school. Mimi and Papaw. Holly had loved them so much, but she'd been too young to understand fully that they weren't coming back.

"No, but she said she wasn't giving up until she found a biological relative. I've thought of hiring a private detective to see what they could uncover, but to what end? Your mother isn't here to receive the news, so I guess it's just silly of me even to consider such a thing."

"Dad, I think it's a wonderful idea! We don't know what Mom might've inherited from her family. Maybe there was a history of heart disease. You should pursue it. And it wouldn't hurt my feelings if I knew what diseases I might face in the future. I'm not getting any younger, you know?"

"I'll see what I can do, old lady. Now, I need to speak to Omar. He's insisting on prime rib for the office Christmas party being held at the Blue Sky tonight. I keep telling him the guests are vegans. I think he likes arguing with me."

Holly grinned. "Sounds just like Omar. Does what he wants, but he should respect the requests of the partygoers. I'll see you tonight."

They said their good-byes. Holly wondered if her mother's relatives had some horrid health history. After the holidays, if Dad didn't hire a detective to locate Mom's family, then she would do it herself.

"Good afternoon, young lady," Marlene said as she entered the office. "We're going to be swamped today."

"And good afternoon to you, too," Holly replied.

Holly nodded. "You're right. We need to get busy."

Five minutes later, Marlene brought to Holly's desk a computer printout and a box of muffins from the bakery downstairs.

"That you insist on bringing that stuff into my office amazes me. I'm not eating any sweets until tonight."

"Doesn't mean I can't," Marlene said, then bit into what

looked like a cranberry-walnut muffin. Holly knew they were to die for, but she was saving her calories for tonight.

"True. Marlene, remember when you were telling me about the countess, Anna something or other, and her friends being involved with a group of vigilantes?"

Between bites, Marlene said, "No, they didn't say it that way. I think they said *they* were the vigilantes."

Holly shook her head. "Okay, of course they are. Seriously, there is a little mystery I'm trying to solve. Do you really believe they're vigilantes? It sounds like something out of a novel, if you want my opinion."

Marlene looked from side to side to make sure no one else was in the room. Then she got up and closed the door to Holly's office. She spoke in a low voice, almost a whisper. "It's been reported in the *Washington Post* that Anna de Silva was involved with a certain group of women who called themselves the Vigilantes and were granted a pardon some years back by the president of the United States. I'm not saying it's true or false, but there is suspicion. She told me she was a Vigilante, and knowing what I know, I feel there is some truth to the story. Of course, she owns the newspaper, so it could be an elaborate hoax."

Holly took a deep breath. Her thoughts were all over the place.

"Listen, I need to step out for a bit. If anyone comes looking for me, tell them I'm . . . at the spa, having a massage. I don't want to be interrupted."

Marlene raised her eyebrows. "Whatever you say. You're the boss."

Chapter 15

Holly held her pass up to the elderly gentleman and waited for him to raise the gate. She needed to make sure Pops and his new friend, Monty, weren't getting themselves involved in something they shouldn't. On the ride over, she had kept telling herself that she was being paranoid. Those women weren't Vigilantes, and her grandfather would never get involved with such nonsense, even if it was true.

She parked in the guest parking lot and raced inside the building to the reception area, which housed the elevators. As soon as she arrived on the third floor, she ran down the long expanse that led to the last condo on the floor. Pops's.

A bit out of breath, she rang the doorbell. No answer. She rang it again and knocked on the door. "Pops, it's me. I need to talk to you." She waited to hear the door being unlocked, but there was no sound coming from the other side of the door. She knocked again, this time putting her ear against the door. Maybe he was in the shower. "Pops," she called out as loudly as she dared. She didn't want the other residents to hear her. She knocked again and rang the bell once more.

He was gone. Where he'd gone, she had no clue. But she

felt secure knowing he wasn't out with a bunch of Vigilante women, whom she had checked on and knew were still back at the inn.

Thirty minutes later, she was in her office.

"That was a quick massage," Marlene said as Holly walked past her desk.

"It was, wasn't it?" Holly said, laughing. "I didn't even have enough time to enjoy it."

"Ava called while you were out. She said to call her immediately. She tried to get you on your cell, too. So you'd better stick to the massage story."

Once she'd taken care of a few e-mails and an urgent call from the temp service agency she'd hired, Holly returned Ava's call. "What's so important?" she asked as soon as Ava picked up the phone.

"Listen, I've just learned something that will totally blow your mind. Are you alone?" Ava asked, her voice lowered like a sleuth's.

"Yes, Ava. I am alone. Marlene is at her desk, so yes, I'm alone. What gives?"

"Go close your door. I'll wait," Ava instructed.

"Good grief! Do you realize how busy I am? Don't answer that. If you did, you wouldn't be asking me to do this." Holly got up from her seat and closed the door. She motioned to her phone when Marlene raised an eyebrow. "Okay, my door is closed. This better be good. I think you have too much time on your hands. You should've stayed at work. At least you wouldn't be bugging me. Now, spit it out. I'm busy."

"Hey, if you're going to act this way, I can always hang up. I have soap operas to watch and romance novels to read, not to mention the millions of baby blogs I need to catch up on. Listen to me, Holly. I've found something out, and it's important. I'm not pulling your leg."

"And it can't wait until tonight?" Holly asked.

"It can, but trust me, you really would strangle me if I kept this juicy piece of news to myself."

"Okay, I'm all ears."

"You know my friend Sandy, the one who loves books?"

"Yes, I remember her. Cute girl. So what's going on with her? Don't tell me she's pregnant, too! Good grief. Is this pregnancy stuff contagious?"

"Would you hush for one minute? And stop jumping to conclusions. Sandy isn't even married."

"Since when does one have to be married in order to get pregnant?" Holly interjected.

"I swear, I am choking you tonight, so don't turn your back on me. Now, shut your mouth and let me talk for two minutes. Can you do that? No, don't answer."

"Again, I'm all ears," Holly repeated. This was getting a bit old.

"Sandy just started waitressing for Draper's two weeks ago. She called me this morning and asked if there were any openings at the inn. Of course, I told her there were, her being a good friend and all. I'm sure Omar or someone can find a position for her. She's very brilliant . . . all those books she reads, but she needs fast money. Tips. You know, a daily supply of cash. She worked a Christmas party last night and said she made only twelve dollars in tips."

"Go on," Holly said. A little bit of gossip about her competitor couldn't hurt.

"Apparently, the owner of Draper's has had to take an outside job in order to keep the place running."

"That's it?"

"I'm not finished. When I pause to catch my breath, you have to be quiet. I'm forty pounds heavier, and I get short of breath when I talk."

"Then you must be short of breath all the time," Holly couldn't help but add. Ava could outtalk an auctioneer, or at least she'd give them a run for their money. *Pun intended,* she thought as she waited for Ava to continue with her story.

"You're mean, Holly. You know that?"

Holly kept quiet. She was grinning from ear to ear.

"So now you're being a smart-ass. Okay, I get it. Whatever. Look, if you don't want to hear what I have to tell you, I'm good with that. You can find out for yourself, and then I can say I could have told you."

"Ava, just tell me, okay? This is fun, but I really have a lot to do before tonight's wreath party. So go on and tell me whatever it is."

"You know, I think I *will* wait until tonight. You have just ticked me off, Ms. Holly Simmons. I will talk to you later." And with that, Ava hung up on her best friend forever.

Rather than being annoyed, Holly was relieved. Ava needed something to occupy herself. Gossiping had its moments, but Ava was taking it too far, and today of all days. She'd apologize to Ava tonight. She wanted to take her time getting ready for the event. After all, it was the first night the guests would see her, and she wanted to make a good impression.

"And that, Holly Simmons, is a crock," she said out loud, thankful her door was closed.

Chapter 16

"I look like a tramp," Toots said. "If Phil saw me in this getup, he'd divorce me."

Annie had provided the clothes for Toots and Sophie to wear. When Toots had seen what she'd been given to wear, she'd almost fainted. "You have to look the part," Annie had said.

Toots remembered Annie saying she wasn't running a prostitution ring, but the outfit she was wearing—a glittery gold sheath dress that barely covered her rear end—seemed to suggest quite the opposite of that reassuring comment. And it was so tight, she couldn't even breathe comfortably. And the high-heeled shoes were nothing but hooker shoes. Matching the gold in her dress, they were at least four inches high. She had a corn on her left toe and would most likely end up having to have it surgically removed after tonight. Toots wondered why she'd ever agreed to submit that questionnaire so she could join this group of crazy women in the first place.

She was happily married. Phil was a dream. She had a beautiful daughter and two grandchildren. She had wealth, love, and, of course, Frankie, Betty, and Barney, those precious little doxies. What more could a woman her age want?

A little voice in her head answered ever so softly, *A little excitement.*

It was true, she thought as she applied blue eye shadow to her lids, as per Annie's instructions. She had a beautiful life, but it had become predictable. Not unhappy, but Toots had always been the kind of woman who needed excitement in her life, challenges, if you will. And, face it, she no longer had anything to do with *The Informer,* and the bakery practically ran itself. Everyone of a certain age in her life was happily married. So what was left? But this time, she thought as she looked at herself in the mirror, she'd probably gone overboard.

Sophie stood at the double sink next to her. "At least you get to wear makeup and look trashy. I, on the other hand, have to dress up as a plain Jane. Look at me! Can you see me wearing this in real life?"

Toots stopped to check out Sophie's outfit. A black wool skirt that hung below her knees and a pale yellow blouse with puffed short sleeves. Toots burst out laughing. "You look like a Pilgrim!" Toots looked at Sophie's feet. She wore sturdy black shoes with fake gold buckles. Toots couldn't stop laughing. "All you're missing is the hat and a ticket for the *Mayflower.*" Toots laughed so hard, her sides hurt.

"I think Annie hates you, or she's mistaken Christmas for Thanksgiving," Toots announced between peals of laughter. "That's the ugliest outfit I've ever seen you in."

"Yeah, well, just wait until this is over. I'm gonna let her have it. I might even kick her in that shapely butt of hers, wearing these orthopedic-looking shoes." Sophic lifted her leg high in the air. "I bet they weigh at least five pounds apiece."

"Stop!" Toots said. "I'm crying off this horrid blue eye shadow. Let's hurry and get this over with. And stop complaining about your shoes. I, after all, may end up being hobbled before the evening's over." She looked at her own feet and burst out laughing.

Toots finished applying her mascara and added the Tangee orange lipstick Annie had provided. She needed updating on what a true slut wore these days, Toots thought as she blotted her orange lips on a tissue.

"Oh, my gawd!" Sophie screamed. "You look like a slut version of Baby Jane!" Sophie laughed so hard, she cried.

Toots cackled so hard, she fell to the floor.

Five minutes later, barely able to stand, Toots sashayed into Monty's living room, where he waited with Rex.

As soon as the two men saw them, they looked at one another a couple of times, and then they doubled over in a fit of laughter.

"By George, I think you two are about the ugliest pair I've laid eyes on in . . . maybe forever," Monty said. Then he asked Rex, "What do you think?"

Rex shook his head but wore a grin a mile wide. "You two are pretty ladies without the costumes, but I have to agree with Monty. You're both mighty ugly."

"Look, us ugly ladies here are gonna catch whoever is screwing around in your pharmacy. We're both wearing a wire, too. Personally, I'm not so sure that pharmacist will even look at me once, let alone let me crawl all over him, as per Annie's instructions, and confess to me. If there's anything to confess," Toots said.

"We won't find out if we don't leave right now. The party starts in fifteen minutes. We need to get there on time so you two girls can home in on your mark," Monty teased.

Ten minutes later, they entered the Goldstar Room, where the Christmas party for the pharmacy employees was just getting started. The employees were decked out in their best holiday attire and Toots spied Norton immediately. He wore a plaid dinner jacket with mustard-colored slacks.

Annie had known exactly what she was doing when she'd picked out their wardrobe for tonight.

Christmas carols played softly in the background. A bar had been set up at the back of the room, and the line for drinks was growing longer by the minute. Toots guessed there were around seventy people in attendance, including spouses and partners. Annie had told her there were thirty-seven employees. Norton was the head pharmacist and manager.

Knowing it was now or never, Toots spoke to Sophie. "Let's hit it, kid. We've got a job to do."

Chapter 17

Holly applied her makeup with an expert hand, then blew her short hair into a flattering style that framed her face. She applied an extra touch of blush, and just because, she added a touch of silver highlights to her cheeks, something she'd seen on YouTube. Her shameless addiction was makeup tutorials. At night, when she should be reading a quality book, she would devour the tutorials. Why, she hadn't a clue, but she had learned a few tips to enhance her looks.

She chose a black velvet skirt for tonight. A red cashmere sweater with a cowl-neck made a perfect mate for her skirt. Plus, the sweater had been a Christmas gift from her mother last year. Holly knew her mother would approve if she were here.

After grabbing a matching black velvet clutch, Holly added a comb, her tube of black honey lip gloss, and her cell phone. She'd parked in her garage, saving herself from the blast of cold wind. The temperatures had dropped into the low forties, and she loved it this time of year. It made it feel just a little bit more special. She drove the mile and a half to the inn and parked in the underground parking area reserved for the employees and, today, the governor and his real family, who had arrived early. Holly was thankful the inn was prepared, but the governor's guests weren't due to arrive until sometime late tomorrow.

She removed the keys from the ignition, tossed them in her clutch, and took the elevator up to the main floor.

Inside, Christmas music flowed from the hidden speakers. The scent of fresh evergreens, mixed with the aroma of right-out-of-the-oven sugar cookies, filled the grand hall. Couples, young and old, were gathered in small groups, some holding a drink, others partaking of the constant supply of cookies the bakery provided.

She was starving and grabbed a cookie before she made her way to the Autumn Room, where the wreath party was being held. The guests weren't due to arrive for another half hour, and Holly wanted to go over a few things with Gannon. She'd asked him to meet her there before she'd left for home.

Staff members rushed around the room, making sure the items the guests would be using were where they should be. A representative from the local craft store would host the wreath making, and Holly, along with Gannon, would mingle with the guests when Ava was not using him for something else. She looked at her watch. Gannon should've been here already.

Holly was walking through the room, admiring the wreaths being used as models for the guests, when she heard her name.

"Good grief. You look like you've swallowed a pig," Holly said and winced. The words had tumbled out of her mouth before she'd had a chance to filter them.

"You are not a nice person," Ava said as she waddled over to a chair and sat down.

"You're right. I'm not, and I'm sorry. For saying that and for today." Holly leaned over, giving her best friend a hug. "Where is Stephen?"

"He's pilfering something from the freezer at Chubs. He

said he's starving, and since I'm no longer employed and bringing home dinner, he had no choice but to fend for himself."

"Why didn't you tell me? I can arrange for something to be delivered for both of you, and for them, too." Holly patted Ava's big belly.

"I can cook. I just haven't felt like it. Stephen is quite capable of making dinner. He needs to get used to it, anyway. Once these two little guys are born, we'll be lucky to have a hot meal."

"Ava, you have to eat right. You're eating for three."

"I know this, and I'm eating right. It's Stephen who isn't. Don't worry. I'm taking care of these guys. If I weren't, I'd be here working right now. I don't know if I'll be able to stand another three months of doing nothing. Maybe I'll write a book."

Holly rolled her eyes. "I can see it all now. Seriously, what was so important this afternoon? You said I needed to know about something. Can you tell me what it is?"

"You're not going to like it, but you need to know, so let's go somewhere private." Ava stood, giving Holly no chance to suggest where. She simply followed her into the ladies' room.

"Sit," Holly ordered. Poor Ava was as big as a house, but she'd already insulted her enough for one day.

Ava did as instructed, sitting on a plush love seat in a small section where one could sit and relax, away from the toilets but still private.

"That guy you hired, Gannon Montgomery. He isn't who you think he is," Ava explained.

Holly sat next to Ava. "So, tell me. Who is he?"

"Are you sure you want to know? I promise it will cause a bit of a problem." Ava took a deep breath, then added, "Here at the inn."

"You've been doing this to me all day, Ava! If there is

really something you think I should know, just tell me. Don't keep dragging it out."

She nodded. "Okay. Gannon Montgomery is the owner of Draper's Lodge."

Holly wasn't sure she'd heard her correctly. "Say that again."

"You heard me the first time. Gannon owns Draper's. He's the grandson. Remember I told you my friend Sandy said the place was as dead as a doornail?"

Holly was stunned. Why would Gannon Montgomery want to work here? And why did he lie to her? To Ava, who'd taken his application?

"Surprised, huh? I was, too. Apparently, they're about to go under, and the guy needed a job. Can't really blame him, though."

"Then why would he pretend to be someone he's not? What's the point? If he needed a job, all he had to do was . . . well, all he had to do was . . ."

"Apply for the job as your new assistant?" Ava said, finishing for her.

"Yes," Holly said softly. "He did, didn't he?" She wasn't really asking Ava. A dozen thoughts ran through her mind, yet none stayed long enough to amount to anything substantial.

She wasn't sure what she was feeling, but she still had an inn to run. "Ava, as Mom would say, 'We'll manage,' and right now, I have to manage the wreath party. Gannon is supposed to act as your . . . assistant tonight. But I think we'll have to change plans, since I need him to work with me." She stopped. What was the problem? "Ava, when you took his application, did he . . . never mind. He's been completely honest, hasn't he?"

"I think you should ask him," Ava said. "Let's go so you can."

As soon as Holly entered the Autumn Room, she spied Gannon with a guest. He wore a black suit and a green tie.

"I thought you said he would wear a red tie."

"I was just being silly, Holly. How would I know what the guy planned to wear? It's the pregnancy hormones. Actually, Stephen thinks they may have kicked in some psychic ability, because I—"

"Find a place to sit down, Ava. I have a job to do."

Holly hurried across the room, and she saw Gannon the moment he saw her. He excused himself and watched as she walked toward him. His blue eyes sparkled as bright as the Christmas tree in the corner.

"Hey," she said, standing beside him.

He looked at her, up and down, then settled on her face. "Hey, yourself. You look fantastic tonight."

"Thanks. You're looking pretty hot, too."

Hot? Did she really just say that? *Hot?*

"Holly, there is something I need to tell you." He looked serious, somber.

"Sure," she said, knowing what he would say but guessing he needed to confess so that he'd feel better about the job deception, even though he hadn't really deceived her. He'd just omitted a few details.

"When I told you I was looking for a change of scenery, the other day when you interviewed me, it was more than that."

She nodded, hoping he took this as a sign to continue.

"Draper's isn't doing well financially. When I heard you were looking for a new assistant, I got this crazy idea. I thought if I could get the job, I could find a way to discover what made the inn so successful, then apply what I'd learned at Draper's. You see, I'm actually the owner, not just an employee. What I've done is dishonest, and if you never speak to me again, I'll understand. I just couldn't continue to play this role.

"I know what makes this place so successful. You like people, you strive to make them happy, and you go out of your way to make this place inviting. For the past year, I've seen our guest list decline. I blamed it all on the inn, because it was so successful, and it was our biggest competition. I was too self-absorbed to admit that it was my managerial skills that were lacking. So, I'll be on my way. I wish you the best, really. And, Holly, have a Merry Christmas."

Holly listened to every word Gannon said. He was down on his luck. He'd tried to do what he thought would work for Draper's. She didn't understand, but who knew what she would do if she were in his position?

"Gannon, tomorrow you can go back to Draper's with this knowledge. Tonight you have a job to do, and I expect you to do it," Holly said, then leaned up and gave him a kiss on the lips.

When she backed away, he began to laugh, the sound rich and warm to her ears. In spite of herself, she chuckled, then pointed to the mistletoe above them.

Gannon's eyes followed her pointing hand; then he pulled her close and gave her a real kiss. "You knew what I was going to say all along, didn't you?"

"I had a bit of an idea," she admitted.

"You're not going to fire me, are you?"

He kissed her a second time.

"I'm not sure. You'll have to give me a reason not to."

He pulled her close and wrapped his arms around her. His kiss was slow and soft. "Is this good enough?"

Holly answered by returning his kiss.

Epilogue

"Look, Norton, I don't think you should be telling me this stuff," Toots said as Norton slobbered against her chest. "You could get in a lot of trouble." She squirmed against the wire, trying to reposition it. Norton's big head kept moving it.

"I don't give a hoot," he mumbled. "Come on. Go with me. I gotta show ya something. You wanna make some money?" He could hardly speak. Toots hoped they were able to pick everything up through the wire.

"Sure," Toots said. She motioned to Sophie.

He looped his arm around her waist and led her outside, to the building next door. "This is it. This is where I work." He didn't sound quite as inebriated. Toots thought the cold air might've sobered him up a bit. He fiddled around in his pocket for a set of keys.

"It's cold out here," Toots said in a whiny voice, playing her part.

Finally, he managed to insert the key in the lock and push the door aside. Greeted by a gush of warm air, Toots couldn't help but feel a bit of relief. If she had to freeze her rear end off just to stay in this group, they could have it. She did not like to freeze. She had no more formed that thought when a swarm of men dressed in black uniforms grabbed Norton and slammed him against the wall. The lights came on, and Toots was yanked aside by one of the men in black.

Frightened, Toots asked in a jittery voice, "What's going on here?"

"We're friends of Annie's. I need you to return to the party to get your friends. Go back to the inn, get rid of this garb you're wearing, and when you see Annie, tell her we said thanks."

"Who are you?"

"Friends of Annie's," the man repeated. "Now, go on back to the party."

Toots raced out of the building, and once outside she saw Sophie, Monty, and Rex. "This is the strangest night I've had in a long time," she said.

"Annie says Monty is right. There is evidence of all kinds of drug tampering, along with a boatload of missing pain medication," Sophie said.

"How does she know this? We were just getting started in there." Toots nodded at the building that housed the pharmacy.

"I gave her my insulin, and she sent it out to be tested. It was diluted with water," Monty said. "I knew I was not going bonkers."

"I say we all go back inside and have a drink," Rex said.

Two minutes later, they rejoined the party. Each accepted a flute of champagne from a passing waiter.

"Toots, let's do that thing we do when we're finished with a project," Sophie urged, setting her flute of champagne down on a nearby table.

"Okay," Toots said and set her flute on the table, next to Sophie's. "You two, join us."

The men placed their flutes of champagne next to Sophie's and Toots's.

"Okay, now follow us," Sophie said. She stuck her hands out, one on top of the other. She motioned for Toots to do the same, then Monty and Rex.

"Okay. On the count of three. Ready. Here we go. One. Two. Three." Sophie threw their hands high in the air and shouted, "When you're good, you're good. Merry Christmas to all!"